Phantasmagorias and Grotesqueries

Brant Danay

Slab of Contents

Beelzebub's Messiah

A horde of termites scuttled up and down Night Beetle's spine as the Parasitique tribesmen hoisted him against the wet wood of the crucifix. With hammers and nails composed of chitin, the Parasitiques spiked the shaman of the Pestilante peoples to the rotten cross. Submerged to the groin in the filthy waters of Crucifix Swamp,yet dangling a few feet above the bottom of the marsh, Night Beetle's chest collapsed and he began to suffocate. The Parastiques quickly tied the entomancer's wrists, torso, and ankles to the wood with ropes of silk and mucus,securely trussing his half-conscious body to the crosspiece to prevent asphyxiation.

A Parasitique priest wearing a gigantic, wooden flea's-head mask stepped forward. In the prosthetic pincers of his left hand he was holding an elaborate, ten-foot long, tubular devicethat looked like a hybrid of giant centipedes and translucent bladders. The Parasitiques fastened the myriad of ring-clasps and tiny grapnels protruding from the sides of the contraption to Night Beetle's flesh, piercing the entire left side of his body, from armpit to ankle, with the pointed, pinching clamp-mechanisms. The device was crowned with a perforated, curling, savagely barbed straw. Chittering a prayer to Venatode, the tapeworm goddess, the Parasitique priest hooked it to the right side of Night Beetle's mouth, driving one curved point through the side of his lip and another through the inside of his cheek. The alveolated tube began to expand and elongate, snaring his gums, tongue, frenulum, palate, and uvula on its hooks before descending through his esophagus and lowering itself into his stomach, then dividing into two, one half plunging through his duodenum like the phallus of a rapist, the other swerving to penetrate his surgically-implanted, giant cockroach gizzard. The sharp spikes dug into his epithelium, stomach lining, and diverticula, burying themselves in his organs and tissues. The straw could not be dislodged, swallowed, expectorated, vomited, or defecated without tearing huge chunks of his digestive system out along with it.

The base of the device was a grilled cubicle that resembled a sewer system. One of the Parasitiques dropped his head beneath the surface of the swamp and anchored it to the mud at the bottom of the marsh. The limp sacs hanging from the side of the device expanded

1

like bladders as the green-brown waters of the swamp came bubbling up, pumping the mire through its tubes in intermittent spasms of peristalsis. It was as if the device were the giant hookah of some dominatrix psychonaut, hanging next to the torture racks and torture wheels in her pleasure chamber/opium den.

The Parasitiques gathered around the crucified Pestilante shaman in a semi-circle. As the priest spoke another prayer to Venatode, they dropped to their knees, then prostrated themselves in the filthy swamp before him. After praying to the tapeworm goddess, they chanted an incantation, blending their voodoo curses and nigromantic hexes with the oral history of the ancient vendetta between the Pestilante and Parasitique tribes. The ritual lasted for several minutes, and then the Parasitiques waded through the marsh, leaving their sacrifice to the tapeworm goddess behind, to contemplate his doom in Crucifix Swamp.

The first splash of swampwater from the force-feeding device surged into Night Beetle's mouth, reviving him from his near-catatonic state. He could taste the rancid, fetid, diseased brine of the entire marsh through the taste buds surgically attached to the soles of his feet. A second later he opened his compound eyes. Through his entomantically grown ommatidia he watched the Parasitiques plodding through the murk and the mire. The silhouette of the large, wooden mask merged with the priest's shadow, and it seemed as though a flea the size of a man were stalking the swamp.

Night Beetle's head-dress of moth and butterfly wings was damp with the moisture of the bog. He shook his bald head and it slid down his face and chest like a mass of wet veils, half-melting the blue paint with which the beetle-markings on his cheeks and forehead and the scarab upon his torso had been daubed. The head-dress floated on the surface of the swamp like a discarded caul, drifting between the satchels of powders, explosives, cantharides, aphrodisiacs, and larvae and the vials of poisons, acids, oils, and quinones that the Parasitiques had torn from his beetle-shell belt and scattered across the mire.

Night Beetle breathed in the mephitic bog-mist and brackish fen-water as he gazed upon the swamp. In the distance, three-headed, olive-colored wooly mammoths were bathing in the fetid marshes while the mahout necromancers riding on their backs cast spells of black voodoo. Bird zombies resurrected from the lethal waters of Lake Avernus by the mahout necromancers were picking the lice from the mangy fur of the pachyderm behemoths. Hippopotami and gorgops were wallowing in the muck and spinning their tails in circles. Green/brown crocodiles floated like piles of verdigris-coated emeralds and moldy opium. Symbiotic harpies cleaned the scum from the crocodiles' teeth in exchange for the sanctuary of their cavernous mouths. Fist-sized tsetse flies, empty botflies, and giant dragonflies buzzed through the moist mists that arose from the waters like the dying breaths of lepers. Hawks sometimes dove from the rotten canopies to catch the flies in their salivating mouths, and ichthyosaurs sometimes snared the hawks with their whip-like tongues as they did so. Cicadas in the tenebrous trees sang stridulating threnodies, triggering Night Beetle's entomantic powers of echolocation.

The crosses from which Crucifix Swamp took its name were interspersed throughout the bog, usually a mile or more apart from one another. Crux ansatas and crux decussatas alike rose from the marsh like the grave markers they were. Some still bore the mildewed skeletons and rotting corpses of the victims that had been sacrificed in days, years, centuries, and millennia past.

The enteral contraption bubbled like a hookah and fed him another mouthful of marsh and miasma. The device kept him nourished and alive with a steady diet of swampwater and all the detritus within it, from flukes and annelids to plankton and prawn, freshly spawned roe and newly hatched larvae to fossilized will-o'-the-wisps and ancient coprolites (which he ground up in his gigantic cockroach gizzard), urine and feces to egg-sacs and milt, etiolated plant-scum and rotten algae to free-floating mud and dredged-up corpse-sludge, the barnacle-ridden flotsam of war canoes and the bait-infested jetsam of hunting rafts to the blood-stained wreckage of legendary hydromachies and the fresh gore of ongoing vendettas.With his heightened shamanic senses Night Beetle could taste everything that dwelled in the noxious swampwater, even the bacteria and microorganisms. Most importantly, he could taste the dead fleas and the unborn tapeworms inside their eggs. He knew he had less than one hundred moons to decrucify himself, escape, and survive. Once the tapeworms had grown to maturity in his guts, the parasite goddess would come to collect her sacrificial offerings and devour his intestines. His eviscerated corpse would be its own cenotaph, his crucifix an open grave.

As a green, flea-ridden swamp sphinx crawled upon the branch over his head and a horde of leeches attached themselves to his inner thighs and genitalia and began squirming up his abdomen, Night Beetle closed his eyes and drifted into a meditative trance. He sifted through all the arcane knowledge stored like ant-food in his brain and soul,conceiving of various methods to decrucify himself.

Telepathically, Night Beetle reached out to the termites infesting the cross. He asked the soldiers guarding the crucifix if they could call upon their brethren to devour the decrepit wood into splinters and dust to free him. The soldiers replied that he would have to ask their Warlord. Night Beetle hopped from the consciousness of one termite to another, working his way down the main tunnel of the cross and below the bottom of the swamp. The end of the crucifix was more than ten feet beneath the ground, where it then opened up into a termite mound. He continued to jump from brain to brain until he found their Warlord, who responded to his query by psychically communicating that the cross was owned by his Princess, and he would have to gain permission from her to initiate its destruction. Night Beetle traveled further into the termite hive, scurrying from mind to mind, traversing now the consciousness of workers and drones, until he reached the chamber of the Princess of the cross upon which he was crucified. He implored her for assistance, but she told him that all of the crucifixes were sacred, and he would have to seek an audience with the Queen. Night Beetle quested through the vast, subterranean labyrinth, and as he wandered he discovered that the termite nest was as long and as wide as all of Crucifix Swamp, and that each of the individual crosses was anchored by a termite mound and ruled by a Princess and her Warlord. At last he came to the royal chamber of the Queen. She was as large as a human, with a gargantuan egg-sac that moved and bulged and rolled as though it were filled with severed heads and interspecies mating balls of of stoneflies and garter snakes. Fresh offspring were crawling over her entire body, and in and out of her crevices and orifices, and flying around the chamber in thick, clustered hordes. Her King lay beside her, his proboscis leashed to her fourth leg, his neck and penis encircled by cangues, his body trapped in three pillories, one for each segment. Night Beetle begged the Queen for aid, but she informed him that the crosses were composed of the eternal wood of the Ashvatha Tree, in which Gaeaphage the Termite Goddess herself had been spawned, and with which she had built her million-storied pagoda in the underworld. The wood could not be devoured, burned, sundered, smashed, or killed. It was the fate of her termite colony to perpetually devour the crucifixes so that they did not grow to the size of trees themselves, for, although coated with rot, the crosses possessed regenerative powers and had cores like stone. This was the reason they had stood for millennia and marked the graves of so many a sacrificial victim, for none had ever been able to decrucify themselves from the living wood.

Night Beetle snapped back into his own body and opened his eyes. He watched the silhouette of a brontosaurus wandering the distant horizon. He unpleasantly remembered a tome which spoke ofdinosaurs bearing hundred-foot long tapeworms in their intestines.

The ba of a scatophiliac skimmed the surface of the marsh, devouring the floating ordure and scum. The tongue of an ichtyosaurus lashed out and snared the ba like a viscid whip, breaking the ba's wings like a garrote while its human head screamed in agony and terror before being bitten off by the dinosaur.

Night Beetle closed his eyes again and drifted into another trance, this time tapping into the Pestilante hive-mind, the collective unconscious of his people that hovered somewhere between the physical and spiritual planes like a continent-sized horde of insects.Climbing through the millennia of wisdom passed down from shaman to shaman, sifting through the histories, memories, and archetypes stored like honey in the Pestilante hive-mind, exploring the entire aggregate of Pestilante knowledge, Night Beetle patiently searched for enlightenment in the Akashic records of his people. Two days later, he opened his eyes.The ancient, arcane, forbidden, hideous means of decrucifixion had been revealed.

Elephantiasis.

As an entomancer, Night Beetle knew that mosquitoes were the vessels which spread elephantiasis, and began to summon a horde of the infected bloodsuckers. From the glands in his armpits and genitals he released a stream of mosquito pheromones, calling them in their chemical language. The scent radiated through Crucifix Swamp, and was soon answered by a piercing, buzzing cacophony. The surrounding marsh began to vibrate. The buzzing continued to intensify and the swamp began to darken, as though from the unnatural gloaming of a mid-day eclipse of the sun, and then, within the span of a single second, thousands of mosquitoes converged upon Night Beetle and covered every centimeter of his flesh.

Their siphons plunged into his skin and it seemed as though he were being recrucified, this time with an infinity of nails impaling his every cell to the wood of the cross. The effect was somewhat akin to being trapped between the halves of a new torture device that was part iron maiden and part crucifix, squeezing him to a perforated pulp. The mosquitoes swarmed and drank, draining his blood until Night Beetle feared they would suck every last drop from his veins. As they fattened they began to fly away, back into the swamps, to digest and breed, until finally they had gone almost as suddenly as they had came, except for the few, red-bellied, bloated corpses who had overindulged and were now floating upon the scummy surface of the swamp.

Night Beetle's flesh looked as though it had erupted into ant-hills and tiny volcanoes. His entire body was swollen, as though from a grotesque congeries of allergic reactions and puncture wounds. The loss of blood soon led to lapses of consciousness. The enteral device hooked into his flank continued to churn and vibrate and gurgle all the while, and his wounds began to fester in the rancid swampwater that bubbled and dripped like liquid vomit from his mouth.

He could sense that the changes were already taking effect in his limbs and genitalia. The mosquitoes had repaid him for the blood with gifts of their own, including fevers and somnolence. The most important gift of all, though, the elephantiasis that would free him from the cross, and allow him to flee Venatode and escape Crucifix Swamp, was one that took months to grow. The acceleration of its development was crucial to Night Beetle's survival, but it was something he could not attain on his own. To escape death at the hands of the tapeworm goddess he would have to seek the benedictions of the Lord of the Flies.

Night Beetle's eyes rolled back in his head as he prayed to

Beelzebub. His lips mumbled spells, his nostrils dilated, his eyelids fluttered, and with the aid of the fevers he began to slumber, and as he slumbered he began to dream, and as he dreamed he astral projected to the netherworld in which Beelzebub dwelled.

Through some stelliferous abyss Night Beetle drifted, journeying further from his physical body than any previous trance had ever taken him, flying through the nocturnal skies, encompassed by one continuous night that glittered with starlight not only above him, but around him and beneath him. There was no earth, there was no moon, there was no sun. There was nought but the mite-sized sparks of distant stars. Like a derelict he floated without volition, his soul suffused with nausea and vertigo as he traversed the unfathomable gulfs of space and time, until finally a shadow appeared within the infinite sphere of the horizon, somehow darker than space itself, and Night Beetle knew that he had entered the realm of the Lord of the Flies.

Like a black star Beelzebub's palace loomed over the ancient void, larger than anything Night Beetle could have ever imagined, and yet somehow it had existed for what he knew to be eons in utter secrecy from his people, too dark or too far or too incomprehensible to the human brain to ever be discovered or even perceived by the antennae of Pestilante astrologers as it floated through its alien and antipodal zodiacs. It drew Night Beetle's soul like a lodestone, sucking his very spirit into its depths as though by some hideous form of osmosis, pulling him like undertow through cold labyrinths of shadow and vacuum and death, then depositing his astrosome inside the throne room of the insect god.

Beelzebub's million eyes were like mirrors of black glass, each one reflecting a different scene of pestilence, torture, and death from somewhere in the universe. Night Beetle spent an eternity trying to decide if the images were reflections of reality or refractions of Beelzebub's mind. He could not determine whether the abominable grotesqueries were histories, happenings, or prestidigitations, or glimpses of worlds, planes, and dimensions beyond any human understanding, or the memories, thoughts and dreams of an omniscient demon. Perhaps they were everything he pondered. Perhaps even more. Looking into the eyes of the perfidious god was like gazing into a congeries of oracles and astrolabes, and Night

Beetle had the cold feeling that the dark deity could see all the way back to the beginning of the universe, and all the way to the end of time, and all the way to the very edges of space, from heaven to hell and all points in-between, be they physical, astral, spiritual, or otherwise.

The Lord of the Flies sat upon an ornate throne composed of some black and alien jewel that was veined with a nebulous species of white quartz. He was juggling a planet in his hands in that peculiar manner with which flies often handle strange and abhorrent artifacts. His chamber was filled with hordes of dipteran demons, buzzing incubi and succubi soaring through the fetid air, crawling along the curved walls, and tunneling through giant heaps of midden. The raw flesh of dead gods hung on meathooks with impossibly long chains, dangling from the dome of the ceiling. The bloody slabs of meat were writhing with maggots and dripping glowing ichor onto the floor. Many of them had been perforated with gaping siphon-holes or carved to jagged pieces with a serrated blade. Night Beetle realized with an ague-like chill that the consumption of godflesh made Beelzebub not only a deiphage, but a cannibal as well. Night Beetle suspected that the loathsome mountains of maggoty ordure piled throughout the throneroom were the feces of the gods.

Night Beetle kneeled down before the throne of Beelzebub, and the Lord of the Flies entered his mind. The Pestilante shaman would remember very little of their communication, only phantasmagoric fragments that lingered like the dreams of a comatose sorceror, images of Beelzebus and his lingering, buzzing, telepathic voice speaking of unholy bargains and abhorrent saviours. As Night Beetle fell back through space and time, he bore with him the strange feeling that he had sold the world for a pittance, and then he slammed back into his physical body with all the force of the infinite miles he had fallen. As he settled back into his flesh, he could already feel the lymph pooling in his limbs and scrotum.

Night Beetle closed his eyes once again and meditated upon the crucifix for fourteen weeks. The enteral contraption of the Parasitiques kept him alive, continuously pouring the swampwater and all the loathsome but nourishing creatures within it down his throat. When he awakened it was in the light of a full moon, with his head lolling and his eyes pointing directly down at his genitalia. His testicles had swollen to the size of severed heads, his distended scrotum bulging like the satchel of a headhunter who had just slain conjoined twins. Beneath them, his legs had grown turgid, like blood-filled lungs that were about to rupture. His ankles had enlarged to such an unnatural degree that the nails impaling them to the cross had been dislodged, and were now resting at the bottom of the swamp. His arms and hands were nearly as tumescent as his legs, and the nails in his palms were beginning to loosen because ofthe rapidly-swelling flesh.

His chest had expanded and torn itself free of the silk and mucus ropes that had tied him to the cross. He was so bloated with lymph that he looked and felt like he might burst apart at any time. His dark skin had grown rugose and scaly, and in certain areas had been completely replaced with a rough, grayish integument. So hideously and permanently disfiguredwas Night Beetle that he no longer recognized his own body. The elephantiasis which the mosquitoes had borne into his flesh had taken hold in a matter of weeks. The Lord of the Flies had answered his black prayers.

A swarm of flies hovered next to a tree a short distance from the cross. Each fly had all six of its legs wrapped around a squirming scarab. Night Beetle could feel them watching him, as palpably as if they were crawling across his flesh; could feel their eye contact as tangibly as if one of them had become entangled in his eyelashes, or trapped beneath one of his eyelids, or imprisoned in one of his optic lobes as though it caught in amber.

In the distance, the last sparks of fleeing will-o'-the-wisps and fireflies disappeared. No animals swam or waded through the bog for miles around. No insects chirped or sang. Every living creature that was able to do so had fled, and the empty trees would have joined them had they the means or the methods of doing so. Nothing remained but the strange horde of flies and their captives, waiting patiently in the humid and viscous air.

A shaft of sallow moonlight illuminated the swamp. Night Beetle's colon was undulating like a giant eel. A bubble floated to the surface of the murky waters, followed by a trail of several more. As they began to burst it was as if the marsh had become a vat of boiling feces. Foul sprays of bogwater fountained through the evening mists. The tapeworm goddess Venatode had come to devour her sacrifice.

Slowly, from beneath the bubbles, Venatode emerged from the swamp. The parasite goddess bore the visage of a woman, with long, blonde hair the color of jaundice and a face as hard and white as bone. She arose from the fen like a cobra, revealing a set of etiolated shoulders, arms, and breasts.Marshwater drained from her skin as she ascended further. Gradually she elongated to her full height, a twenty-foot tall abomination. She was segmented like a tapeworm, but those segments were human torsoes with bulbous breasts.Some of her nipples were more than a foot long and resembled pale termite mounds. Her middle segment bore a gaping vagina. Her skin was a strange shade of alabaster, all at once reminiscent of eggs and scorpions and albinos and virgins and skeletons. Her face was beautiful, yet horned like a demon's and covered in suctorial organs. Brown and green juices poured from her smiling mandibles, dripped from her vampire fangs, and runneled across the wicked pincers that jutted from both sides of her mouth. Her every fang itself was a tiny maw, ringed all-around with pointed teeth, extending to the back of her throat in rows of three and writhing like worms on barbed wire. Her fingertips bore miniature replicas of her mouth, gnashing and salivating and chewing on the air in anticipation of flesh and blood. They began to sing.

Night Beetle felt another wrench in his guts. He struggled to free himself from the crucifix, but still could not tear his tumid hands from the chitinous nails. As he writhed in place his abdomen began to distend even further, like that of a pregnant woman. He could see things writhing beneath his skin. A tapeworm crawled out of his rectum and slithered down his leg in a spiraling descent. Another slowly dropped from the tip of his penis, while three more emerged from his mouth and four more from his nostrils and ears. They landed in the swamp with the sound of flesh slapping water, then began swimming and wriggling toward the parasite goddess.

Night Beetle pulled and felt the rotten wood of the cross start to loosen. He lurched and shook and tried to tear his swollen hands free. The horned head of a tapeworm burst through his naval with a tiny explosion of blood, then squirmed out segment by segment until its entire ten-foot long body was dangling in the bog. It finally detached and began swimming towards Venatode with its brethren.

Night Beetle was shaking from side to side now, trying to rip each hand free in alternating spasms, jerking first to one side and then to the other. The crucifix was creaking and flaking and pieces of damp wood were starting to fall from the crosspiece. As he lurched to and fro his stomach inflated even more, its skin stretched as tightly as that of a tom-tom. As the mouths in her fingertips continued to sing, Venatode began calling out with her mouth, summoning forth her minions in the eldritch and grotesque language of the helminthes. The flesh over Night Beetle's stomach began to bubble, first slowly, gradually increasing until it seemed as though it were blistering, and then his intestines unwound, his torso shattered, and in an explosion of blood and feces all manner of tapeworms, hookworms, pinworms, and roundworms rained down upon the waters of Crucifix Swamp. As the parasites were making their gory egress Night Beetle screamed and made one final heave against the cross. The nails ripped through his palms with a sound like papyrus being shredded by the claws of a sphinx. Night Beetle fell face-first into the swamp and floated motionlessly in the ensanguined waters.

Venatode was wallowing in her sacrificial feast. She draped the tapeworms over her shoulders, caressed them, embraced them. She shoved one of the tapeworms facefirst into her vagina and used it to masturbate with. The hooked, suctorial organs upon its head tore her womb to bloody shreds. She slurped another tapeworm into her mouth, then swallowed an entire fistful. The tapeworms were a mere prelude to the ultimate sacrifice. When she had finished with them, she would devour Night Beetle's intestines from his sundered belly.

Distracted by the live offerings of the Parasitique priests, Venatode gave no attention to the swarm of flies that were rolling Night Beetle onto his back. The Pestilante shaman's eyes were fluttering, and through them he could see the goddess as she made her grisly repast. The flies were dropping the scarabs into Night Beetle's open torso. The dung beetles immediately burrowed into the fecal matter of his sundered intestines. Night Beetle combined his entomantic sorceries with the scarabs' energies to heal himself, sealing them inside his guts and then knitting his intestines and flesh back together. After the scarabs had fed, they crawled all through his digestive system and unhooked the barbed straw from his innards, so that it could be safely removed.

As Night Beetle was healing the flies were rearranging themselves, flying in eccentric orbits and mounting one another as if they were mating. After several minutes they had taken on the form of a gigantic caddisfly, with a three-foot long ovipositor. Through this ovipositor a large, black egg slowly descended. It looked uncannily like the planet Beelzebub had been juggling between his forelegs in his accursed throneroom. Night Beetle flashed back to his phantasmagoric encounter with the Lord of the Flies. Beelzebub's avatar dropped the egg of the eldritch deity into the hole of Night Beetle's abdomen just before the skin sealed itself shut. The strange entity then ascended straight upwards into the night, with neither the slightest arc nor hint of curvature, as though it were directly bound for the moon and the stars and beyond.

Night Beetle slowly gathered up his discarded vials and pouches. As Venatode remained oblivious to his revival, consumed by her own orgy of bingeing and masturbation, Night Beetle pulled the broken straw from his digestive system and out his mouth. Gastric juices hissed as they met the rancid swampwater. He removed the enteral device from his side, then opened a bottle of formic acid,and poured its contents into the chambers of the feeding contraption. Night Beetle raised the device high over his head and charged, breaking it into pieces over Venatode's head and splattering her with the corrosive beetle-secretions with which he had filled it. The tapeworm goddess screeched, looked up, and lunged in one fluid motion. Just before Venatode buried her fang-mouthed fingertips in his flesh, Night Beetle saw that each one was a living hookworm. A moment later their concentric circles of teeth were tunneling, suckling, masticating, feeding, feasting. Night Beetle pounded Venatode's hands and wrists with his engorged arms until the hookworm-fingers detached, many leaving their fangs behind, embedded in his wrinkled skin.

Venatode charged the Pestilante shaman, goring him with the horns and suctorial organs upon her head, driving him onto his back in the marshwaters and landing heavily atop his deformed body.Night Beetle spied the nails of chitin lying in the swampbed. He reached out with a bulbous arm and placed them in one of his pouches, even as the tapeworm bitch-goddess smothered him against the bottom of the bog. Night Beetle wrestled her like an animal, fought to his feet and, with the newfound strength of his enlarged body, lifted Venatode into the air and rammed her against the crucifix which he had hung from for three months. He let her long body slump down into the swamp until her head was even with the top of the cross, then drove the nails into her uppermost hands. As she thrashed about on the cross and a hundred hookworms plunged their mouths into his skin, Night Beetle pulled a handful of dung-bombs from another of his pouches. He sparked them by grinding two coprolites together, then shoved them one by one into the womb of the crucified goddess. Venatode screamed an instant later as her middle segment exploded, tearing her in two. Her upper half, still nailed to the cross, burst into flames, the tapeworms dangling from her flesh and mouth sizzling and burning to a crisp. Her lower half sank down briefly into the marsh, then floated back to the surface, spasming and bleeding and splashing in the water. Venatode watched her severed body twitch and writhe like a sundered basilisk tail as she burned on the cross,expending its every reflex until finally submerging itself in the filthy waters and descending back into the depths of Crucifix Swamp, leaving a ring of bubbles in its wake, the same bubbles which had augured Venatode's coming. As Venatode thrashed violently upon the crucifix, her head and the remainder of her body still aflame, Night Beetle lit another dung-bomb and tossed it down her throat while she was shrieking. An instant later the parasite goddess exploded, and the swamp was once again showered with helminthes, tiny comets of burning tapeworms and flaming hookworms and blazing pinworms and sparking roundworms. The shrapnel rained all around, chunks of blackened tapeworm meat and entire organs smoldering like embers. Flaming, severed breasts floated gruesomely through the bog, their tall nipples burning down like candle-wicks. Night Beetle stood, his massive chest heaving, his brain spinning with fever, gazing upon the drifting carnage until, gradually,the burning shrapnel dwindled and disintegrated, the waters grew still, and the creatures of Crucifix Swamp began emerging from their sanctuaries and returning from their exoduses.

Night Beetle retrieved his damp head-dress of butterfly and moth wings and placed it back upon his skull, then fastened his belt of beetle-shells around his waist and balanced its pouches over his grotesquely swollen genitalia. With his turgid scrotum painfully dragging the green and brown waters of Crucifix Swamp, and his fevered mind half-thinking and half-dreaming about his pact with the Lord of the Flies, Night Beetle began the long journey home. Beneath the light of the full moon he carried the unfamiliar girth of his elephantiasis-ridden body through the marsh like a beast of burden, a beast who's burden was its own flesh, blood, soul, and karma, for Night Beetle knew that he bore the burden of the Lord of the Flies along with it, and he could already feel the black maggot of Beelzebub's messiah squirming in his entrails.

The Orrery Man

He had possessed the greatest orrery on Earth, the greatest orrery known to man, but he, his sculpture of the solar system, and the comatose human race were Terrans no longer. As his monastery/observatory/spaceship, the Psi-Orbitron, launched through Earth's ionosphere and into the sidereal beyond, the Orrery Man meditated inside an incandescent replica of the Sun. Confined to the sphere of fire opal and molten gold, the Orrery Man was enlightened by a pulsating continuum of claustrophobias and claustrophilias. Like a hybrid of sensory deprivation chambers and sweat lodges, the calescent, womb-like isolation of the hollow pseudo-sun heightened his consciousness, until he could feel the rest of the orrery spinning around him, the mechanical orbits of the nine artificial planets and their one-hundred and seventy-five moons cycling through the planetarium chamber, energizing the Psi-Orbitron with their gyroscopic and astromantic forces and serving as the fuel for the metaluminal/juxtatemporal space/time-drive of the starship.

Beyond the walls of the Psi-Orbitron and the transparent black glass of the planetarium ceiling, the gravitational pull and blazing quanta of the Alpha Centauri system grew stronger and brighter. Visions of the future flashed through the Orrery Man's brain, like images from the optic lobes of God. He pictured the instant, mere hours away, when he would become the first astronomer to create an orrery of an extrasolar system. Eventually he would expand his masterpiece into a simulation of the Milky Way, and then the entire universe, at long last ending the war between art/sorcery/genesis and science/technology/eschatology.Just as the great philosophers and astronomers of the past had rewritten the one-dimensional starcharts of their times and, thusly, the minds of men, so too would he augment his four-dimensional orrery into a replication of the entire cosmos and rewire the very gestalts of the human brain.

The sound of one of his acolytes knocking on the exterior of the model Sun awakened the Orrery Man from his trance. An instant later, the glowing sphere in which he meditated unfolded into four separate pieces, like the flaming labia of Lilith dilating to give birth to Satan himself.

The Orrery Man slowly arose from the lotus position. Seven feet tall was the Orrery Man, with more than four-hundred pounds of musculature wrapped around his powerful frame. His biceps were as massive as his head. Every centimeter of his body had been tattooed the exact color and shade of outer space and, like palimpsests in a tome of astrophotography, his skin had been further decorated with layers of constellations and zodiacs, each star drawn with the tip of a glowing moonbeam, a masterpiece of minimalist pointillism. His back was covered by a cyanescent, photorealistic tattoo of the Hourglass Nebula, etched into his flesh with spacedust, and his arms and legs shimmered with renderings of luminous nebulae, as well. His penis had been dipped in liquid sunlight and reshaped to resemble a comet. Its head and glans had been surgically enlarged, then pierced with ampullangs and apodydoes forged in solar eclipses, giving it the appearance of a blazing coma. His bald head was completely devoid of tattoos and modifications, for it symbolized a black hole.

The scrotum of the Orrery Man had been cut away and his testes replaced with spermiferous neuticles, one a sculpture of the moon, the other the sun. Connected to his groin by prosthetic gonads, each neuticle possessed a hot, churning core that generated more semen than a priapic anakim in musth. On each of his nine fingers he wore a ring of black gold, and each ring held a jewel that had been carved, engraved, and shaded to resemble one of the planets of the solar system, beginning with Mercury on his right pinky and proceeding, in order, to Pluto on his left ringfinger. His left pinky had been severed for numerological and astrological reasons. Miniature replicas of all the planets' satellites had been threaded together to form a long string of pleasure beads, which were permanently housed inside his rectum.

The atramentous eyes of the Orrery Man opened as the model sun closed. He removed his black, floor-length cape from the scaffolding of the orrery, draped it over his shoulders, and fastened the links of its tiny chain around his taurean neck. A complete map of the Milky

Way Galaxy had been woven into the back of the cape with glittering starlight. The tiny tapestries of microstars sparkled just like those of the stelliferous robe of Ahura Mazda, the Zoroastrian god whom the Orrery Man had once worshipped.

The Orrery Man looked down into the face of Jove, Demiurge of Chemigenics and one of the ten High Astrolaters aboard the Psi-Orbitron. Just like the orrery and jewelry of his master, Jove's head had been sculpted by the hands and Aesthetimantic powers of the Orrery Man, surgically altered to resemble the planet Jupiter. His skull was gibbous and misshapen, like that of a retarded child. His left eye had been replaced with an artificial one that looked just like the Great Red Spot. His right eye had been removed and filled in with a gobbet of striated red, orange, and white flesh, the same flesh which covered the rest of his body.

Two of Jove's scions stood behind him. Io had been mutated to resemble the moon he was named for. His head was covered with mountain-shaped protuberances of flesh that periodically ejaculated blood from their suppurating calderas, just like the volcanoes of Io fountained lava and magma. His volcano-like penis frequently did the same. Europa was the antithesis of Io. His head had also been crowned with spires of flesh, but immediately after the deforming surgeries he had been frozen into a state of semi-liquidity. Beneath his frost-rimed skin his flesh and organs were like snow, his bodily fluids a slow-moving slush, his skeleton coated with ice. His skull was a grotesque parody of Europa's cryovolcanism, erupting with streams of crimson sleet that poured down his face and body like the cataracts of an ensanguined Cocytus. His chilblained, icicle-like phallus often dripped the same scarlet slush from its urethra.

Jove kneeled down before his master. His scions dropped to their knees a moment later.

"Speak." The voice of the Orrery Man was booming and ominous, as heavy as a neutron star and dripping with doom.

"Supreme Cosmogonarch, we have arrived at the Centauri system."

A flash of euphoria electrified the Orrery Man's brain. At last, the first step on the intergalactic path of destiny had been taken. The augmentation of his masterpiece had begun. When finished, his life's mission would be complete. The exact count of galaxies, stars, planets, and moons in the universe would no longer be a mystery, no longer an indeterminate quantity ambiguously spoken of in tones of wonder and awe, or symbolized with blasphemous euphemisms like "infinite" and "eternal" by the brainwashed heretics who refused to forsake God and worship the universe itself. No longer would the cosmium/chronium invented by Jove and Kronos be thought of as an endless cornucopia which could never be quantified with human mathematics.

"Have the Voyeur Dome prepared and disperse the acolytes to their stations," commanded the Orrery Man. "The death of the myth of infinity has begun."

*

The Orrery Man lay supine in the transparent, gyroscopic Voyeur Dome as it made a slow tour of the Centauri system. Like a drugged Grigori he gazed upon Centauri's three suns, forty-two planets, and two-hundred seventy-one moons. Their orbits and rotations aroused the astrophiliac lust he had first developed as a Zoroastrian stylite. He began to masturbate as the Voyeur Dome rotated and tilted and slowly flipped over. His sperm spread and floated through the low-gravity chamber, and he used his aesthetimantic powers to mold it into a sculpture of the Milky Way more perfect than anything ever wrought in marble and more realistic than any image ever captured by a camera. The comet tattoo covering his penis glowed even more intensely as he ran his planet-ringed fist over its effulgence.

While in the trances of his hour-long orgasms, he was capable of seeing farther into space than any camera, telescope, or astrograph. With his brain amplified and his mind expanded through his rituals of autoerotic enlightenment, the Orrery Man stored every physical detail of the planets and their satellites in his eidetic memory. With his powers of psychic astrophotography, he telepathically beamed those images back into the body of his star-vessel, one at a time. His acolytes channeled his memories into the ship's computer, then printed them on sheaves of smooth papyrus.

After several hours of observation, the Orrery Man telekinetically guided the Voyeur Dome back to the Psi-Orbitron and docked the womblike cosmosphere in the anterior hangar of the monastery/observatory/spaceship, then made his way to the planetarium, where one-hundred and seventy-five of his acolytes awaited his presence on bended knee. Like Jove, the heads, faces, and skulls of every one of his minions had been surgically altered to resemble one of the solar system's planets or moons. The gathering was a grotesque parody of the annual science summits they had once celebrated on Earth, before being mutated and enslaved by the Orrery Man.

The Orrery Man called the nine High Astrolaters present to step forward. They did so and knelt before him in a single row that began with Hermes and ended with Hades.

"What is thy bidding, Cosmogonarch?" they said as one, their voices as mellifluous and synchronized as the Music of the Spheres, which had been injected into their throats during synesthetic trances where sounds took on the form of matter.

"Hermes, Cytherea and Gaiea, cultivate and deliver three spectrumites of gems from the Jewel Incubator.Mons, Ouronos and Oceanus construct the scaffolding for the Centauri system.Jove and Kronos, commence expansion of the planetarium. Hades, set course for Sirius. Together, we shall construct a model of the entire universe. I will sculpt your very minds and souls,as surely as I aestheticized your bodies with my sorcerous surgeries and sacred cephaloplasties. When we arrive at the center of the cosmos and my orrery is complete, you will all realize the sins of your sophistry-riddled theorems, your superstitious equations and your primitive laws of physics. You shall worship the cosmos and I, not science and God, as the true Lords of the Universe."

"Yes, Cosmogonarch," the High Astrolaters replied as one, then rose to their feet and left the Orrery Man's presence, their moon-headed scions following behind them.

The Orrery Man departed the planetarium and entered the hub ofthe Psi-Orbitron. The Orrery Man walked through the circular corridor to Ra's laboratory. Ra was his one-hundred and seventy-sixth acolyte, tenth High Astrolater, and wife. She sensed the approach of the Orrery Man with her psychic powers and telekinetically opened the door to the chamber when he arrived.

As the Orrery Man entered the laboratory, Ra turned from the tank of black, viscous, steaming liquid over which she toiled and looked briefly into the abyss-like eyes of her husband. The sweet, cyanide-like smell of cosmium/chronium swirled around the room, rising like smoke as Ra cooked and stirred it in the space/time generator.

Ra had been tattooed orange, doused in flammable gases extracted from the core of the sun, and set afire by solar winds. Her head was grotesquely swollen, like the skull of a deformed fetus. Her eyes and mouth had been replaced with sunspots, and her head erupted with solar flares every time she spoke. Her vagina roiled and gyrated like a hellmouth.

Ra rose from her chair and knelt down before her husband. "What is thy bidding, Cosmogonarch?"

"Generate one-hundred and sixteen parsectites of cosmium and chronium."

The formula for channeling space/time into elemental forms had been first been postulated by Ra, the Queen of Nuclear Physics, and then actualized by Jove and Kronos. The Orrery Man had constructed the Psi-Orbitron from the newly invented elements.It was Ra's Sisyphean duty to generate the cosmium/chronium as a single substance, then separate it into its two manifestations.

The one-hundred sixteen parsectites of space/time would enlarge the Psi-Orbitron, allowing it to accomodate the new model of the Centauri system, as well as keep the Orrery Man, his crew, and the torpid human race, packed like living contraband in the incubators of the starship's hull, free from the effects of ageing during the metaluminal/juxtatemporal voyage to Sirius. The cosmium would also provide the morphmatter to create the gargantuan jewels, gems and stones from which the additions to the orrery would be sculpted, and provide the raw materials for oxygen, food, water and other amenities for the crew and passengers.

Ra worked side-by-side with Jove and Kronos, both of whom now entered the laboratory and took their places at the space/time converter. Seated to the right of Ra, Kronos' pale green head bobbed over the vat of steaming chronium as he toiled. The neutronium replicas of Saturn's rings bolted into the skull of the Emperor of Hyperchemistry began collecting an inky condensation, as did the ringed neuticles dangling from his crotch. Jove sat at Ra's left, slaving over his own vat, which contained a whirlpool of cosmium.

If ingested in its raw, fluid form, the elemental space/time caused permanent and irreversible immortality, mutating flesh and tissues into a substance as indestructible as neutronium, and rendering death obsolete.Therefore, it was the task of Jove to harden the cosmium into morphmatter, and of Kronos to vaporize the chronium into harmless wisps of gas.

The Orrery Man exited the laboratory and checked briefly upon the progress of the Jewel Incubator. The Jewel Incubator consisted of two artificially conjoined mutants, with heads surgically deformed to resemble their namesakes, the asteroids Ceres and Eris. The skin and flesh of their heads had been turned to rock and then cratered with a jackhammer.

Ceres dangled from the ceiling by a tube that had been hooked through her lips and welded to her face. feeding her a continuous supply of liquid coal and molten rainbows. The tangible spectrum flowed through her body, transforming into raw, semi-liquid, colored magma before being excreted through her colon, which had been surgically extended several feet beyond her anus. Her elongated intestine had been interwoven with the retrograde umbilical cord of Eris, which had been turned inside-out, reversed, and drawn up through her intestines, stomach, and esophagus to protrude several feet beyond her mouth. The two tubes of flesh were braided and welded together. The liquid jewel-ylem poured directly into Eris' womb. There, it solidified into rocks and gems before being dropped from her bloody uterus like babies and feces and long-lost, extravagant sex toys that had been lodged in the infected vaginas of lapiphiliacs for decades. Beneath her frogtied body, suspended from the ceiling in a squatting position by flechettes and chains, the falling jewels formed a wet pile of sparkling rubble, like the afterbirth of a rainbow goddess.

The Orrery Man returned to the planetarium. His acolytes had already begun constructing the Alpha Centauri System.Once the massive piles of jewelry had been aligned, melded, proportioned, and hollowed out, the Orrery Man would sculpt them into exact replicas of the planets and stars stored in his computer-like memory.

The Orrery Man ignored his toiling slaves and strode directly to the tilted, emerald-and-jade sculpture of Saturn. The miniature planet unfolded like a Venus flytrap in the Garden of Eden. The Orrery Man placed his cape on the adjacent scaffold, stepped inside the model planet, seated himself in the lotus position, and began to meditate. Confined to the orb of emerald and jade, a continuum of chronophobias and chronophilias enlightened the Orrery Man. Like a hybrid of sensory deprivation chamber and time machine, the simulacrum of Saturn delivered him to a higher state of consciousness, where his memories surrounded him like the virtual reality of a dying cyber-solipsist watching his pseudo-life flash before his misdirected eyes...

As an Aesthetimancer's prodigy he had taught himself the creative euphorias of painting and sculpture. As a Solipsist anchorite he had discovered the tao of orgasm. As an Existential cenobite he had been initiated into the arts of sadomasochism, bondage, discipline and domination. As a Hindu acolyte he had learned the ways of tantrism. As a Buddhist monk he had taken a vow of celibacy. As a Zoroastrian stylite, stargazing atop dokhmas, he had replaced that celibacy with a meditative form of onanism. As a Niezschean priest he had channeled his fetish for celestial bodies and his sexual obsession with the cosmos into erotipotent trances of reason, enlightenment, and euphoria. As the Orrery Man he had mastered the mystical, fourfold continuum of space/time/sex/death known as Cosmogony,and used his newfound sorcerous powers to construct his orrery and conquer the human race...

Like a chrononaut, the Orrery Man drifted through his own memories until his devotees had completed their tasks, then emerged from the replica of Saturn and feverishly sculpted a photorealistic, meticulous, working model of the Alpha Centauri System.

*

The minions of the Orrery Man were gathered in the large basilica at the rear of the spaceship, resting and celebrating after their hours of toil. Mons, Warlord of the Cyborg Corps, and Hades, Chief Pioneer of Necronautics, were sharing a bottle of neon absinthe. The maroon head of Mons had been outfitted with spikes like the mountains of Mars, and his testicles had been replaced with neuticles that were tiny sculptures of Deimos and Phobos. Hades' had been subjected to ancient headshrinking techniques and then turned into a living snowglobe, with a transparent body and skull through which his organs could be seen floating amidst flurries of dry ice.

Ouronos and Oceanus, the incestuous Overshamans of Astropharmaceutics, were sprawled upon the floor in a drugged, quasi-sentient torpor. Identical twins before suffering the Orrery Man's surgeries, their formerly matching heads and bodies were now grotesqueries of their namesake planets, with prosthetic rings like those of Kronos, but much thinner and lighter in color. The green smoke of cancer-curing cannabis and psychosis-curing opium billowed around them. Hookahs filled with liquid uranium and plutonium lay strewn around their bodies, along with empty vials of somnosthesia, the soporific which had been used to induce the mass coma of the human race. It was the tiny dropper of Lethe betwixt the brothers, however, which had induced their lucid hibernation. A liquefied black hole, a mere drop of Lethe was enough to repress a day's worth of memories. Two drops induced a fugue state. An overdose resulted in complete memory erasure, leaving the user in an eternally plant-like state of existential perception, with no connective thoughts or feelings to link experiences and sensations together.

In one corner of the room lay Hermes, King of Chronicity, inventor of the metaluminal/juxtatemporal space/time-drive which allowed the Psi-Orbitron to travel through the vacuums lying next to time at a speed far greater than that of light. Hermes was making love to his wife Cytherea, Queen of Neuralerotica and inventor of the tantra microchip. In yet another corner Gaiea, Mother of Biogenetics and one-time saviour of the Earth's environment, made love to her husband Kronos. A few feet away her moon-headed daughter, Luna, stroked the crater between her legs with two silver-gray fingers.

The Orrery Man entered the basilica. Paying no mind to the various debaucheries of his minions, he simply asked Ra for an updated chart of the Sirius system. From her table at the back of the room, where she binged on cocaine and studied her multitude of scientific tomes, she focused her eyes upon the grimoire the Orrery Man desired and, with the gravity of the Sun, telekinetically guided it through the air and into the waiting hand of her husband. The

Orrery Man closed his fist around the book, then turned and exited the room without a sound.

*

As the eons passed, the orrery grew decillions of times larger, as tall as it was wide, with billions of galaxies and googleplexes of stars, planets, and moons circumnavigating the planetarium, all connected by a labyrinth of catwalks, rampways, and scaffolding.The Psi-Orbitron had become so vast that it could only be navigated through the wormholes which now tunneled through it like alveolated nihilism. All of the tiny space-warps were replicas of actual wormholes, sculpted from white diamond and crystallized teleportation portals, and arranged throughout the orrery in the same locations as their cosmic counterparts. In addition to the wormholes, the Orrery Man had further augmented his masterpiece with quasars, pulsars, blazars, and collapsars. Nearly the entire universe was represented. The metaluminal/juxtatemporal space/time-drive of the Psi-Orbitron had allowed the Orrery Man to travel the byways of the cosmos for several trillennia, while a mere few millennia had passed in the tangible universe. Now, after epochs of labor, there was but one last set of celestial bodies to be added to the orrery.

The Orrery Man meditated inside a sphere of amethyst, ruby and hematite, a sculpture of a crimson and indigo planet from a recently-visited solar system. Deep in trance, the Orrery Man could feel the gravitational force of Omnigen, the supermassive black hole spinning at the nexus of the universe, calling to his soul.Omnigen was the source of the Big Bang, from which all of space and time had exploded in the meta-moment of genesis. Omnigen was also the destination of the Big Crunch, and would crush all space and time back into a singularity at the escha-moment of armageddon. In a synergic reflection of the cosmic life cycle, the primary celestial body of the universe would be the final effigy in his orrery.

The Orrery Man was stirred from his reveries by the sudden presence of his acolyte Mons, who had beamed himself across several miles of planetarium through a wormhole and was knocking upon the exterior of the sculpture.The red and purple planet burst like the orgasm of a vampire leviathan spreading across an ocean of nocturnium.

"Supreme Cosmogonarch," said Mons, kneeling and bowing his maroon, spiked head. The tip of the sculpture of Olympus Mons which had been screwed into his skull like an animal horn touched the ground as he knelt. His two scions, Deimos and Phobos, dropped to their knees behind him.

"The Omnigen system is within viewing range."

A surge of ecstasy blasted through the Orrery Man's brain.

"Prepare the Voyeur Dome and assemble the crew in the planetarium. Begin construction of the Omnigen system immediately after I beam down the first mnemograph, then prepare to awaken the human race. The time of the final ritual draws nigh. When I return, I shall assume my rightful place as the messiah of space/time/sex/death."

*

The Orrery Man reclined in the Voyeur Dome in a state of sexual euphoria. Below him, at the center of the universe, spun the supermassive black hole Omnigen. Omnigen was orbited by seven black suns, each of which were orbited by seven black planets, each of which, in turn, were orbited by seven black moons. A sudden remembrance of obscure numerology ascended from the Orrery Man's subconscious, but uncharacteristically slipped back to the bottom of his brain just as quickly as it had risen.

The Stygian celestial bodies possessed just enough anti-gravity in their cores to keep them from crossing Omnigen's event horizon. When they inevitably did so, it would signal the end of the universe's expansion and the beginning of the Big Crunch. .

All three septets of celestial bodies were resonating with the seven chakras of the Orrery Man. His spine felt as though it had been transformed into the axis mundi of the universe as he meditated above the very spot where the Big Bang had initiated space and time. His rings, neuticles and pleasure beads were humming and vibrating.

Throughout the course of an orgasm that lasted seven hours, the Orrery Man beamed his photographic memories back to the Psi-Orbitron, where his acolytes received them and laid the groundwork for the completion of his mind-blowing, four-dimensional mandala.

*

The Orrery Man slowly walked amongst his sculptures of the Omnigen system, admiring his own handiwork. He had masterfully crafted the seven solar systems of the Omnigen system, and now had only to add a simulacrum of Omigen itself to his orrery. The final victory of art over science had been achieved. He was a visionary who had seen his own prestidigitations made manifest, a philosopher who had achieved eudaimonia. He had quantified the entire universe, and would now become the messiah of space/time/sex/death. The mega-moment to take his place at the nexus of his ultimate effigy of astrolatry had arrived.

Preparing to become one with his supernal temple of the almighty universe, the Orrery Man seated himself in the lotus position at the nexus of the planetarium, at the exact spot where the final sculpture, the sculpture of Omnigen, the primeval black hole at the center of the cosmos, was to be placed. After several hours of meditation he drifted into a lucid dream state, fantasizing about the ritual to come...

Between his folded legs a long, golden, gyroscopic spike was slowly spinning beneath his chin like a needle-shaped drill. The Orrery Man reached into the inner pockets of his cape, withdrew a neutronium machete, and slowly raised it to his throat. A tiny droplet of blood ran down the edge of the blade, like a freshly-skinned lamia crossing a Chinvat bridge...

Hermes suddenly burst through a space/time portal, his gray, metallic, wrinkled, beetled head bobbing upon his heaving shoulders.

"My lord," he said, rousing the Orrery Man from his reveries, "Omnigen is not a black hole."

*

The Orrery Man and Hermes entered the cockpit of the Psi-Orbitron. Hades and Charon were seated at the command console. Charon served as the Psi-Orbitron's pilot, guiding the vessel through space just like his mythological namesake had once been said to ferry the souls of the dead across the river Styx. Hades served as the navigator. Both were transfixed by the atramentous abyss beyond the console window.

The Orrery Man walked across the cockpit. "Speak," the Orrery Man demanded, looming over his acolytes.

"Supreme Cosmogonarch," said Hades, "forgive me, but Omnigen is not a black hole." He bowed the tiny snowglobe which had replaced his head. White flurries of dry ice dervished around his brain. "Tis a wormhole, my lord."

"It's too big to be a wormhole."

The sweet, cold, cyanogenic, comet-tail scent of cosmium/chronium drifted into the Orrery Man's lungs as Ra entered the chamber. She held the ship's main computer in the palm of her hand.

"The computer verifies the readings, my lord," said Ra, telekinetically sending the tiny machine across the room to her husband. "For lack of a better term... it's a supermassive wormhole."

The Orrery Man pondered the readings on the console, then looked directly into Omnigen itself with his meta-vision.

"A supermassive wormhole..." the Orrery Man mused, sexually mesmerized by the concept for a brief moment before once again assuming his imperious demeanor. "Where does it lead?"

"The sensors can't decipher its destination vector," replied Hades.

The Orrery Man paused for the briefest of moments, simultaneously calculating millions of equations in his mind before determining a course of action.

"Fly into it," the Orrery Man commanded Charon.

"Cosmogonarch?" Charon's voice quaked.

"Fly into it!" the Orrery Man yelled.

"Yes, Cosmogonarch."

Charon sailed the Psi-Orbitron into the Stygian depths of the wormhole like an astronaut psychopomp, an intergalactic doppelganger of his namesake. A raw, pulsating vacuum devoured the star-vessel, but the space-tunnel lacked the usual blackout of an interspatial void, for it was illuminated by a blinding white light at its terminus. As the Orrery Man and his minions soared through the wormhole, the sensations in their stomachs and souls were not of forward motion, but of ascension. They were floating upwards through the vibrating tunnel, upwards to the white light. It was as though the Psi-Orbitron were having a near-death experience, and they were all trapped inside it, like bacteria or parasites or embryos in the flesh of a comatose or dying saint, empathically and vicariously experiencing the epiphanies and thaumaturgical phenomena with their host.

The Psi-Orbitron re-emerged from the white hole like an entire universe turning itself inside-out. The Orrery Man and his acolytes gazed in wonder upon a vast and alien cosmos.

The blinding glow of a nearby sun forced the Orrery Man to recalibrate his meta-vision. He blinked and focused on the massive sphere of white fire. His psychic senses were vibrating like alarums. The celestial body was much too far away to appear as large and bright as it did.

"The mathematics of this universe are absurd," the Orrery Man said. "Ra, what are the computer-readings? How large is that star in front of us?"

"The computer can't quite decipher it, my lord...but it's vigintillions of light years long."

"It's bigger than a galaxy," the Orrery Man said incredulously. "How can a star be bigger than a galaxy? Hades, run a complete cosmographic analysis."

Hades pressed a series of buttons, then carefully studied the holographic, four-dimensional star-map that arose from the command console like a wraith. The chasms of his eyes grew wide, as did the eyes of the other scions.

"It's exactly like our universe," Charon stuttered in disbelief, "but infini..."

Before Charon could finish his blasphemous proclamation his severed head was flying across the room . As Charon's decapitated body slumped down in its chair and the back of the Orrery Man's fist reached the endpoint ofits lethal trajectory, Charon's head bounced off the far wall, leaving a stain like a red and black supernova in its wake, and fell to the floor.

The Orrery Man turned to Ra. "Gather the others and prepare the Voyeur Dome. I'll annihilate this riddle myself."

*

Another cosmos hung over the Orrery Man, googolplexes of times larger than the nanoverse he had previously inhabited. It was filled with planets the size of galaxies, and stars a million times brighter than the combined effulgence of every sun he had ever gazed upon.The albedo of a single moon outshone any star the

Orrery Man had ever seen. The zenith of the strange universe was comprised entirely of blinding white light, shining down over all of the celestial bodies. The nadir was lit only by the interdimensional portal, within which could be seen the entire universe from which he had come, like a tiny planetarium, or an astronomer's oubliette.

The Orrery Man's meta-vision flashed through the alien planets and stars. After twice sweeping his gaze across the bulging galaxies, the Orrery Man zeroed in on a group ofsmall objects floating amongst the white hole from which the Psi-Orbitron had arisen. They wore white robes, decorated with the same star-patterns as his own cape. Their heads were ringed like Saturn, only the rings were gold. The Saturn-headed creatures were fluttering around the white hole, gazing into the universe beyond it, the universe from which the Orrery Man had come. With the aid of astrolabes and abacuses, elaborate starcharts were being etched by the Saturnheads. Calculations were being made and zodiacs were being observed. Lessons were being learned.

As the Orrery Man's senses heightened, his ears suddenly began to ring, not with the familiar OM and the Music of the Spheres from his universe, but some strange combination of mellifluous mantras and harpstrings. Suddenly, the significance of the Omnigen System blasted his brain like a supernova. Seven suns, seven planets, seven moons...777...

The Orrery Man's eyes expanded like cannibalistic black holes gorging themselves on other collapsars. His gaze flashed frantically from tiny universe to massive universe, over and over, and then, suddenly, he found his eyes transfixed on the white light above, the omniscient, omnipotent, omnipathic white light above, and he realized that he did not possess the greatest orrery in the universe.He did not possess an orrery of the universe at all, only an orrery of an orrery. All of his eons of toil had been in vain, all of his dreams false prophecies, his very destiny a dead-end in a labyrinth of nullity, for the universe he had inhabited was not the universe at all, but God's orrery, a model of the real universe constructed by His omnipotent hands, far greater and larger than his, scaled to size and inhabited by sentient beings.The Orrery Man had only created a replica of a replica, a clone of a clone, a tertiary refraction of the true cosmos.He dropped to his knees and screamed, then began to weep and sob and shudder and babble and gibber, a failed messiah driven to insanity by his own disgrace, as the pure, invincible white light of God shone down like a spotlight over the wreckage ofhis mind and soul.

*

"Tis still an orrery of the universe, Cosmogonarch," said Hades. "Inferior only in size, if inferiority that be."

"God's orrery is not only superior in mass, you fool. It's scaled to perfection. It can be destroyed and remade at his whim. It can be replicated as often as He desires. It will exist for as long as He wills it. It's eternal and infinite." The Orrery Man fell to his knees as he spoke the accursed words he had forbidden as blasphemies. "Ah, my devotee, do not you comprehend the prime ratio of pleasure to pain, of enlightenment to ignorance, of omniscience to subjugation? Half the heaven is twice the hell!"

The Orrery Man grabbed Hades by the throat, stood, lifted him into the air, and began to strangle him. A few seconds later, the Orrery Man rammed his own skull into the snowglobe of Hades' head, smashing it into thousands of bloody shards. Hades' head exploded like a window through which a nephilim had been defenestrated. His brain landed atop the broken glass in one piece and continued to tremblefor several minutes, slowly twitching across the floor like the bloody, discarded vibrator of a gonorrhea-ridden cyborg succubus quarantined to eternal solitude upon an uninhabited Lazaret planet.

Hermes fled the cockpit as Ra screamed at the Orrery Man to stop. The Orrery Man dropped the decapitated corpse of Hades, turned, and backfisted her. Her head erupted with solar flares as she fell to her knees. He struck her again, then lifted her over his head and heaved her across the cockpit. She landed atop the command console. The Orrery Man pounced upon her like a panther and punched her in the clitoris, then drove his hand into her womb, his rings shredding her labia while her vaginal walls burned his arm like brimstone, and fistfucked her like a misogynistic, pugilistic, incubus cyborg inquisitor/alastor who had tracked Eve across the universe, hellbent on avenging the human race she had damned with her sins, and finally cornered her on an uncharted planet to exact long-sought sexual vengeance.

The Orrery Man felt something squirming against his fingers, something moist and sentient.He grabbed it and ripped his hand from Ra's womb. A bloody embryo quivered in his fist.

The Orrery Man roared and squeezed it to a pulp, letting the blood rain down over Ra's downcast face.

"Which one of my devotees has betrayed me?"

"None, my lord," she sobbed."I've known no other lover than you, and you've not touched me since the Grand Syzygy. I knew not that I was with child, and know not why or how..." Ra wept, tears of magma flowing from her sunspot eyes.

"If you didn't know you were with child, then why do you weep for it when it dies?"

"It was still my child...if only for a moment...you'll never understand, never comprehend..."

The Orrery Man grabbed her by the hair and dragged her through the ship to the Jewel Incubator. He ripped Eris free of Ceres and shoved Ceres' extended colon into Ra's vagina. Molten gems poured out and then hardened, filling her womb and hermetically sealing her vaginal entrance, forming an irremovable chastity device ofdiamonds, rubies, sapphires, and amethysts.

The Orrery Man stormed into the cabin of Kronos and Cytherea as they made love. He grabbed Kronos by the rings in his skull, yanking him free of Cytherea's womb and into the air. Kronos jabbered and denied the Orrery Man's accusations.

"Lies," roared the Orrery Man. "All lies. Betrayal. Mutiny. My devotees have turned against their god...". Like a living strappado device, the Orrery Man abruptly lowered Kronos to the floor. Still holding him by the rings in his skull, the Orrery Man suddenly twisted Kronos' head from his neck with one mighty, wrenching motion. As Cytherea screamed, the Orrery Man tossed the severed head of her lover into her lap and abandoned her to her agony.

The Orrery Man burst next into the bedchambers of Ouronos and Oceanus. Engaged in an act of tantric sodomy, with their backs to the door, neither one noticed his presence. The Orrery Man strode across the room, grabbed the part of Ouronos' ring that protruded from his forehead, and peeled his scalp from his skull. He yanked harder, until all the skin and flesh of Ouronos' head came off. His exposed brain pulsated and seemed to suckle upon the air.

Oceanus fell quivering into a corner as the Orrery Man stalked him. The Orrery Man lifted him to his feet by the rings and then yanked the rings downwards, ripping them from his skull and pulling them down around his neck. The Orrery Man's muscles bulged as he bent the neutronium rings like a garrote around Oceanus' throat. As he was strangling Oceanus with his own mutilated prosthetics, he noticed a bottle of Lethe amongst the various vials and drug paraphernalia lining the shelves of the chamber. He stared at it for several moments, then released Oceanus from his grip. Oceanus fell to his knees, coughing up blood.

The Orrery Man walked to the shelf and lifted the bottle of caliginous fluid. "Lethe," the Orrery Man said to himself. "With this Lethe I shall nullify my memory. I'll forget this megaverse ever existed."

The Orrery Man placed the bottle of Lethe in the inside pocket of his cape.

"Oceanus, tell Mons, Deimos, and Phobos to assume control of the cockpit, fly back through the wormhole, and set course for the edge of the universe." His voice was completely devoid of its usual, nearly-palpable mass, and the fury which had driven his rampage against the other males of the ship had suddenly dissolved. "Gather the other High Astrolaters and soak the entire ship with liquid chronium and cosmium. I want the Psi-Orbitron hermetically sealed. Nothing shall ever again enter or leave our sanctum. Have the scions awaken the human race, then detonate the hull of the ship. I want everyone gathered in the planetarium within the next one hundred hours. The final ritual shall proceed as planned, but must now be witnessed by all if I'm to retain any vestige of peace."

*

Over the eons, the Orrery Man had surgically altered the heads of every comatose human to resemble one of the alien planets he had discovered. Now, mankind awakened in shock and horror to its own mass-mutation. They screamed and wept as the High Astrolaters and their scions led them into the planetarium, driving them like a gargantuan herd of posthumans to a cannibal's slaughterhouse. Controlled by telepathic implants and bound by neutronium chains, protonium handcuffs, electronium fetters, bosonium collars, fermionium genital piercings, gravitonium mind-stabilizers and tachyonium soul-gibbets, the totality of mankind moved like beasts of burden through the orrery. A continuous, miles-long umbilical cord had been woven through the eyes, ears, noses, mouths, vaginas, anuses, and urethras of every man, woman, child, clone and cyborg, tying the entire human race into a single Gordian knot of living flesh.

The Orrery Man's High Astrolaters and their scions arranged the billions amongst the planets, telepathically commanding them to intersperse themselves throughout the orrery, close enough to its nexus to observe the final ritual. After positioning the human race they knelt before the freshly sculpted replica of Omnigen and awaited the emergence of the Orrery Man. A large, golden, gyroscopic contraption, surrounded by an impenetrable forcefield, spun slowly above the sphere of black diamond. On a platform beside it was a large bottle filled with liquid cosmium/chronium, over which the Orrery Man's cape had been partially laid.

After several hours, The Orrery Man emerged. The giant sphere of black diamond opened in four pieces, like the cloaca of Kali dropping the dark underworlds of Erebus and Tartarus into the Abyss at the bottom of the universe. Once it had completely opened, the replica of Omnigen disintegrated into black diamond-dust.

The Orrery Man picked up the vial of cosmium/chronium, placed it in Ra's mouth, and forcibly closed her flaming jaws around it. Glass shattered and black spit bubbled from her lips as she reflexively swallowed the dark, viscous fluid. The contents of the vial poured down her throat, into her stomach, and through the umbilical cords connecting her to the rest of the High Astrolaters. Gradually, the liquid space/time would saturate the entire human race, making them immortal, allowing them to break free from the umbilical cords and the other devices which bound them, forcing them to spend the rest of existence within his idol of the cosmos, imprisoned in the custom-made heaven of their master.

The Orrery Man donned his cape, then lowered the gyroscope around his head. Long golden spikes extended from the inner ring of the device and pierced his skull, holding his head in place. He removed the vial of Lethe from one of the inner pockets of his cape. After drinking the mind-cleansing potion, the Orrery Man pulled a machete from his other pocket, raised it to his neck, and slit his own throat repeatedly, using the knife like a hacksaw to cut through tendons and ligaments, jugular veins and carotid arteries, esophagus and trachea, and, finally, cervix and spinal cord. Although the sacred ritual of self-decapitation had taken on the pall of seppuku, the Orrery Man still felt a tiny surge of ecstasy, for he knew that the Lethe was saturating his brain, and he would never again be burdened with the knowledge that his destiny had been a perverted mutation and his philosophies a mass illusion.

Through his decapitory hari-kari the Orrery Man slowly rid himself of his atavistic limbs and his human, all too human torso. As his body fell away, the gyroscope lifted his severed head into the air. Spinning and tilting and flipping over, the device let him observe his orrery from every angle. He could still taste the Lethe on his tongue. It tasted sweet, sweet like the apples of Eden. His mind, dripping with Lethe, would never remember the other universe, the real universe. Protected by the forcefield surrounding the gyroscopic contraption, his severed head would spin in the nexus of his beloved orrery forever, and never again would he know that his life's mission had been an apocalyptic failure.

As the Orrery Man waited for the Lethe to cleanse his tormentous memories, he recognized the familiar scent of cyanide, rising like smoke from his tongue and penetrating his mucous membranes. It was the scent of raw fruit, the scent of cyanide, the scent of a comet, the scent of Ra...

It was the scent of cosmium/chronium.

As his head began to swell and mutate, like the skull of one of his minions, the Orrery Man screamed in agony. The raw stuff of space and time coursed up and down his brain stem like an amphisbenic cataract. He looked out over the faces of his High Astrolaters. They were completely devoid of expression, their eyes like voids and vacuums. The rest of the human race, in all their billions, bore the same, nullity-like faces, the faces of Lethean zombies.

Ra slipped free of her bondage devices. As she began to wander about, a vial filled with black liquid, identical to the vial which the Orrery Man had just drank, slowly emerged from her rectum. It descended by tiny degrees, then fell to the floor and shattered. Amidst the broken glass, apuddle of inky fluid pooled about Ra's feet like the necrotic amnion of an anal birth. The Orrery Man immediately recognized the inky fluid as Lethe, and realized that Ra had used her telekinetic powers to replace the vial of Lethe in the pocket of his cape with a vial of cosmium and chronium. It was liquid space/time, not Lethe, which the Orrery Man had ingested.

As the Orrery Man continued to scream, his brain bulged as though with some cerebral and neurological strain of elephantiasis. All of mankind now wandered through the orrery, oblivious to the spinning planets, the godlike craftsmanship, the eons of labor it took to construct it. Their minds were empty, too empty to ever comprehend the theories he had proven and disproven, too hollowed-out to even conceive of the concepts of eternity and infinity, too vacuous to appreciate his genius and dominance. The human race had transformed into the mindless acolytes of nullity which the Orrery Man had always perceived them to be.

As the hours passed, his head grew until it was three times the size of the largest stars in his orrery, dislodging and destroying the nearby sculptures.Enraged, the Orrery Man wrapped his now-anaconda sized tongue around Ra as she wandered by and pulled her into his mouth, enwombing her like the black hole of her own vagina, even as her burning flesh glowed inside him like his own comet-penis. His skull continued to spin and roll inside the gyroscope, as though it had been impaled on an elaborate spit and was slowly roasting over the fires of Gehenna. The gyroscope was enlarging along with it, imbued with the same cosmium and chronium that flowed through the Orrery Man's flesh.

With his metascopic vision he could see all the hand-made galaxies, spinning lazily around one another as though in some combination of mating ritual and danse macabre. Like God overlooking all of Creation, the Orrery Man gazed upon his insignificant microverse and the humans wandering through it like walking vegetables. Mentally and spiritually, the human race had become extinct, abandoning the Orrery Man to his custom-made Malebolge. They would never appreciate his deification, for they were as numb and mindless as broken androids, and would do nought but venture aimlessly through his psuedoverse until the end of time.

As the eons passed, the Orrery Man's skull continued to expand like the black hole it had symbolized for so long, destroying everything in its path, swelling until it crushed the entire human race into a dripping, incarnadine ichor against the walls of the planetarium, then bursting from the Psi-Orbitron and ejecting through the void until it reached the very rim of space and time, and there he remained, a sentient planet circumnavigating the cosmos in a decaying orbit, a living incarnation of a celestial body, an unwilling avatar of the cosmos whose worship had delivered him to this hyperkarmic doom. The Orrery Man spun in agony, for epoch upon epoch, until the Big Crunch began. The death of space and time swirled him in a downward spiral the size of a trillion galaxies, faster and faster, until kalpas became nanoseconds and parsecs became nanometers, and the totality of everything was vacuumed into the nexus of armageddon. The Orrery Man closed his eyes and screamed as the abyss of Omigen sucked his severed head back into the real universe, the infinitely divisible heaven of the real universe which would eternally multiply his exponential hell.

The Ascent to Forever

1

The angel and demon made love beneath the purple starlit skies. The clouds before the moon thinned and parted, allowing it to splendidly spotlight their forbidden love. Their bodies shimmered with every delicate motion, every touch and kiss glowing through the surrounding purple nocturne. Cavyn stroked Lyssa's golden hair with his clawed hand as he entered her gently trembling skin.

The night was untouched by their innocence; as untouched as it was by the dark clouds which drifted through its warm shroud; as untouched as it would have been by Cavyn and Lyssa's births, deaths, or rebirths. Lyssa noticed this with beautiful eyes widened, gazing upwards as if entranced. It did not disturb her. She smiled at Cavyn. He returned her kiss with a faintly curling lip. His eyes were flashing bloodshot, the way they did in battle. He noticed, also, the silent night, untouched by the beauty of their first love. It did not disturb him either.

Together, they closed their eyes. Her goodness, his evil, the very things which separated Lyssa and Cavyn and had forbidden them from one another's embrace, now seemed to melt together. Now their exile became real, their true freedom attained, in their lovemaking. Virginity lost, Lyssa could never return to her people, would never be accepted as an angel again, and Cavyn would be executed by his demon brethren should they learn of his heresy. Now, it was as though they were the only two spirits in the Infiniverse.

A gentle trickle of crimson ran down Lyssa's thigh as their movements became one. They surrendered their innocence together. It was a moment in time they shared, a moment in time all their own. The night was untouched by this also. This time, they did notice.

2

Lyssa smiled as, hand in hand, she and Cavyn soared through the airy morning. Cavyn's great ebon wings wrapped playful shadows around Lyssa's body, which her small wings of creamy gold returned with gentle glitterings, falling lightly upon his dark skin, illuminating it for the barest moments, then sparkling once more and disappearing. The skies were cool and soothing to their slowly softening wings. Lyssa and Cavyn had chosen to make their exile by foot rather than flight, for fear of being sighted by either of their peoples. Their wings had grown tense and stiff throughout their journey, but had nearly regained their full strength and rhythm now, and Lyssa and Cavyn flew together in sweeping ellipses and circles, rising and falling in dizzying spins, their wings beating together in perfect synchronicity throughout their whimsical flight.

The clouds above shimmered in the dawn's light, forming prisms that criss-crossed Lyssa and Cavyn's darting bodies with sparkling silvers and immaculate golds, ashen blues and scintillant pinks and damson shades of violet. The colors flashed and faded and burst and melted, forever changing, never growing still. Lyssa and Cavyn, nearly out of breath, ceased their flight and hovered together in the tinctured sunlight, shivering against one another's naked bodies. Cavyn's midnight hair floated on the anxious air, brushing against Lyssa's beautiful face.

Together they gazed upon the sweep of the forest. Its murmuring trees stretched to every horizon, glowing with deep, reflective greens as they absorbed the light of the rising sun and brought the forest its first warmth of the morning. The forest was protective and mothering to everything within its trees, from the arboreal dragons which wandered its darkest passages, to the unicorns that fled from even the gentlest of noises, to the giant butterflies that danced in dappled sunlight around brightly colored flowers which brought euphoria, sleep, and death to those who breathed their perfumes for too long. Lyssa and Cavyn had found the forest just as accepting when they had fled through it, and it seemed strange to gaze upon it from above . The spring which they had followed for the last few days seemed still from this height, but they knew that it was not, for they could hear its sparkling whisper as it became a small but captivating waterfall flowing into a bubbling pond. Just below lay the meadow where they had made love the previous night, crystalled with dew and barely recognizable now.

Lyssa pointed in the direction of her homeland, then Cavyn's, both far beyond their sight even from this height. She did this with a sorrow in her eyes that held no regret, and Cavyn followed her gesture with a similar expression. Though both longed for their childhoods at this moment, neither longed for their races. They understood this about each other, intuitively and empathically, with no need to speak of it.

"It's so cold up here."

Lyssa's voice faded as gently as a shadow. Dawn had brought a curling wind as well as the sun, furthering the chill they already felt from their height.

Cavyn gripped Lyssa's silken, trembling hand and they flew directly, gracefully upward, through the brightly swirling clouds, far above the wind. They were bathed now in warm sunlight, their bodies golden against the azure skies that deepened into darker cerulean shades as the sun rose even higher. Their eyes flickered in the caressing beams, as did the many scars on both their bodies, not usually visible except in direct, blinding light. They weren't unsightly scars, and neither gave much attention to them. Some they had given to one another. Others they couldn't remember anything about. All were pale and of a faintly pink hue, the type which, in normal light, could be seen only by chance; never when looked for.

Cavyn's slightly slanted eyes, dark with melancholia and sensuality, gazed upon a scar gleaming on Lyssa's thigh, and he traced its path with one clawed finger. Lyssa smiled, caressing his face as his hand wandered past the scar. For a brief hour, they kissed and stroked one another's silken skin, hovering in one another's arms beneath the sighing skies.

The winds had grown stronger, carrying the iridescent clouds on jetstreams of auroras and rainbows. The winds were blowing in the direction of Lyssa and Cavyn's flight, and it occurred to Lyssa and Cavyn that they could ride the clouds into another dimension. Tenderly, Cavyn lay Lyssa down upon the blue-pink mists of the largest one, then landed softly atop her, entering her skin as he did so.

In a flash of sunlight, upon their coasting cloud, they began to make love again. Lyssa reached like a small child into the wispy cloud as they did so, smiling at its softness. Their silhouettes were weak against the cloud, and became as blue and pink as it, vague and beautiful. The soft mists contoured around their bodies, gently embracing them as they sank down into its billowy blanket.

The blue-pink cloud carried them swiftly over the forest, shy unicorns and dancing centaurs staring upwards upon the lovers with wide eyes as it did so, enchanted by their sweet innocence. Lyssa and Cavyn looked sometimes upon them as they kissed, with as much fascination and wonder as they. Deeper within the forest they glimpsed a flock of beautiful birds whose feathers formed deep mazy patterns that immediately dissipated when glanced at, as if they were eternally disappearing. The birds flew alongside Lyssa and Cavyn's cloud, and sometimes landed upon it, allowing Lyssa and Cavyn to touch their feathers before being frightened away by the occasional pegasus which came to nuzzle Lyssa's hand.

Their lovemaking lasted throughout the entire day, as their cloud carried them deeper into the forest, agleam with diamond sparklings as the sun reached its zenith, then beginning to darken with the stirrings of another purple evening. Lyssa and Cavyn kissed as their cloud carried them into the next plane, watching with some sadness the trees fading beneath them, and the purple night in which they had first loved one another suddenly blackening behind them, then disappearing almost violently.

3

Darkness surrounded Cavyn's mind as he descended into sorcerous meditation. Within the sable silence he imagined a perfect image of himself, every rippling of his muscles, every tapering of his face. He could feel God's presence, raw, bulging, beyond and within him, electrifying the conduit of his flesh with terrifying energies.

Sitting beside him, Lyssa empathically knew the agonies of her soulmate. She had abandoned prayer as a cherub, and sorcery as a seraph, because of her fear of God. Unlike Cavyn, she sometimes felt God's presence when she did not wish to.

The spell was rapidly coalescing now, and something like nausea was creeping into Cavyn's chest. A quick paranoia wove through his mind, and with it, a burning sensation, as if he and Lyssa had become engulfed in flame, dying in one another's arms, enjoying one last pleasure as their flesh melted together.

Cavyn's eyes flashed open as his spell transported Lyssa and him into another plane. The Abyss surrounded them, alive with writhing shadows, crawling with reeking smoke, and moist, moist not like a cave or a fog, but moist like a body.

They began to float within the Abyss, their hearts numbed by their strange driftings. Whether they were rising or falling, they could not tell. Lyssa beat her wings once, instinctively, before Cavyn quickly stifled her. Their motions were dreamlike in the thick air.

"Don't resist," Cavyn explained with his smooth voice. His words were soft and quiet, nearly lost in the encompassing silence. "You must let the Abyss guide you. If you try to guide yourself, you will become lost."

As Cavyn alluded to, the Abyss was teeming with confused souls who had become disoriented within its infinite blackness, creatures who had been trapped for so long that their eyes had become shrunken and pale, and their flesh hung in tendrils from their skeletons. Others had taken refuge in the crevices which lined it and never emerged, forever gazing from their sanctuaries with glowing eyes, their sanity sacrificed to the Abyss.

Cavyn wrapped his arms tightly around Lyssa's torso. With Lyssa secure in his embrace, Cavyn guided the two of them through the encompassing shadows and voids. The Abyss was a nexus of planes, the omphalos of the Infiniverse. It was also something of a hybrid reality, simultaneously physical and spiritual.Its very duality made the Abyss dangerous, dangerous in its confusing nature, and hated by both materialists and spiritualists alike. However, it was also a pathway between dimensions, the quickest way to traverse the planes of the Infiniverse for those skilled enough to navigate it.Cavyn knew that it was the surest way for he and Lyssa to continue their escape, and had not entered it sooner only because his people traversed it frequently, and he had wished to enter it at a point far from his homeland.

Lyssa was cautious of her eerie environs, and Cavyn smiled to ease her trepidation, his shadowed, arching smile that was mysterious without being frightening. Lyssa returned his smile as Cavyn began to tell her the history and mythology of the Abyss, to distract her from the very thing of which he spoke . He explained that some felt there where many Abysses, while others felt there was but one continuous Abyss, running to every plane. Some felt the Abyss would one day absorb the entire Infiniverse, while others stated that if one were to travel to the Abyss's very end, they would discover Hell.

Their minds were now beginning to empty as they floated, emptied by the enwombing silences and darknesses, the surreal peace of the Abyss, bringing the forced meditation which was another of the Abyss's dangers.

A sweet fragrance melted in the air as they drifted through a narrow, shadowy corridor. A golden flower, beautiful and roselike but infinitely more layered, stretched beneath a dank orifice upon the black wall. Lyssa gasped and showed Cavyn, who immediately glided over to it. Lyssa grasped it gently, and it seemed to lift gratefully into her hand. She smiled, and placed it in her hair as Cavyn resumed their flight.

Lyssa's gaze slowly filled with horror as they floated onwards, her innocent blue eyes stunned by the grotesque, twisted creatures which lurked in the shadows, some relatives of Cavyn's race. Cavyn's touch reassured her, however, and she knew he was accustomed to the Abyss's dark ways. He continued smiling as he guided her through it , feeding her its strange berries and showing her its every curiosity.

The Abyss widened once again as they drifted, kissing and embracing, into a more populated area. Bats flew all around them, raping and murdering one another, spilling their dank crimson blood across the darkness, to float and whisk and separate upon the surging air. An uncolored, nearly translucent creature was floating near to them. His limbs were hideously stunted, and he had only wrinkled skin and white hairs where his eyes should have been. Cavyn recognized him immediately as one who had stayed too long within the Abyss, one who had been blinded and aged beyond death by it, one who had become so adapted and acclimated to it that he would actually die if he ever found his way out. He was reaching toward Lyssa with a gnarled hand, cackling as he did so.

Cavyn's hand shot out in a blur. Even within the thick and stifling atmosphere of the Abyss his single strike was too fast to be seen. The mutated creature howled as blood floated from his face in four sheets, and immediately retreated.

Lyssa gasped and looked away, with sympathy for the mutant, but knowing that his intent had been harmful or Cavyn would not have struck him. He had probably never encountered anything like her within this never-ending pit.Lyssa suddenly realized that she was the first angel to ever travel the Abyss, and became uneasy with the thought. She did not belong here.

Cavyn continued to guide their driftings, flowing with the Abyss as he used to with his demon brothers so long ago, in curious youthful explorations or sadistic hunts for lost souls and mutants to battle and torture. They had reached the place where Cavyn intended to disembark, but he was now driven to continue, to travel further within the Abyss, to planes as far away from their homelands as possible.

More sickly, diseased creatures were confronting Lyssa now, hypnotized by her angel's eyes, her beautiful face, her glimmering wings. They implored her with twisted, gaping mouths, drooling blood and pus that lingered in the murky air. Cavyn slashed each one to pieces before their decaying fingers touched her skin.

Lyssa closed her eyes, fearful of the creatures and the dizzying way in which she and Cavyn now floated through the Abyss. Cavyn's eyes were dark red, bloodshot nearly to blackness. His lip curled determinedly as they traveled deeper still into the Abyss.

More creatures approached Lyssa, and were instantly maimed by Cavyn. They seemed to be coming faster now, and in greater numbers, swirling relentlessly around the two of them. Cavyn's heart was thundering; Lyssa could feel it in her spine. She closed her eyes again as the air seemed to pour around her, wondering if they would ever escape the Abyss. She could feel God haunting her, and thought with a silent gasp thatperhaps not Hell, but God, lay at the Abyss's end, waiting to take their souls.

Entrances to a myriad of planes flashed before Cavyn's eyes. They flickered and taunted him, but he could not bring himself to leave the Abyss for any of them. He floated to one, peering upon its vast, frigid wasteland. He began to pass their bodies through its entrance, then paused, suspended halfway between the Abyss and the wintry plane. With a snarling lip, he reentered the Abyss.

Lyssa was shivering now, wanting only to escape. She wondered if Cavyn felt secure here, if his homeland were similar to this. She knew that she would die here if she ever came alone, and so would every other angel who dared to do so. This thought brought her a knifing fear of Cavyn's evil race.

Cavyn hovered again upon the edge of a plane. This one was warmer than the other, bathing in sunlight. It smelled of trees and long, wondrous summers, of blooming poppies and exquisite skies. The summers of Cavyn's homeland had been like these, and memories flooded his mind, memories both pleasant and hateful. He withdrew instantly from the plane, tangled with the rushings of memories he had so delicately hidden. He hoped Lyssa had not noticed the summer of this plane which was so like their own.

Cavyn returned to his mad floatings, half-entering countless planes, only to retreat for vague reasons, all the while slashing at Lyssa's admirers. His eyes were bloodshot and effulgent, dangerously driven. Lyssa noticed that some of the attacking creatures possessed crimson eyes as well, and shuddered as she likened them to Cavyn's, thinking of his relation to these evil cousins of his which he now battled. In their love, Lyssa no longer thought of Cavyn as a demon, nor of herself as an angel, and had nearly forgotten the hatred of their two races. These separations returned to her now, however, and she feared Cavyn would become possessed by this place. Stark images gripped her, of Cavyn attacking her with his glinting claws, the way he now attacked the creatures which came too near her, and of her and Cavyn becoming lost in the Abyss, mutating like the hideous creatures, remaining together as they decayed until they finally succumbed to their angel and demon natures and murdered their sweet love. Lyssa shuddered, and swore to herself to love Cavyn forever, no matter what his evils brought her, no matter how primitive and insane the Abyss might make them.

The Abyss swarmed and breathed, and seemed to multiply. It fueled fear and obsession alike, a drop at a time, with maddening measure. It attacked them on both physical and spiritual levels. It was a haunting glimpse of the world beyond death, a terrible torture to the physical body, ultimately disorienting the entire soul, dismantling the spirit piece by piece and forcing them to gaze with writhing inner eyes upon the wreckage of the very stuff they were made of.

Lyssa screamed. Cavyn snarled and, with a flash of his bloodshot eyes, suppressed his distorted mind. He focused his power as a giant, festering creature flew towards them, a gargantuan monster seemingly composed of hundreds of spiders and scorpions that had been packed together into one seething mating ball. It reached with a multitude of ragged pincers for Lyssa's breasts and vagina. A great burst of flame then ignited the Abyss, shriveling every creature within its radius and exploding the monstrosity. As he cast the spell, Cavyn backed into a nearby entrance to another plane. The putrid, massing smoke of his pyromancy warped Lyssa's scream, clenching Cavyn's heart and echoing its every note throughout the dark halls of the Abyss.

*

Lyssa opened her eyes and met Cavyn's tender gaze. They had tumbled in each other's arms into another dimension, and lay now upon the gossamer grasses of a redly sunlit hill. She sighed and placed her head upon his chest, warmed and consumed and relieved by the love in his eyes. Cavyn stroked her damp hair, and removed the golden rose. It had died in the passing from the Abyss, and lay twitching and oozing. Cavyn closed his hand over it, crumbling it to a fine dust. It turned the still air around them a pale shade of gold as it disintegrated, hypnotically perfuming Lyssa's exhausted body with its dying breath.

4

Lyssa awoke one morning from a dream she could not recall, but which had imbued her heart with a longing and a sorrow. Cavyn slept still, motionless except for the rhythmic risings of his muscular chest. They had passed through many planes, and were now in the midst of a lush world of great oceans and tranquil lakes, The Graveyard Of Every Tear Ever Cried.

Lyssa rose and made her way to the small pool in which they had bathed the previous night. She sat upon the grassy edge, her feet touching the water, warmed and caressed by the bubbling hotsprings. Brightly colored fish played in the water, creating proud fountains anda mild tide, and became mesmerized by Lyssa's reflection when they swam near her.

A droplet of blood ran down Lyssa's shoulder, where Cavyn's claw had scratched her, and another down her thigh, as her body was still accustomed to virginity. She had found both wounds pleasurable during their lovemaking, and neither disturbed her now. Her scars had grown somewhat darker, crimson and brooding purple, and she noticed this with some distress. She had watched Cavyn's deepen throughout their lovemakings, and had imagined that hers had also, but had not expected the darkenings to remain. She gazed upon them, one at a time. She had forgotten she had so many.

Her beautiful, sad eyes lingered upon the scar on her wrist, the only scar she had given herself. She thought about her suicide attempt, and her and Cavyn's exile, and wondered just how similar the two were.

Lyssa constricted with the touch of Cavyn's lips upon her neck. He still possessed the stalking skills of a demon; she hadn't heard any part of his approach. He smiled as he sat beside her, though immediately sensing her sorrow.He, too, had had troubled dreams, though not as real as hers. They sat in silence for several moments, watching the opposite shore.

"Have you ever wanted to die?"

Cavyn's voice was as delicate as a whisper, though he spoke aloud.

Lyssa wondered if, somewhere, Cavyn knew her thoughts. She was enchanted by the notion, not unfearingly.

"No."

She paused.

" I just didn't want to live."

Cavyn cradled her head to his chest andkissed her once. They remained in silence for some time, seized by black thoughts. They were learning a despair along with their love for one another, and over the next few weeks, they gradually learned to combine the two.

5

Blood covered and warmed their bodies, protecting them from the cold of the snowstorm above. Blood made a sucking noise when their bodies came together, and again when they parted. Blood ran from old and new wounds alike, drawn by claws and teeth, stone daggers and roses' thorns, and vines and lianas used as whips.

Lyssa kissed Cavyn's chest, tasting his blood upon her tongue. It was thicker than hers, but just as sweet. She wrapped her arms around his neck as he rubbed his penis in a wound upon her thigh, spreading his black semen within it. Their scars were pulsing, and seemed to shift in their beds, exalting in Lyssa and Cavyn's newfound form of lovemaking.

Lyssa opened Cavyn's flesh with her dagger, then healed it with her angel's hand, then slashed it once again. Cavyn shuddered while she repeated this act, continually, over and over for several minutes. Somehow, both the sting of thedagger and the soft caress of her healing hand seemed a relief. He shredded her back with his claws as she did this, with all the glee he had known in battle, though taking care not to wound her too deeply.

The snow came now in violent torrents, irritating their cuts, melting into them and allowing them to bleed more freely. The snow was soft and neither warm nor cold as itmelted upon them, relaxing their muscles and bringing them strength. Cavyn kissed away the snowflakes on Lyssa's face and neck. Peals of thunder, each building on the previous, rang out with a macabre ecstasy, shaking their bodies and bringing a gentle vertigo.

Lightning arched across the sky. Illumination came screamingly to this sunless plane, briefly severing the eternal night and seeming to shrivel the dark, snowed ground beneath it. The sudden light gave Lyssa and Cavyn their first glimpse of their surroundings, before seen only by faint starlight. Cavyn entered Lyssa's body as another blast of lighting tore the skies. Their scars perfectly imitated its near-white golden hue, and seemed enormous throughout the lightning's reign. Lyssa was beautiful in the violent light, her damp hair sparkling with snow-diamonds.

Their blood ran together and into each others bodies as they made love. Every wound seemed alive, as imploring as it had been when freshly carved. Orgasm came quickly, and lasted many moments, for time was unusual within the umbrousplane known as The Winters Of Pleasure And Pain.

They lay in one another's embrace for many moments, massaged by the snow which now fell gently across them. As Lyssa removed her arm from Cavyn's neck, she gaspedwhen she saw what it had left. The scar on her wrist, which she had created as a child with her mother's knife, was firmly implanted upon Cavyn's throat. She knew it instantly, for she knew every edge of that scar, every discoloration. Upon her wrist, where the scar had lain just moments earlier, was white, undistorted flesh.

Cavyn only smiled when she showed him, accepting it as a gift of love. Both had observed the strange nature of their scars throughout the last weeks, and Lyssa took it, also, as a giving of herself, and secretly, asa symbol of their new life.

Neither spoke again that night, but remained in one another's arms, lovingly pondering the scar's movement.The soft sounds of the falling snow tenderly lulled them to sleep, and thankfully took the place of dreams.

6

Lyssa and Cavyn walked hand in hand, sometimes gliding, through the splendid wreckage strewn throughout The Floating Gardens Of The Abandoned Heaven. It had been centuries since God had left the souls of this once-great paradise to live their afterlives in misery and perpetual waste. A few half-torn towers remained, as well as some broken halls of what had once been vast palaces, their colors as soft and unfading as the petals of amaranthine flowers, even in decay. The debris lay upon the lush ground like dead bodies, dignified in its destruction. Twisting gold stairways and perfectly tapered spires spoke of ancient and intricate architectures, now forever lost.

The gardens grew around the ruins in comfort, completely unaffected, in colors too deep to fully comprehend, a wild mixture of infinite flowers that grew in harmony with one another, teeming with butterflies whose wings' bright patterns changed like kaleidoscopic mandalas before Lyssa and Cavyn's unbelieving eyes. Most breathtaking of all were the dreamlike cycles of the gardens, which carried Lyssa and Cavyn even as they flew amongst them. The entire fallen paradise floated and drifted, rising and falling andcircling, continually separating in new places and rejoining in others, as smoothly as the imagery of a dream.

"This place must have been beautiful, to be so lovely even in ruin." Lyssa spoke in a whisper, as if fearful of further torturing the gardens.

"Perhaps it is more beautiful in ruin, and that is why it fell." Cavyn's reply was spoken in a whisper, as well.

The shimmering palaces, though demolished, were full of life, as Lyssa and Cavyn soon discovered. Humans like they, though pale and bent, still wandered the caved-in chambers, with movements as fluid as the garden's own. They seemed sick and half-starved, and their forlorn eyes looked upon Lyssa andCavyn without emotion, and but briefly, before they returned to their travels. They were haunted by memories of their former heaven, and seemed to be always searching, though what they searched for was unclear, and they did not themselves seem to know. They communicated in whispers, but were mostly alone, and paused their hopeless quests frequently to eat of the garden's sweet fruits and bathe in its many-colored fountains.

Lyssa and Cavyn explored the forgotten heaven for some time, and became saddened for its disgraced beauty. Sometimes they made attempts to talk with the sad creatures, but they seemed unable to understand, or did not care to. A few spoke of other heavens, perhaps wishing to escape to them, or speaking of God's forsaking of their heaven for newly created afterlives.

Many made love with empty eyes, in flowerbeds and gurgling baths, often switching partners or becoming separated by the garden's gentle breakages. They never seemedto receive any pleasure from their lovemaking. Sometimes there were great orgies, which Lyssa and Cavyn were often invited to join, but refused with curious mouths. The motions of the creatures were weak and uneven, and their lovemaking went without kisses or embraces. It was merely a sweet remembrance for them now, which brought an end to the encompassing ennui and aided the spreading of their vast and numerous diseases, one of which, each hoped, might put an end to their suffering.

Some lay motionless throughout the lush grounds, pretending to be dead, hoping that if they pretended long enough, their wish would be delivered. Many had lost all sanity in doing this, and had come to believe their deaths true, laying starved and decrepit, barely breathing, beneath their blanketing fantasies. They paid no heed to Lyssa and Cavyn, and were senseless to flowers which fell upon them from gardens floating above, or the nudgings of other lost souls around them.

Lyssa and Cavyn observed the forsaken heaven quietly, despairing for its damned inhabitants but likewise enthralled by its beauty. They flew on, pondering God's abandonment of the paradise and the terrible afterlife of its people, an afterlife which could not be escaped. Perhaps the wretched souls were now beyond death, having perished once in coming here. Perhaps they could die but once, and were now doomed to eternal melancholy within the floating gardens.

Further within the plane, Lyssa and Cavyn received a glimpse of the ruined heaven's future. At some spots, the trees were dead and flaking, the flowers putrid and rotted. It seemed that the garden itself was capable of dying, and its inhabitants would eventually be forced to live upon its dank corpse, its every fruit soured, its every perfume nauseating, coated with layers of filth and disease.

Lyssa and Cavyn flew immediately from the blackened foliage, soaring now above the heaven. The sun was rich and golden, and melted into Lyssa's hair, which was the exact hue of its effulgent beams. Lyssa thought with a sigh that the sun, too, would one day blacken over the gardens, its rays becoming unbearably warm, or perhaps frozen and clenching. Lyssa and Cavyn grasped one another as they flew on.

Theynow ascended the tiers of a hanging garden, an oblivion of color and perfume which writhed and swayed about them. Between the embracing midst of flowers at the hanging garden's zenith sat a woman, legs folded in the lotus position, deep in meditation. Her body was mutilated, torn apart by her own hands in a desperate hope for death, and her skeleton flashed white in several areas. She was blind by her own hand, but sensed Lyssa and Cavyn's presence and gestured to them. She had severed her own tongue, so she dipped her fingers into an open wound on her breast and scrawled a message in blood on her thigh.

"Help me."

Lyssa kneeled beside her and healed her wounds and illnesses as best she could, warmth radiating from her soft white hands. The woman remained tattered, but was assuaged of her pain and no longer crippled. Her tongue had grown back.

"Why did you do this to yourself?" Lyssa asked as she passed her hands across the woman.

"I could no longer bear to see my heaven wither before me. I was once a great sorceress, and felt sure that I could find some salvation through self-mutilation. Perhaps I was merely imitating the destruction of my beloved gardens," she said, gesturing across her wounded body, and chuckling weakly as she spoke. "I think it was for the best, after all. Without eyes, you cannot weep. Without a tongue, you cannot scream. Without flesh, you cannot bleed. Without a heart, you cannot dream."

The woman sighed as Lyssa ended her healings, restored to mobility and sanity. She turned her blind eyes toward Cavyn, and her voice cracked, "I've been waiting for you."

She stretched her newly healed body, re-exploring it. For the first time in centuries, her heart beat again. Now that she had been resurrected, she had one more imploring.

"Kill me."

She reached out for Cavyn with one scarred hand, still radiant with the energy of Lyssa's healing.

"You are healed," Lyssa said, her voice sad and full of wonder. "Why now do you wish to die?"

"There is a peace, as delicate and balanced as you two lovers. O, you are the highest equilibrium, a peace encompassing more than any other. I too, require peace, within my body and my soul. As I lived in mutilation, I must now die with my body restored."

"You're rambling in your senescence," Cavyn said.

"On the contrary. It took the healing powers of your angelic soulmate to restore my sanity and I realize now that I and my gardens number among the damned. There is no hope whatsoever, for either of us."

"The dead cannot die again. None have died here for centuries, and never will."

Cavyn spoke intently. He had been pondering this since their arrival in the floating gardens.

"If any can commit murder in a heaven, it is you, my fair demon. Your peace with your angel lover gives you more power than you know. You must try. I will help you."

Cavyn closed his eyes, against Lyssa's pleading wishes, and drew upon his evils. He would have to nullify the woman, completely and utterly destroy her soul. It was a simple matter of logic, as afterlives cannot have their own afterlives. Breathing deeply, Cavyn channeled God and cast the nullification spell. The woman began to die immediately, her spirit gradually being erased from the Infiniverse. Her death was a slow one, but Cavyn was able to deliver it to her.

She spoke to them as she faded, telling them of all the former glory of the heaven, how it had been blessed by God, and how she had been a sorceress and a sibyl and a prophet before she losing her powers to the decay. She had regained many of her powers through Lyssa's healing, and demonstrated them now, in a continuous, raving manner.

The woman's mind was expanding as she died, and tangibilized around Lyssa and Cavyn with pulsating intensity. Images flowed from Lyssa's body, flashing colors and geometric patterns forming inchoate faces and exotic mandalas before the darkness flowing from Cavyn destroyed them. The force of creation and the force of destruction, battling at first though tenderly merging, joining as Lyssa and Cavyn seemed to join. Together, they watched the realizations unfold between them. The two were one.

Lyssa and Cavyn seemed to rise and fall before one another now, drawing ever closer, righting one another until they were side by side, stilled with peace. An image of the two of them, joined, with four arms, four eyes, their hair and faces combined, as one single beautied entity, hovered above them.

The old woman had died, but her mouth continued to speak even after her soul had been nullified. "Good and evil are more than you know, but you have greater peace than any before you. Remember the balance, and go now from this damned heaven with my blessings, O' inheritors of every innocence ever lost."

Before leaving, Cavyn and Lyssa paused upon the edge of the plane, looking upon The Floating Gardens Of The Abandoned Heaven with tears in their eyes. Cavyn shut his eyelids as they drifted away, and the entire plane exploded into flame. The smoke which curled towards them was beautiful, carrying the sweet and narcotic scents of the flaming flowers. Cavyn knew not whether this would nullify the souls of the derelict heaven or simply force them to live amongst the ashes that remained. He watched their bodies burn and disappear, hopefully into nullity. He saw that their destructions were of a much more painful fashion than the one he had bestowed upon the sorceress, but he also knew that, ultimately, they would be better off for it.

"Why did you destroy them? They might have been saved one

day." Lyssa was crying as Cavyn took her hand into his strong grip and they floated from the burning heaven into yet another plane.

Cavyn's voice was cold and tortured with emotion. "Some things are beyond salvation."

7

Lyssa shuddered in Cavyn's arms. She could feel God watching them; observing them; spying upon them. God had been haunting her more frequently than ever before since the day they had begun their flight, and she could feel his presence growing stronger on this night, terrifying her while the sky patiently blackened outside the cave where Cavyn and her had taken refuge from the violent winds of the Mountains Of Enlightenment.

Cavyn whispered a reassurance as he entered Lyssa's trembling body. He could feel God also, but was angered rather than fearful. Lyssa could feel God in different parts of her body, sometimes her face, sometimes her breasts, sometimes her heart. Now, he was creeping into her womb, darkly along bloodstreams and bones, leaving them tingling as if his travel left a residue behind. The darkness came, and with it, the paranoia.

Tears came slowly from Lyssa's eyes, with hints of silver as they passed between her long lashes to streak her delicate cheeks. Darkness swirled against her, every emotion lashed her. Terror circled around her skull, faster every moment, unstoppable, insatiable, tearing her brain apart thought by thought, dream by dream. She was sweating now, and her heart raced and palpitated, seeming to shred itself upon her ribs. She felt as if she had been this way for days, paralyzed with dread, limp in Cavyn's arms.

Cavyn began casting spells to comfort her, rapidly and to exhaustion. The darkness was as thick and vibrant as a muscle. God's presence came weakly to him. It was as though God's all-seeing eyes were completely focused upon Lyssa, temporarily ignoring the rest of the Infiniverse. Cavyn no longer feared God, no longer believed in his omnipotence, and sought to confront him.

Lyssa focused on Cavyn's touch, which was all that kept her from screaming, his rockings which seemed to bring her back to her body, his whisperings which she couldn't comprehend but calmed her anyhow. She opened her tearful eyes. All was black landscape before her dilated pupils, the sunset outside the cave corrupted and betraying. Cavyn whispered another spell, and looked into her eyes to reassure her. His eyes were the only life and color before her black vision, and she felt protected by his vicious demon's gaze.

Cavyn's spells were bringing her warmth and comfort, and he had begun to make love to her again. Now, she returned his lovemaking, seeming to cleanse herself of God with every motion. Together, they drove God away with every touch, every push, every kiss, Cavyn's whispers giving Lyssa strength and hope. God's presence began to withdraw from her flesh, leaving it pale and quivering. Cavyn pushed again, and Lyssa was consumed in orgasm, no longer aware of God's hauntings. She gripped Cavyn with unusual strength, bruising his dark skin.

They lay together, still joined, for some time. It was many moments before Lyssa's skin regained its color and her heart its rhythm. Cavyn's eyes were distant, and remained red as he brooded upon Lyssa's haunting.

"God is a voyeur". Cavyn's voice flowed as evenly as his blood. "He created the Infiniverse to watch. He watches certain parts more than others, whichever parts best fulfill his needs. Good and evil are only things he created for his own pleasures. Everyone is an exhibitionist for God."

Cavyn's words were chilling, chilling to the very heart of the mind, the very mind of the soul, the very soul of the heart. Lyssa forced herself to forget them. They remained joined throughout the night, fearful of parting and allowing God to reappear, at length falling asleep in one another's sanctuary.

8

Lyssa and Cavyn gazed in awe upon the plane which sloped before them. It was filled with mist and seemed as if it could disappear at any moment. They recognized it immediately; it was a plane from the folklore of both their races.

"The Valley Of Wasted Dreams," Lyssa breathed almost silently, her whisper faint with disbelief.

They descended together into the ephemeral plane, rejoicing in its existence, shocked that the myths of their races held at least one truth. They parted ways briefly, as their every dream, every childhood whim, returned to their heads and was played out before them.

They ran like children throughout the mists, collecting their long-lost thoughts and possessing dreams-never-dreamt. Dreams they didn't share merged until they belonged to both of them. Lyssa and Cavyn made love as a princess and prince, an avatar and deity, beyond good and evil. There was no God now, and they had only their love to worship. There were sweet flowers and purple nights, and they made love in golden ponds, in silver snowy skies, and on silken stars overlooking the entire Infiniverse.

Lyssa and Cavy clasped hands and noticed with wide eyes that many of their dreams were one, even those from early childhood. For hours they played in the swirling mists, living their every fantasy. Finally, The Valley Of Wasted Dreams passed through them. They left the ephemeral plane in peace, angel and demon as one. Their lovemaking that evening was joyous, and they still played like children throughout the night, assured more than ever of the strength of their love.

9

Cavyn writhed beneath the crippling weight in his head like a snake dying in its sleep, tearing open fresh wounds and bleeding upon the moors of The Golden Badlands. Lyssa struggled to comfort him, leaning him against one of the plane's dead and petrified trees and placing a hand upon his chest. She asked him what was happening, but he spoke no more.

Cavyn knew what was happening, the answer loomed in his throbbing mind, but he hoped to win his internal battle quickly, without frightening Lyssa. Demons were a possessive and vengeful race. His brethren had searched for them in the astral plane, as he had known they would, and had inevitably tracked him down. Now, they were repossessing his evils, and possibly his soul.

He could hear their laughter through the darkness, and knew the voices from his childhood. They were entering his mind now, exploring its corridors,tampering with his thoughts. Cavyn cast spells to protect himself and drive them away. He wondered if he could survive if they merely took his evils and nothing else, or if those evils were an integral and vital part of his soul.

Cavyn struggled to remain beyond the grasp of their cackling hands. He knew now that more than one attacked him, but he knew not how many more. They, too, were casting spells, and Cavyn had to fight them to channel God's power. Fainting seemed close to his clenched body, and he was continually tearing himself away from its death-grasp.

The stinging gravity in his head seemed to relent before his spells, though his vision remained hazy. It seemed as though the demons had retreated. His eyes were milky, and rolled into his head. His breaths were shallow, and came in strangles and clutches. He wondered if he had won.

"Are you all right?" Lyssa asked.

"Yes," Cavyn replied quickly, though he still felt somewhat dazed. He kissed Lyssa to reassure her, and soon they were making love in a nearby green and purple flowerbed.

Cavyn's embrace was more powerful than usual, and his eyes were hateful. Lyssa was unable to breathe, and struggled beneath his body. His movements were filling her with pain,pain which, unlike other times, was not pleasurable. She was less concerned with this, however, than her smothering and sense of being trapped. She screamed for Cavyn to stop.

Cavyn rose to his knees above her, snarled once, then struck her in the face. For one moment he paused with shock, then was overcome by the darkness. He felt as if he were in a trance. He wondered if he had possessed by his demon kin.

Cavyn placed a hand over Lyssa's mouth, suffocating her. Her blood and tears mixed and collected against the veins and pulsing scars of his clawed hand. As the darkness began to settle in his skull, he reentered Lyssa's body with a growling sigh.

"Do you love me?"

Cavyn thrust violently into Lyssa's vagina as he spoke, creating a spattering of crimson upon the flowers beneath her spread legs.

The image of Cavyn's question burned in Lyssa's mind. She imagined herself alone, and found only emptiness. She imagined herself with Cavyn, and found her soul. She was Cavyn.

"Yes."

Lyssa answered in both truth and fear.

"Do you worship only me?"

Cavyn thrust into Lyssa again. He was lost in darkness, nearly possessed fully by the demons. He was unable to control his body, but his words were his own. The presence of his people was stimulating his own evils, evils which he thought he had transcended long ago. He was at war with them now, and he was losing. He was forever a demon.

Cavyn's question burned in Lyssa's mind again, and she imagined herself kneeling at his feet in the temple of his love. She imagined herself using his power for her spells. He was more than God to her, and she drank a slow communion of his soul from a golden chalice in his hand.

"Yes."

The blood flowing through her womb seemed to enable Cavyn to drive deeper into her body. She felt as if he would rip her in two.

"Would you sin for me?"

Cavyn rended Lyssa's flesh once again. His voice swelled into the darkness, then rotted into him. Thoughts were like razor blades, leaving his mind in quivering pieces on the floor of his skull. He destroyed them. He waited with a snarl for Lyssa's answer.

Lyssa imagined herself the demon, and Cavyn the angel. She found it to be remarkably easy, for they seemed to be one and the same. Their roles were unimportant, and she would use evil to protect him, the same way she used her good.

"Yes."

She could feel God watching, creeping into her bloody womb, reveling in its every wound, weakening her even further. Her fear doubled rather than divide itself.

"Would you sacrifice everything, the Infiniverse itself and all that lives within it, for me?"

Cavyn's movement now brought a nausea to his chest, and with it, a falling sensation, like a dove with a severed wing, watching the earth speed towards him, nearly regaining flight, then beginning to flip uncontrollably.

Lyssa imagined herself as God, creating Cavyn from the blood of her heart and the pure white of her soul, allowing him to fill the entire Infiniverse until he became even more powerful than she and love itself, slaying every other living creature in existence. The Infiniverse disintegrated until there was only Cavyn.

"Yes"

Her vagina was red and could bleed no more. She could feel God haunting Cavyn through the darkness as well, and the demons channeling God's power in their attack. She opened her eyes. All was black again,but she was able to discern Cavyn's outline above her, his body wracked with spasms as the two forces fought to control it. She began to weep.

"Would you die for me?"

Cavyn had retreated to a part of his mind that he had never known. He could hear the laughter of the demons in the darkness, sadistically triumphant. He didn't feel the sperm rush from his body.

This time, Lyssa needed no imaginings, only the reality of Cavyn's possession and torment. If he was dying, she would willingly give all her energy, all her lifeblood to him so that he might live, and surrender herself to the demons in his place.

"Yes."

Lyssa's voice was barely audible. The warmth of Cavyn's sperm relieved her as the force of his final thrust screamed into her every nerve and tore away her last remnants of consciousness. She convulsed once, then slipped into a God-haunted coma.

Cavyn moaned beneath the weight in his head, struggling to control his fingers. The demons had used his body to rape Lyssa, and now they sought to kill her with his hands. His arms began to reach for her throat, slowly, with a million tremblings. With all that remained of his life, he was able to keep from strangling her. He rose from Lyssa's limp body, stumbled a few steps, then collapsed into the flowers with his head in his hands. The demons were taking his soul.

Lyssa could feel Cavyn's soul through the darkness. The demons flew above him, howling in delight as they tormented him. He was dying. She knew that if the demons possessed his soul, he would be tortured for all eternity. Risking a similar destiny, and allowing God greater entry into her body than ever before, she floated to him. Their souls merged like two teardrops. Together, they combined their waning strength and cast several continuous spells, driving the demons to a confused scattering.

*

Cavyn awoke to blinding, hammering memories. Lyssa lay near him, unconscious, but neither dead nor possessed as he had feared. He had regained his evils; they were resettling like maggots into his soul. His crimson eyes were seething with rage as he remembered his possession by the demons, his rape of Lyssa, and their shared salvation in the darkness.

Cavyn closed his bloodshot eyes. God's presence was still near, and he channeled it violently, with all his demonic wrath. He searched madly through the darkness, harnessing a tremendous and mind-twisting power. He cast his spell, and the three demons that had used his body to rape Lyssa and tried to possess their souls were instantly transported into The Golden Badlands.

The first two died before they realized where they were, their throats torn out and laying in quivering tendrils amongst the flowers. The third made some feeble defenses before being sliced halfway up his chest. Cavyn then grasped him by the face, embedding his claws in his skull, and rammed the back of his head into the trunk of a petrified tree, again and again and again. A sickly mash of blood and brains oozed to the gnarled roots below.

Only when he ceased did Cavyn stop to recognize the three demons. He had known them all, but he couldn't remember their names anymore. In his dreams and imaginings, he had expected to feel sorrow if ever forced to slay members of his own race. He felt nothing but hatred. He now possessed evils beyond those of his people, for he had learned the power of betrayal and fratricide.

Cavyn knelt beside Lyssa and embraced her limp body. Her heartbeat was weak against his chest, her breath shallow. Cavyn knew that they'd be searched for, and that they must take flight again. A single teardrop fell upon her ashen face as Cavyn lifted her high and swore his love to her. Cradling Lyssa in his arms, sick with guilt, Cavyn flew into the night.

10

Cavyn made love to Lyssa as she slept, begging her forgiveness and kissing her continually. He prayed to himself that she would awaken, and felt that he would die if she did not.

Lyssa's body twitched with God's hauntings. She lay suspended in the darkness, and felt as if her very soul was being ripped from her body. Continually she implored God, asking him why he haunted her, but she never received an answer, and throughout her coma, was never able to determine a reason. It was as Cavyn had spoken that threatful night. God was a voyeur, and she his unwilling exhibitionist. She accepted his hauntings now, and knew that she would never be free of them. Every moment of her long sleep, he gained greater entry into her body. The fear never left, but she was able to conquer it, so that despair alone dwelled within her sad heart.

Cavyn's sperm rushed into Lyssa, and he hoped that it would somehow revive her. He looked into her eyes for many minutes, expecting them to open. Finally, he fell away from her limp body and began to weep.

Cavyn spent much time in meditation as he awaited Lyssa's awakening. He blamed himself for her coma, and feared that it would last forever. He gazed upon the small, tortured writhings of her body as God coursed through it, and thought occasionally to take her life, to assuage her of her misery. Perhaps, if he did not, she would be haunted by God for all eternity. His murder would be merciful, as it had been to the sorceress in the Floating Gardens Of The Abandoned Heaven.

The Shadows Of Love were playing across her now, and Cavyn gazed upon her as they did so, covering and revealing her gently closed eyes, her red lips, her golden hair and wings, her perfectly formed breasts and silken vagina. He began to cry again.

Their souls reached for one another in the darkness, and they were able to calm themselves as they exchanged thoughts. Cavyn felt pawned by his evils, and he knew they were an inherent part of him, never to be overcome. He tried to cast spells to bring Lyssa back to life, but none were successful. God's presence was mocking, and it seemed to Cavyn he was stealing Lyssa from him.

"Cavyn..."

Lyssa's voice floated into Cavyn's soul, a reassurance.

"Lyssa..."

Cavyn returned Lyssa's call in the darkness. They floated as if resting upon thrones of flower petals, and their souls spoke softly and vaguely to one another. The silent words were neither his nor hers, but belonged to them both, and they spoke them together.

"Death is not to be feared, and its difference from life is as subtle and misunderstood as the difference between good and evil. Death is the only salvation, for life is only suffering and sorrow. Death bows to love alone, and is the ruler of all else. There may be Gods other than ours, but even a God benevolent to his Infiniverse would want his subjects to worship love above him. Love is the answer to every question, and to cherish it is to be divine. Our love is our salvation. Our love will light the way to forever."

Raindrops began to fall through the sliding, dancing shadows, a manifestation of Lyssa and Cavyn's love. The warm, serene rain grew stronger every moment, casting even more Shadows Of Love across the skies. Each fell alone, and sighed as it struck the ground.

The rainfall born of their love was great and continued for three days, rapidly flooding the plane. Lyssa's awakening was slow, and Cavyn guided her through it. The rain helped to revive her, and she embraced Cavyn with great strength. Upon her awakening, they became instantly aware of their shared hopelessness. Their lovemaking was sweet and violent, and they knew that, this time, it would lead to their death.

11

The surf sighed wistfully upon The Shores Of Life And Death, purpling with the sinking nightfall and reddening with the blood of Lyssa and Cavyn's slow suicide. The stars were out and shining upon the velvet sands of the beach, and cast a golden pall upon the waves which crashed against the shore. Rainbows stretched all across the ocean, disappearing and reappearing with tranquil whimsy, some small, some great, some touching ground near Lyssa and Cavyn. The air was warm and silent, disturbed by neither clouds nor winds, and was filled with the sweet fragrances of underwater foliage.

Lyssa and Cavyn's bloodletting lasted for many hours, and they continued to make love throughout. They performed it as delicately as if it were a ritual, two heretics creating their own private religion. Suicide by sexual torture. It was, they realized, what they had been doing all along.

Lyssa slowly pulled the dagger across Cavyn's chest. He kissed her breast as blood welled from the cut, then scratched it with his teeth. As always, each enjoyed the givings and receivings of pain, and felt a pleasant calm as their death drew near. Their scars were flickering with millions of colors, and murmured to themselves, seeming somehow aware of the suicide. A pool of crimson surrounded them, more blood than they had ever imagined their bodies contained, too great to be absorbed into the sand. They were rapidly losing consciousness, and now possessed more than enough wounds to assure their death.

Lyssa and Cavyn made love for the final time. Their lovemaking was as graceful as the waves which rushed upon the beach and brushed against them, mixing with their lifeblood, bathing them in it, and then carrying it away to the ocean. Each gentle push brought them closer to death. They kissed as the darkness returned, this time eternally. Their souls joined again, as they had just days before while battling the demons.

Cavyn's last orgasm was painful, and he withdrew from Lyssa's body before it was complete. Not sperm, but blood coursed from his penis, splattering Lyssa's already crimsoned torso. He groaned with its violent departure, his upper lip curling over his sharp teeth.

Their scars began to throb, and then burst with thin gasps, spraying even more blood across the ensanguined sands, hastening Lyssa and Cavyn's imminent death. Lyssa and Cavyn noticed this in a detached way. It relieved them. Now, they possessed no scars, only wounds. Now, there was no past.

Their soul was halfway out of their bodies, rising into the purple skies. Planes swirled and switched around them, and they entered each one as their bodies lay dying upon the beach. An infinity of heavens, hells, and purgatories flashed before their eyes, each imploring to be Lyssa and Cavyn's chosen afterlife.

The planes were drawing them, now, with their spiritual gravity. They pulled, and Lyssa and Cavyn flowed between them. They hovered upon the edge of one, filled with damned souls frantically torturing one another, or weeping into their own hands. This was the hell for those who had committed suicide, and it sucked at Lyssa and Cavyn, trying to pull them in. For an instant, Lyssa and Cavyn feared it had possessed them, but they broke free from its grasp with a rush and floated onward. Their death was only partly suicide, for it was also partly murder. Lyssa and Cavyn searched for a fate perhaps not unlike the one they had delivered to the sorceress. It seemed the only way to be free of God, and good and evil.

They floated forever upwards, holding onto one another in fear of being swallowed by the heavens and hells surrounding them. They were drawing near to God, and strained desperately to peer beyond him

Lyssa and Cavyn found it impossible to completely perceive what they saw beyond God, but they knew it to be beautiful and calm.

Perhaps it was an afterlife just for them. Perhaps it was nullification. It didn't matter.

God reached violently towards them as they passed through his soul. Both Lyssa and Cavyn found that, within God, they were no longer haunted by him. Their love overwhelmed him, and his presence slowly dissipated as they rose past him. God disappeared.

Back on the beach, in their physical bodies, Cavyn smiled as Lyssa opened her beautiful eyes. His entire body was trembling with his love for her. He took Lyssa into his arms, and they tranquilly awaited their death, Cavyn sometimes whispering his love with his dying breaths. They gazed upon the ocean, imagining its waves washing over their corpses, eroding their flesh from their skeletons, burying them in one shared lovers' tomb upon the dreaming beach.

Silken light irradiated the pool of blood as the moon rose above the ocean. Lyssa and Cavyn could see themselves in the surrounding scarlet, its surface shining beneath golden moonbeams. They watched their reflection in silence, their bodies tattered and pale, each enraptured by the other's beauty. Their heartbeat became faint, and pumped nothing but air through their veins. Finally, it ceased completely.

With a tear and an embrace, still gazing upon their beautiful reflection in the mirror of blood, Lyssa and Cavyn died as one. Just like the night of their first lovemaking, it was a moment in time they shared, a moment in time all their own. This time, it lasted forever.

The Anchorites of Armageddon

Part One
Genocide Tryst

Still holding the Chronodagger with which he had slain the human race, the Eschaphiliac began the long journey back to the Westpalace.The jihad of genocide was over. Mankind had been assassinated.

The Eschaphiliac had smeared the blood of every stabbed, slashed, and sundered corpse across his body and wore each blood cell as a souvenir, an aggregate of microscopic mementos combining to form one giant trophy.The collective lifeblood of the entire species was drying upon the Chronodagger. Their hemoglobin was clotting on his skin, their plasma was seeping into his flesh, their erythrocytes and leucocytes were flowing through his arteries, veins, and capillaries. Their blood was coagulating into a single, continuous, gargantuan scab that covered his entire body like a crimson exoskeleton. He was no longer a part of the human race. The human race was a part of him

Like a homunculus composed of badlands and scoria, the Eschaphiliac walked through a Shangri-La of death, a mass grave the size of a planet, the charnel house which had once been called earth. The world was his possession now, was his to christen as though it were his newborn child. He decided to name it The Elysian Aceldamas.

Atop Mount Malebolge, overlooking the Avernal Sea, the Westpalace glittered like a pile of raw jewelry, all jagged pyramids and paralyzed scintilla. As the Eschaphiliac scaled the corpse-littered mountain passes the Westpalace slowly dropped from view, descending beneath the horizon like the sinking sun of twilight. As he neared the peak of Mount Malebolge the Westpalace slowly re-emerged, rising like a flailing god, its twisted minarets and corbels shimmering in the sun. His soulmate, Innocence, was waiting for him beneath the portcullis like a taxidermied Venus, straddling the horizon like a chroniade masturbating with the edge of time, a cosmiade fucking an event horizon with a black hole of her own. Blinking the blood from his eyes, the Eschaphiliac gazed upon her crepuscular-hued silhouette and the star-colored hair that flowed to her feet, and he fell in love with her once more, just as he had so long ago, in that abhorrent time before time itself stopped.

The Eschaphiliac climbed to the zenith of the corpse-strewn mountain, then kneeled down before the Westpalace. He reversed his grip upon the Chronodagger, then plunged it into the stone of the mountain. As he released its hilt from his grasp, time restarted and began to flow once more.

He knew not if the Chronodagger stopped the very universe from moving, or if it placed him in his own little bathysphere outside of time, like an inside-out sensory deprivation chamber. Trying to determine whether the Chronodagger's effects were internal or external was like trying to prove or disprove solipsism: impossible yet addictive. He had christened the placeless place Time's Antechamber, for it was like spying on the entire universe through a one-way window, like a peeping god, and yet, like a suit of armor, he could travel within it, completely unnoticed by the frozen life surrounding him, completely unaffected by everything the blade did not touch. With its anti-temporal powers and its razor-sharp arete it was the Chronodagger which had enabled him to slay the human race like the double-edged blade it was. Now it was time to enjoy the tranquilities of genocide.

The Eschaphiliac rose to his feet. Innocence ran across the drawbridge and leapt into his arms. They kissed and embraced, then danced like Citipati upon the corpses, still moist and warm beneath them. The scabs which had formed over the Eschaphiliac's bodily orifices began to flake and fall away in pieces. His mouth stretched open, his nostrils flared, and his ears re-opened like roses and lotuses. He carried Innocence into the Westpalace and laid her down within their bedchamber.

The Eschaphiliac's erection caused the caked plasma encasing his penis like a lobster-shell to crack into faultlines reminiscent of Marsquakes. Tiny chips of crimson rubble rolled and tumbled away like the red boulders of a sudden avalanche on Olympus Mons. When he ejaculated, the jetstream of sperm shattered the rock-hard scab that had grown over the tip of his penis into a million pieces. The shrapnel of clotted blood decorated the inside of Innocence's womb like art. The heat of her vagina melted most of the blood covering his phallus, but a layer of crimson crust still remained after his withdrawal.

He tried to whittle and chisel the dried blood from his skin over the next few days, but the scab was a permanent part of his body now, an eternal symbol of his royalty.It was irremovable, but he would soon discover that, when moistened, it could be sculpted...

*

The Eschaphiliac scraped his newly fashioned claws down Innocence's spine as he massaged her labia with his freshly-grown horns. He bit her clitoris with his fangs and partook of cunnilingus with his forked tongue, then rose to his cloven-hooved feet, stabbed his barbed phallus into her vagina, and drove her into the bloodstained sands. Upon the shores and in the tides of the Avernal Sea they writhed, making loveas severed body parts and excised organs washed up on the beach. Hours later, as they sat in one another's arms and watched the sun set in a flood of convulsive purples, Innocence kissed the tip of the Chronodagger and tasted the blood of the human race, and the Eschaphiliac gently whispered into her ear,

"Now we can be alone."

Part Two
Suicide Sacrifice

Seated high atop the throne of bodily orifices that overlooked the utopian necropolis, the Eschaphiliac maneuvered the ropes of human hair to which his flesh-puppets and necro-dolls were bound. His clawed fingers danced and directed the decomposing marionettes to leap and pirouette,fly and fall, battle and fornicate. Gangrenous extremities and pieces of maggot-laced rot shook free of the bodies as he played, forming human compost heaps and piles of death in the city streets below.

Inside the Westpalace, Innocence lit a cigarette of perennial lotus and watched her soulmate perform his grotesque comedies and merry tragedies. The Eschaphiliac had been dangling his dead toys from the stone dais built into the side of Mount Malebolge for over three hundred hours. Innocence's gaze drifted to the rest of the utopian necropolis. Built on the shores of the Avernal Sea, it was a labyrinth of mausoleums and cenotaphs, with crematoriums for energy plants and graveyards for parks. The beasts of burden which had been used to construct the city were still wandering along the bone-paved streets, sometimes feasting on the broken morsels of flesh that rained down from the corpse-show above. The city was one gigantic, twisted, morbid dollhouse.

There was an hourglass filled with cocaine upon the table of fontanels at Innocence's side. Both a symbol and a symptom of the Eschaphiliac's fetish, the hourglass had not been turned over in years. Next to it was a stalled clepsydra filled with absinthe, and next to that a broken clock with a giant peyote button for a face. At the far end of the table, completely shrouded in shadows, was a sundial with a needle dipped in opium for a gnomon.

These drug-filled timepieces had once been the playthings of the Eschaphiliac and Innocence alike, but the Eschaphiliac had grown bored of them and abandoned them, discarding them like broken toys and tattered dolls. Innocence suddenly realized that she, like the drugs, had been replaced by the utopian necropolis. With tears in her eyes she lifted the hourglass of cocaine and smashed it upon the floor, then inhaled every last grain of cocaine and broken glass through a fossilized fallopian tube. With blood dripping from her nose and down her throat, and jagged shards of shattered glass puncturing her lungs, esophagus, stomach, and intestines, Innocence drank all the absinthe from the clepsydra with a single swallow, devoured the entire face of the peyote clock, and jabbed the gnomon filled with opium into her left breast. As the drugs began to course through her brain, she staggered from the bedchamber and down the spinning hallway.

*

The Eschaphiliac awakened after a sudden eternity and everlasting instant to the clatter of steel striking stone. After a moment of vertigo he gazed once more over the streets of the utopian necropolis. The beasts of burden were all dead. The maggots in the corpses had stopped writhing, as though paralyzed. The flora and fauna surrounding the city were decaying. Something had exterminated all the plants and animals of The Elysian Aceldamas. The Eschaphiliac's planet had been transformed into a menagerie of carcasses.

The Eschaphiliac glanced down to find the Chronodagger lying beneath his feet, at the base of his throne. It was the Chronodagger that had made the sound. Right next to the time-knife was the limp hand of Innocence. The Eschaphiliac dragged his gaze along the ensanguined arm of his soulmate to find the rest of her body sprawled across the dais. Blood was pooling around her supine form and fountaining in jetstreams from her mutilated wrists, lacerated jugular vein, and severed carotid artery. Upon her breasts and pregnant abdomen she had carved her own epitaph with the Chronodagger.

"Now you can be alone."

Part Three
Prolicide Apocalypse

Black tsunamis crashed through the utopian necropolis as the Avernal Sea vomited itself beneath the churning skies. The Eschaphiliac ran through the streets, dodging the onrushing waves and shrapnel of collapsing buildings. He clambered up the side of Mount Malebolge just as the entire city was submerged in the Stygian waters of Avernus.

Mount Malebolge was crumbling as well, dropping huge boulders all around him as though it had grown sentient and desired to lapidate him. The Eschaphiliac scrambled into the Westpalace and up the stairways. He burst into the weapons gallery as the floor started to fall away beneath him. As the roof caved in he lunged for the Chronodagger. The Westpalace fell apart as he grasped the hilt of the blade. With a large, jagged piece of ceiling six inches from the crown of his skull, and a quaking floor opening like a trap-door over the giant abyss beneath his feet, time suddenly stopped, paralyzing the collapsing Westpalace in mid-destruction.

The Eschaphiliac made his way through the rubble and extricated himself from his half-destroyed castle. Another black tsunami, this one taller than Mount Malebolge, had been frozen just as it was cresting over the minarets and corbels of the Westpalace. To the north, south, and east lay nothing but annihilation and cataclysm. Long, ragged faultlines had torn open the surface of the planet. Bolts of lightning and giant meteors hung suspended in mid-air. Huge fires with flames a mile high were glowing in the fields and forests. The Eschaphiliac gripped the Chronodagger with all of his might, for he knew that if he ever released it from his grasp, both he and The Elysian Aceldamas would be destroyed, as surely as the Westpalace and the utopian necropolis had been.

Still holding the Chronodagger with which he had saved the planet, the Eschaphiliac began the long pilgrimage to the Eastpalace.A strange combination of dawn and mushroom clouds formed the skies and the horizon. The sunrise had been halted, the sun trapped in space as though it were part of a broken orrery, rusting in an ancient observatory beneath an anachronistic zodiac.

As the Eschaphiliac marched through the wastelands and debris, the sunlight began to flicker and shimmer. Neither celestial bodies nor quanta could move when he held the Chronodagger. Mirages were impossible, but perhaps hallucinations were not. Gazing through his transparent time-cocoon, the Eschaphiliac fixed his eyes directly upon the disc of the sun. He walked slowly now, squinting into the blinding light. The sunbeams were intensifying and radiating a strange, otherworldly heat. The sun was glowing brighter and brighter, transforming from luminous to chatoyant to phosphorescent and back again. It metamorphosed into a glowing eyeball with a white hole for a pupil. It blinked.

The sky around the sun began to coalesce into something incarnadine and tangible. The Eschaphiliac shielded his eyes with his clawed hand and stared directly into the face of God.

As he stood, mesmerized by revelations and hypnotized by epiphanies, the Chronodagger slowly floated from his hand and into the beam of white light. Time remained frozen, even though the Chronodagger was no longer in the Eschaphiliac's hand. The knife disappeared into the tunnel of light for an instant, then came hurtling back with its blade pointed at the Eschaphiliac's chest and plunged into his heart.

As the Eschaphiliac died, the Chronodagger melted and the voice of God rattled the universe. The Eschaphiliac knew not whether God spoke to the Chronodagger or him.

"You have served me well. Now I can be alone."

Riddle of the Loveghouls

The virgin goths walked hand-in-hand through the cemetery gates.As the sun slowly set like a severed head sinking into a cauldron of blue and purple, viscous Lethe, they stripped off their black garments and began making love amongst the tenebrous gravestones.The imprints of their naked bodies in the dirt marked the death of their virginity with a shallow grave, an inverted, sex-shaped barrow.

Behind the two goths, the white moon rose as stealthily as a thief, its light ambushing and cold. It gazed down upon them like the eye of a cyclopean voyeur. Ashen moonbeams cascaded across the tombstones, scattering the shadows of twilight and illuminating the epitaphs. The shivering lovers found themselves unable to keep their gaze from wandering to the suddenly-visible necroglyphics, and reading the brief eulogies and elegies. Dread settled into their minds and squatted.

"Let's leave this place."

Diamond's serpentine voice, a lisping susurrus due to her recently-pierced tongue, leaked past her black lipstick and seemed to sink into the dirt around her white-painted face and partly-shaved head.It seemed as though it were being drawn downwards into the burial grounds by the gravity of death.She was growing more and more apprehensive oftheir eerie environs, and was not finding her first lovemaking to be as magical as she had always imagined.

"Just a few more seconds," Scorpio said breathlessly, pushing sweat-laden strands of jet-black and purple-dyed hair from his eyes. He had been waiting for this moment for years, and wasn't about to sacrifice it to superstitions. Besides which, the other goths all said that orgasms were ten times as powerful in cemeteries. He wasn't about to take Diamond somewhere else.

"Hurry up," Diamond said, her eyes opening wider while Scorpio's closed.

Scorpio shoved upwards into Diamond with increasing intensity. Orgasm continually tantalized him, but somehow never arrived. He sighed, frustrated and embarrassed. Such vexations had never occurred during his masturbations.The graveyard was exerting a strange and supernatural influence over the two of them.

Diamond's eyes rolled slowly from side to side, becoming slippery in their sockets as she bit her lip with pain. The looming tombstones seemed to move before her, to sway and pulse as if ready to crumble, and the earth seemed to bulge and rise around her. She dismissed the movements as mere hallucinations of her red agony.

Scorpio pushed determinedly onward, chasing the elusive orgasm which would finally complete the impromptu coming-of-age ceremony. He knew that he had not chosen the most romantic location to spontaneously seduce Diamond, but he had felt that the brilliance of his lovemaking would compensate for it. He breathed in gasps and felt as though he might collapse, but continued to struggle regardless, his pride and will as strong as his name suggested.

Meanwhile, the sensations of movement continued to haunt Diamond. With disturbed blue eyes she watched as the graves heaved and crashed around them, and the soil beneath began to bulge and separate. She slowly realized that she was neither hallucinating nor suffering from irrational fear. She screamed.

Scorpio remained oblivious to the tremors of the cemetery as the tension between his legs grew. He snarled as he forced the sperm from his body. At the exact instant of orgasm, Diamond's scream tore his eyelids apart. He gasped as he saw the cadavers rising from their graves, watching in horror even while he trembled in the rapture of his long-awaited ecstasy.

The living corpses were twisted with strange patterns of decay. Forsaking their humanity, they had evolved and mutated into incubi and succubi. They moved tentatively, with weak legs and violent tremblings, as it had been some time since their evil souls had been drawn back to their former bodies. Their genitals were enormous and bloodshot, their eyes perverted and distant. They had been ravished upon the dark side of love. They were beyond death. They were Loveghouls, and their libidos hungered for souls.

The undead fiends formed a circle around the two joined bodies, floating several inches above the ground, cackling and howling as they watched the two lose their virginity. Their souls were rising partway from their bodies, with creeping illuminations, and they dripped rotting flesh onto the grass and soil below.

"Get off me," Diamond screamed, squirming across the quaking ground as she tried to escape.

Scorpio pulled himself backwards through her womb, but was unable to completely remove his member from her clutches. He tried again, but, with a sharp twinge of pain in his groin, his withdrawal attempt was abruptly halted once more. Scorpio could not free himself from Diamond's flesh. Their bodies had somehow been locked together.

"I can't," he yelled, now as frantic as she.

Diamond convulsed her body, bracing herself against the ground, tearing her sweat-drenched thighs. She tried desperately to dislodge Scorpio's phallus from her flesh, pulling and tugging at it until Scorpio feared it would be severed from his groin and remain inside her. The Loveghouls laughed loudly, gesturing and joking amongst themselves as they watched the two bloody their crotches. Their ghosts drifted within their own bodies, ricocheting against their chipped skeletons, their bones visible where pieces of decaying and maggoty flesh had fallen or been eaten away. Their death wounds and diseases remained with them still, festering in the moonlight, steaming with contagion. Their stench was like demonshit being boiled in the fires of Hell.

"What have you done to us?" Scorpio demanded, his voice faltering midway through the sentence.

The Loveghouls cackled, and the vibrating muscles of their skinless throats shimmered in the starlight. Their lengthy cachinnations caused even more gore to spill upon the ground, in conjoined piles of blood, pus,gangrene, leprosy, and rot.

Scorpio made another futile attempt to pull free of Diamond while she looked upon the hideous, floating corpses. "What do you want?" she implored with a half-choked voice. "Just let us go and leave us alone." Diamond began to sob.

The Loveghouls laughed again, then one, with a cockroach nestled in one eye socket and crimson cancers lacing through his chest, answered with frothing lips," One of you may go free...."

He paused and smiled, and a barrage of yellow teeth rained down upon Scorpio and Diamond. He then faded into the background and another Loveghoul glided forth to take his place. This one had a cranium like shattered glass. A black bandanna had been fastened around his cracked head to hold his brains in, and to keep the crepitating shards of skull-bone from collapsing and falling apart as well.

The second Loveghoul completed the sentence and decreed, "...but only when one of you dies."

Laughter once again consumed the Loveghouls, and they slapped each other across their flaking backs, sometimes spraying blood through the air and dislodging organs to land with wet sucking noises on the ground.

"What do you mean?" Scorpio's cry was desperate.

The Chief of the Loveghouls then flew forward. His death had been one of fire in the scalding flames of Hell. Long wisps of burnt hair fluttered around his shoulders. He wore a dark cape which rippled like a nocturnal heat-vision in the air behind him. His eyeballs were still intact, and his glance struck like nitrous. As he glided nearer, black scabs and ashes floated from his charred skeleton and whirled upon the tortured winds.

"We have waited many centuries for this moment, young ones." His voice whistled and splintered. "One of you must join our undead love circle. You will lay, locked together, slowly maddening, until one of you murders the other. The sacrificed will become one of us. The other shall be freed." He threw his head back, hislaughter echoing through every nook and cranny of his seared skull.

"What if we die at the exact same moment? What if we grow old and one of us dies naturally, in our sleep or of a heart attack? What if one of us takes ill? Won't we starve to death or something?" Diamond sobbed, searching desperately for some loophole, some salvation from this horrid fate. She wondered how many lovers had been damned this way in the past. Perhaps the Loveghouls which tortured them now had all been victims of the same curse.

"My voodoos and necromancies will ensure that such unfortunate calamities do not occur."

The Chief of the Loveghouls spoke in a drawn-out manner, with the elegance of a somniloquist poet, then returned to hover amongst his brethren. The perverted eyes of the Loveghouls remained fastened upon Scorpio and Diamond, and many of them engaged in sickening copulations and orgies throughout the cemetery as they awaited the sacrifice, exchanging maggots and worms and venereal diseases.

"We'll just stay this way forever then," Diamond whispered to Scorpio, hoping the Loveghouls wouldn't hear her words. "We have each other; that's all we need. I love you, Scorpio."

Diamond began to cry.

"I love you, too," Scorpio replied, scraping gently against the walls of her womb. A surge rose in the lowest pits of his stomach, and they began to make love again. At least they could still fuck, Scorpio thought to himself. Perhaps this fate would not be as dire as he had first anticipated.

For many weeks they remained with flesh locked together at the crotch, making love, whispering reassurances, surviving upon the food and water which was forced down their throats when they tried to refuse it. The Loveghouls remained throughout, hovering patiently above them. They stared with voyeur fascination when the two made love, sometimes masturbating to the sight of their thrusting bodies and rubbing rancid flesh from their penises and vaginas to fall upon the ground as they did so. A few accidentally castrated themselves in this manner, scattering their twitching, severed phalluses and clitorises across the cemetery lawn.

Scorpio and Diamond could not break the spell of the Loveghouls, no matter how intently they sought to. Sometimes, they attempted to roll to freedom, but were never able to pass through the boundaries of the cemetery. The graveyard was surrounded by an invisible and inpenetrable circle of containment. Diamond prayed every night for their salvation, but never received an answer. Still, she maintained a glimmer of hope in her eyes, sustained by her love for Scorpio, knowing in her heart that she could never murder him, and that he could never murder her. This cured her fear some, and, as madness deepened,she even began to consider their curse somewhat romantic.

For months they lay joined, their bodies wasting against each other, goaded and cackled at by the ubiquitous Loveghouls, forever anticipating the moment when they would receive fresh meat to torture in their perverted orgies, a fresh soul to eternally corrupt and damn.

Gradually, Scorpio was falling out of love with Diamond. Her beauty had slowly dissipated throughout their months of supernatural bondage. Unable to bathe herself, her flesh had become foul and sticky. Her breath and excrement reeked all around him, and her legs and underarms were now covered in hair. She had endured the same filth from his body, he knew, had borne his urine in her vagina quietly, had breathed his stenches without a whimper. He knew this, but it no longer mattered to him. He had now witnessed her true nature, and found it hideous and repugnant. Scorpio now felt ashamed to have ever wanted to make love to Diamond, to have ever lusted for a creature so foul and grotesque.

He pondered the murder for many days, playing with concepts of good and evil, pondering the true nature of love and sin. He longed desperately for freedom, and had frequently come close to performing the sacrifice, before growing nauseated with emotion and guilt and eventually passing out in meditative agony.

One night, after a particularly thick and miasmic menstruation had spilled over his crotch and onto his thighs,hardening around his testicles and drawing forth his vomit with its emetic stench, he decided at last to rid himself of the bestial monstrosity that he had once loved.

Scorpio waited until Diamond slept, then strangled her to the cheers of the encircling Loveghouls. He was surprised at the small smile which came to his lips as he did so, but was relieved when her final spasm flattened beneath him and she lay dead.

With a sigh, Scorpio finally withdrew from Diamond's festering vagina, wiping the sweat from his brow as he rose above her corpse. He stretched his stiffened and atrophied muscles. He sighed once more, then brushed his overgrown hair from his eyes. The sacrifice was complete, and he was free. He turned and headed for the cemetery gates.

Scorpio didn't notice for many moments the blackening of his flesh, nor the way it fell about him, as he walkedtowards the edge of the graveyard. The Loveghouls were floating in his wake close behind. Eventually, he grew apprehensive of the way in which they followed him, and halted his stride to confront them.When he turned to face them, the Chief of the Loveghouls merely smiled and pointed with one black finger into the sidereal firmament of the night.Scorpio's mouth flared into a horrified gape of realization as he focused upon the white misty substance rising gently through the darkness.The laughter of the undead love circle pounded his rotting head as they swarmed around him, and he screamed, longly and with terrible mutations of cacophany, as he watched Diamond's soul knife through the skies towards heaven, and a cold cankered penis slipped slowly between his sweating buttocks.

Synpathodrome

"For you who would know about love..."

At first there was only the motion. Just an abstract sensation of raw kinetics. Still floating in the event horizon between consciousness and unconsciousness, his resurrecting sentience was a chaos of anatta and paramnesia, pulling him through a thousand strange awakenings which acted as one. Gradually, in what could have been a moment or an eternity, his thoughts went fluttering and fascinated to the vertigo the motion brought, the dread the vertigo brought, and the nausea the dread brought. The nausea spread through his body like a sentient, polymorphous mass, awakening his nervous system and slowly delivering him into higher and higher states of awareness, his mind alternately imploding and exploding like a miniature universe undergoing an endless cycle of Big Crunches and Big Bangs within his skull.

Time and space formed suddenly around him, with a tremendous but silent jolt. He awoke in a sensory deprivation chamber the size of the universe. He opened his eyes and saw darkness. He gradually became aware of his body on a tactile level. There was a large, hard ring driven through the top of his skull. The ring was linked to a giant chain, and from this chain he swung through an unfathomable void.

His regalvanized sense of touch spread through his flesh, then across his skin. He had been completely shaved, from head to pubes, for aerodynamic purposes. A cock-and-ball device held his depilated genitals in place. His hands were bound behind his back and his feet were fettered to one another. A ball gag had been placed inside his mouth and secured with a garrote-like strap. His flesh was racing before him, dragging him along while he struggled to keep up.

His blood bubbled with turbulence. The force of his flight crushed his organs together. His heartbeat and breathing were no longer functions of his autonomic nervous system. Consciously breathing in and out was Zenlike. Consciously forcing his heart to dilate and contract was Hellish. He wondered if the motion was to be his torturer and executioner, if the excruciating physics of the void would abrade and erode him into a mutilated corpse, his flesh torn from his bones, his muscles blown away layer by layer, his skeleton loosened by the vicious friction and then systematically unhinged.

His body angled upwards for a few moments, then the chain in his skull yanked him violently back. He was flying in reverse now, the sucking winds stealing the breath from his lungs. With soft wet noises and considerable discomfort, his organs were readjusting and clamoring away from his spine to rest against the inner walls of his torso. The pulp of his brain shifted also, gathering itself from the back of his skull and squirming to the front. He could feel its weight against his face, as well as an unsettling emptiness in the parts of his skull it had abandoned. Miniscule tendrils of brain were wisping from his nostrils and eustachian tubes, and a few loose brain cells fell down the back of his throat and onto his tongue. He could taste his own brain. He swallowed.

Knowing not where he came from, he had nothing to compare a possible destination to, and thusly found it difficult to conceive of one. He knew the universe-sized sensory deprivation chamber was a torture device. He wondered if it were some type of womb or negaverse. Having no recollection of his past existence, assuming he had one, he was unable to determine the evil deeds which had led to his punishment. Perhaps it was self-bestowed, perhaps wrought by an enemy, perhaps just a natural function of the universe.Perhaps it was some horrid form of enlightenment. Perhaps this itself was the torture, he thought, eternal, mind-twisting, nauseating contemplation in a void where nothing could be proven.

He swung backwards through the void, unto a second zenith, and then, just as before, followed the same trajectory in the opposite direction. As his organs made the painful shift within his body again, slamming against his spine and the insides of his back, a thought crept through his brain like a living, pulsing, creeping, slimy hole. Cold realization blasted him like an epileptic seizure.

He was a pendulum.

And so the chain continued to bear him, forward and backward, for eternity after eternity.He wondered if this was to be the torture, a torture of endless repetition in an empty purgatory.

A slave of both kinetics and time, he began to adapt to the ways of his masters. His very thoughts and bloodflow took on a pendulous motion. He created his own private system of mathematics to predict how far and long it would be to his next rise and subsequent fall. He knew what particular point of the trajectory he inhabited at all times. He had developeda firm sense of balance in all things, and, in fact, could no longer even conceive of random occurrences.

Thusly,he was startled in a manner that was physically painful when he saw her.

A dim glow, the first light he'd ever seen, burning at the edges of his vision as he approached his forward apogee, growing smaller, then fading away. He was sure it was not an illusion, and, for the duration of the next cycle, wondered if he would see her again. He did, and he was a little closer to her this time, but then she rapidly disappeared from view once more. The third time he caught her gaze, the gaze of the other, in a synesthesia of nausea, dread and eye contact.

The next few cycles of the pendulous swing brought the two still closer, and it was apparent that she had noticed him, as well. She was a pendulum, too, but swinging with a slightly different rhythm.

Like he, she had been bound, gagged and handcuffed. Her feet were tightly wrapped in strips of black cloth. Because of the foot binding, her feet and ankles were deformed and unnaturally small. A tight leather corsette held her breasts up to keep them from bouncing and ricocheting off one another. Her long, blonde hair had been shaved into a topknot and then braided to her chain. The rest of her body had been completely depilated, just like his own. A chainsaw epiosotomy/historectomy/vivisection had expanded her vagina all the way to her cleavage, leaving a raw red wound held open by tiny pins.

As time dragged on they swung closer and closer, until he was able to make out her facial features, and she his. Flying nearer every time, he knew that their pendulums would eventually swing in perfect synchronicity. He anticipated the conjoinment with the familiar combination of nausea and dread, and soon found himself besieged by angst as well. Perhaps, when they met, it would signify the end of the torture, and she would execute him. Perhaps she was the dominatrix who had orchestrated the ordeal, waiting to deliver him to higher tiers of suffering. Gradually, though, his theories softened, as he began to see that she was very similar to himself, fearful of the motion and powerless to control it, anguished by her own thoughts. He could see the torment in her expression, feel the torture in their eye contact. Her fate was the same as his. He hoped that, somehow, they would be one another's salvation, that the inevitable touch of flesh to flesh would free them both to a universe where motion and time did not exist.

Every unendurably long cycle saw them draw closer and closer, until he could feel the breeze of her passage as she fell past him, breathe the scent of her body, study her beautiful face. They communicated with a language of eye contact and pheromones. They reached for one another, but their trajectories did not yet coincide. They waited. The rest of the cycle was no longer meaningful, had become nonexistent. The moment was nearing, the moment of joining, the moment of oneness, and, perhaps, the moment of salvation.

Finally, their pendulums swung together in perfect synchronicity. They flew together at an astonishing speed, and he feared his destiny now, hoped more than ever for salvation, and shrank from images of their bodies crashing violently together and mangling as their skeletons interlocked, but more than all of this he desired her, desired her the way he desired freedom, desired her the same way he had desired his own death when first becoming purgatory's pendulum.

As they attained the sacred moment of synergy, that interval of hesitation where they both seemed to free-float in the void, his penis swelled against the restraints of its cock-and-ball device and slammed into her surgically enlarged vagina. In the moment that followed he possessed the stillness he longed for. The motion was forgotten now, in this one eternal instant. He was floating in his own inner void, his own inner vacuum, a replica of the one without. The power of love vibrated through him as he became possessed by the adoration and worship of a woman who had endured the motion just like he, a soulmate who was now lost in the trance of orgasm along with him. Their spirits were joined, arising in bliss with one another. In a world of nothingness, they were the only substance, the only truth ever known, the genesis of beauty. There was light all around, forceful, immense, and their faces floating in it, a millionfold, and a smell of the birth of the universe, and a taste of its death. There were colors and beautiful sounds, and the entire universe poured through them and was theirs to make love upon, and as he exploded within the heaven of his les petits mal, the voice of Existentiala fell from blackest nowhere and whispered in his ear, "Hell is other people."

Then, just as suddenly as they had joined, they were torn apart by the pendulous rhythms of the abyss. The ring in his skull jerked him out of her flesh and back onto his invisible track. He felt a pain in his heart as he watched her disappear. His newfound inner void and vacuum became as black and lonely as the one without. His cycle seemed interminably long the next time, as he hoped that their pendulums would swing together in perfect synchronicity once more.

Their next meeting was close, but not as close as they desired. They touched, with tears and longing, but their pendulums were no longer synchronized. He sighed as he fell away from his love. She was the only meaning he had ever known, the only meaning he could ever know as a pawn of this massive void.

He knew that, at some moment in the future, after another eternity of pendulous cycles, their rhythms would join once again and they would share a second experience of peace and bliss. Then, at some point even further in the future, they would have another, and then another, and then another. He also knew that, from now on, they would exist solely for those moments, dreaming of them as they hurtled through the infinite blackness. It wasn't exactly hope, and it encompassed an infinity of aspects. He began to weep.

In that one moment of little death, everything and nothing had changed. There was still the physical torment of flesh, chain and kinetics; still the monotony, tedium and ennui of infinity, eternity and immortality. There was still the sadistic irony of being a living pendulum swinging through a timeless void, and the longing for a stillness that would never be. There was still the nausea, the dread, the angst, the pain and the motion, the terrible, vertiginous, punishing, excruciating motion which would never cease.

But all that was only half the torture now.

The Nether-Womb of Nihilistika

As Harquebus Acidicus III ejaculated, the countenance of Aphrodite suddenly mutated from one of ecstasy to one of torment. A series of clicking noises reverberated through the pleasure chamber as her orgasm triggered the Necrogram. The death-device shot from Harquebus' penis and into her womb, a tiny, straight piece of wire connected to the innards of his testicles that grew after emerging from his urethra, elongating and expanding, sprouting hooks and branching through her flesh like killer dendrites. Like a concatenation of heat-seeking missiles, the lethal network of jointed barbed-wire spread through her vitals and sunk its prongs into her every organ, connecting them like needle-thin scaffolding.

The Necrogram contorted into surgical matrixes and gestalts of excruciating accupuncture, turning her into a living, inside-out voodoo doll. Harquebus smiled to himself as he watched the beauty draining from her face. He always enjoyed watching their facial expressions as they died, the simultaneous eros and thanatos, the exquisite combination of id and epiphany. He liked to imagine their psychological reactions, in that final instant between life and death, when they realized that love, souls, and the afterlife were but illusions to which they had been addicted.

With one cataclysmic lurch, Harquebus withdrew from Aphrodite's flesh. As his tantrically strengthened phallus tore free from the oubliette of her vagina, so too did the tapestry of sexual barbed-wire, its miniature hooks dragging every organ of her body through her uterus and into the open air. As Harquebus backed away from the bed, her entire digestive, respiratory, and reproductive systems slapped the tessellated floor. Her intestines unwound and followed. Her still-beating heart and still-pulsing lungs were twitching and squirming across the tiles, while her esophagus and trachea undulated like copulating earthworms in pools of their own mucus. Tongue and eyeballs were wrenched all the way from skull to crotch, and then, finally, the crown jewel, the glistening mass of her brain, passed through the narrow tunnel of her neck, through the torn membranes and tissues of her thoracic cavity, through her hernia-laden abdomen, and out of her lacerated womb in one sudden motion, completing the inside-out anatomical model of innards and vitals.

Harquebus pulled another three feet of Necrogram from his urethra, then severed the excess length of deadly filament with his rapier. Like retrograde ejaculation, the Necrogram immediately recoiled back into his flesh, rolling into itself like a mating ball of hookworms, winding itself into tinier and tinier spheres of string until it was small enough to crawl back into the tiny caves of his testicles and regenerate.

Harquebus quickly readorned his white, ruffled, Gothique Inc. designer shirt and his black leather pants, then pulled on his dragonskin boots. He tied his belt around his waist, inserted his rapier in its sheath, checked the pistol in his holster, then gathered up the slack end of the Necrogram and flung the concatenation of organs over his shoulder. As the sun set he stole silently through the mansion, out the double doors, across the front porch, and into the cobblestone street. He climbed into his carriage, lashed two of the six stallions which drew it, and disappeared into the twilight, leaving the organless corpse of Aphrodite to be discovered by her chambermaids, devotees, disciples and priests in the morning.

'Goddess of Love,' the tantric assassin thought to himself with a smirk as he rode towards the pink sunset. Aphrodite's epithet had been both an oxymoron and a two-pronged lie. Her death would be a boon for bourgeois and philosophers alike.

*

Harquebus strode through Cabal Cantina, winding his way through the throngs of philosophers, Epicureans, hedonists, maenads, lotophagi, psychonauts, apothecaries, procurers, prostitutes, dominatrices, fetishists, sexual deviants, mercenaries, bounty hunters, serial killers, fallen angels, extraterrestrials, and demiurges. Deftly maneuvering through labyrinths of gluttony and revelry, he spotted his patron seated at a table in a tenebrous corner, dining on . Harquebus slung the entire, connected mass of Aphrodite's excised organs across the table. Hermes looked up and Harquebus held his hand out.

Moments later, with a pouch filled with one hundred gold pieces hanging from his belt, Harquebus crossed to the other side of the cantina. As he walked past two naked, pyrophiliac, Siamese twin albinesses seated upon a marble bench, he spotted his fellow members of Necrofuck, Inc. at their regular booth along the far wall, accompanied by a solipsistic lesbian, an altruistic odalisque, and an atheistic geisha.

Harqeubus made his way towards his comrades, passing a deep-set nook where a gang of four hebephrenic anarchists dressed in white were imbibing liquid amphetamines. One of the youths tipped his cup to him. Harquebus pointed at the youth in acknowledgment as he walked past.

As Harquebus approached the booth where he and the other Deathfuckers always sat, he threw his newly-acquired sack of gold down on the table. . "Absinthe's on me," he said.

"Another false god slain?" asked Chainsaw Rapemeister, looking up from his plate of sauteed swan genitals.

"Goddess," Harquebus clarified.

"Pope Abaddon hires you so much I'm starting to think you're in the Inquisition," said Hydrahead Shrapnelizer.

"It wasn't the Pope this time, actually. Just a pissed-off husband. And you know Father Azrael and General Astaroth would never let me serve in the Inquisition."

"They still mad about that bitch you saved from burning?" asked Ophiucus Planewalker.

"Among other things, my friend. Among other things."

"Whatever happened to her?"

"Pope Abaddon cleared all the charges against her and called off the hunt. She's working in live S & M shows, last I heard. I ought to look her up again. Her pussy was like a garrote. I thought my Necrogram was going to short-circuit and kill her."

Harquebus lit a cigarette, leaned back, put his feet up on the table, and placed an order with a waitress whose every bodily orifice was a vagina, except for her vagina, which was a face. Baubo returned in her stead, a neckless, torsoless, waistless sexling with a tray of drinks balanced atop her flat skull. With a broad smile stretching across her entire face, Baubo raised the stubby arms protruding from the sides of her head and placed a bottle of absinthe on the table, followed by two tankards of wine. Several wine-glasses immediately followed, each with a telamone or a caryatid for a stem.

Baubo smiled again and her pudenda, a mere three inches below her gibbous mouth, seemed to smile as well. Harquebus placed a coin in her vagina and thanked her. She returned his pleasantries and waddled back into the crowd.

Several minutes later, with a half-empty glass of white wine to his left and a half-full glass of red wine to his right, Harquebus snorted a line of cocaine and powdered rhinoceros horn through a straw of filigreed gold. As he did so, two nymphomaniacs made their way to the table, sipping chocolate absinthe from crystal goblets. Harquebus looked up as they seated themselves beside him.

"What exactly are Deathfuckers," asked one, crawling into his lap. "Lovers of death, or slayers of love?"

"Love is for fools and sycophants," he replied, "and cannot be made or killed any more than God or evil or any other illusion. We're sexual assassins... though not averse to trysts between tantramachies."

Deathfuckers weren't usually this forthcoming, but Harquebus' limbic system was floating in warm oceans of wine and the nymphomaniac's question suggested that she already suspected his profession. At any rate, the nymphomaniacs seemed too drugged to recall the conversation in the morning, and if they did he could always execute them.

"Tantramachies?" asked the second girl.

"Sex wars," Harquebus replied. "The art of erotic murder, if you will." He lit another cigarette and took a drag. "We deal in both little deaths and big deaths alike." His witticism regarding le petit mals, orgasms and dying caused an uproar of laughter from everyone at the table.

"I, too, can send a lover to heaven," giggled the first.

"There is no heaven, my dear, nor hell, nor purgatory, nor any afterlife whatsoever. Much like love, such fancies are the refuge of the weak-minded and the sexually ill."

Laughing, the nymphomaniacs kissed him, running their fingers through his long, dark hair, playing with the gold chains and diamond necklaces hanging around his neck, hand-feeding him oysters from the beaches of Lesbos and mushrooms from the fungus forests of Cockaigne.

"Why don't you just kill with your rapier or your pistol?"

"Tis primitive and gauche, my dear. Tantramachy is elegance made lethal."

"Why do you carry weapons, then?"

"Solely for self-defense, I assure you. If I'm attacked by a pack of succubi in an alleyway, I can't very well fuck them all to death, now can I?"

"What happens when someone wants a man assassinated?"

"They hire Chainsaw."

"Fuck you," Chainsaw said, reaching over and cuffing him on the side the head while Hydrahead laughed.

"We have a Kali Division for man-hunting. The bisexual ones kill male and female alike. And we have a Monster Corps for bestial assignments."

As the nymphomaniacs caressed and fondled him, a bald existentialist with a missing eye approached the table. He was flanked by twin ubermensch. The gigantic ubermensch had been completely shaved, making their bald heads, bulbous torsoes, chiseled arms and powerful thighs seem even larger. They wore spiked leather harnesses and girdles, and ironclad chastity belts from which a plethora of hooked weapons dangled. Their genitals were bound up in cock-and-ball devices, and were visible through the large keyholes in their chastity belts. The key was dangling on a gold chain around the existentialist's neck.

The existentialist sat down uninvited, and each of the ubermensch dropped an enormous sack of gold coins on the table. Both bags were more than fifty times the size of the pouch Harquebus had received from his last mission.

Harquebus disentangled himself from the arms of the nymphomaniacs and raised a single eyebrow in inquiry.

"Nihilistika," the man simply stated. "And no questions asked."

"I never ask questions, friend," Harquebus replied, "but 'twill cost you two more bags like those to spur me after prey that deadly."

"This," the existentialist said, sweeping his arm over the bags of gold, "is but an advance. Three times this bounty awaits you once you've assassinated the bitch."

Harquebus considered the offer for several seconds. Few had ever seen Nihilistika, for she was a recluse who never left her palace. She was said to be a sorceress, a vampiress, a succubus and a psychopomp. The last didn't concern him, but the other legends were enough to turn his genitals cold. He thought about all the bounty hunters and assassins who had visited her palace in the past: Hydrahead Shrapnelizer and his detachable, exploding penis; Chainsaw Rapemeister and his mutilatory sex-toys; Electric Siren and her sixteen-megavolt vibrator;Romeo Venom and his cyanide sperm; Kama Thuggee and her cock-and-ball rumel; Pestilus Max and his neurovenereal diseases;Ophiucus Planewalker and his interdimensional serpentiary; Venus Venoma and her living, poisonous, amphisbenic double-dildo/familiar; Castellanand her inner portcullis;Slaughteresse and her abattoir womb; Mistress Vesta the virgin dominatrix and her portable torture chamber; Procrustea and her Deathbed; Shamanique Brainperfume and her mind-altering pheromones; Proteus Rex and his claylike, sarcogenic, womb-filling, flesh-bursting, organ-rupturing, eyeball-popping, skull-breaking, shape-shifting phallus. None of the sexual assassins had returned.

Harquebus shook his head.

"Nay, friend. Tis a suicide mission. There's not enough gold in the world to buy back one's life once it's been spent."

"Quadruple," the man countered. "You'll never have to work again."

Harquebus pursed his lips. Fantasies were flashing in his brain, visions of ménages a trois with mermaids in swimming pools filled with wine; of orgies with a thousand virgins in bathhouses of gold; of a trillion-square foot castle brimming with sex and drugs and wealth and power. Just one last tantramachy, one final bounty, and he could retire in the prime of his youth.

"Quintuple," said the existentialist. "If you won't do it, I'll find somebody else. Quite frankly, they'll probably disappear like the others. That's why I've sought you out. You're the best in the business, but this is all the gold I have. Once its been spent on other assassins, be they successful or unsuccessful, t'will be gone forever. Tis the opportunity of a lifetime, my friend."

Harquebus reached across the table and took the bags of gold. "Give me your address. I'll have her organs on your front porch by sunrise."

*

He had considered fleeing with the gold, taking up residence in some other realm, but the allure of lifelong riches was too great, and by midnight he found himself trekking through the aphrodisiac jungles surrounding Nihilistika's palace.

Along a winding path he strode, betwixt giant mandrakes and towering gingko plants, through glades where lounging lotophagi stargazed, oblivious to the green beetles which sometimes scurried over their bodies. He passed through purple meadows where hornless rhinoceroses grazed; crossed bridges of sandalwood over ponds of liquid attar where castrated swans swam about in strange patterns; and all the while, in the shadows of the forest, he could hear the sounds of copulating beasts, and the rustling of satyrs chasing woodsprites, and the rumblings of teratonymphs chasing satyrs. Through the strange flora and fauna he walked for nearly an hour, until at last he came to the rose-colored palace of Nihilistika.

Harquebus gazed upon the ithyphallic parapets and minarets, the hemi-orchid crenellations and corbels, as he made his approach. As he crossed the moat of sperm, he observed that the palace had no windows. Other than the pink, irising portal at the end of the drawbridge, it was completely devoid of entrances and egresses.

The portal dilated as he approached, as if it had been expecting him. Harquebus stepped into the palace, glancing warily from side to side. As he made his way through the entrance hall, he wondered how many victims had crossed its tesselated floor before him, never to return.

He drew his rapier and pistol as he navigated the twisted halls of the palace, halls which ran hurtling like severed veins toward some pouring wound. Wandering circular labyrinths, he neither saw nor heard any sign of life. He ascending a helixing stairwell and entered a library of curiosa. Pausing to open some of the pornographic tomes that lined the bookshelves, he discovered descriptions and pictures of sexual acts and tantramachies more arcane and complex than any he had ever learned, or even knew existed. Several copies of the Kama Sutra, including versions translated into German, Enochian, Transylvanian, and Atlantean, were amongst the books lining the library shelves. Thinking of Nihilistika, he found the various volumes simultaneously thrilling and foreboding, wondering how many of the techniques she had mastered.

Leaving the library behind, Harquebus navigated through mazes of pleasure domes, saunas, balinea, wineries and opium dens, finally finding Nihilistika's secret bedchambers at the exact nexus of the palace. He tested the door and, finding it unlocked, silently entered the room.

From the golden bed with its silk blankets to the pink curtains and the creamy carpet, from the perfumed air to the twin, curving stairways and the balcony overlooking the room from behind a railing of filigreed baberies, the bedchambers of Nihilistika were filled with love, nothing but love, pure, tangible, immediately jarring him into a higher state of consciousness. Harquebus' muscles relaxed and his fists unclenched. He barely noticed the sound of his rapier and pistol striking the floor.

"Welcome to my chamber."

The voice came from everywhere and nowhere at once. Glancing upwards, Harquebus espied Nihilistika leaning over the ithyphallic damascenes and pornographic bas-reliefs that comprised the balcony railing. Her hair was black as Acheron; her skin was white as angel's milk; her lips were red as lacerations. She turned and, like smoke and shadows, languorously descended one of the convex stairways. As she walked towards his paralyzed body her cheeks and labia blushed like heliotropic roses in the morn. Her nipples and clitoris were stiffening like rigor mortis in the sun, and her pupils and vagina were dilating like interdimensional portals at midnight.The pheromones wafting from her marmoreal skin were soporific incense, immediately jarring him into a lower state of consciousness.

"My chamber has been expecting you." Her lips turned black as she spoke, her eyelids turned black as she made eye contact, her nipples turned black as she approached, and her labia turned black as a tiny drip of semen leaked from Harquebus' semi-erect phallus.

His genitals turned cold. Seized by an unpleasant combination of ague and horripilation, Harquebus wondered how and why Nihilistika had known he was coming. He tried to respond but couldn't speak, for his tongue was swollen like an erection.

He stared into her eyes. One of her eyeballs was like an abyss; the other an atramentous sphere. Her pupils alternately dilated and constricted, forming a hypnotic rhythm that entranced him like the stare of a cobra. His member hardened like a man turned to stone by Medusa's gaze. Though his instincts were telling him to flee the palace, Harquebus was possessed by a raw, atavistic lust. His desire to make love to Nihilistika was equal to his desire to murder her. A strange equilibrium of eros and thanatos was balancing his body with his mind, and a bizarre syzygy of id, ego and superego was aligning in his psyche. He could no more leave the palace without fulfilling his obsession than he could without completing his mission. Neither death nor love alone would do... he had to have them both.

His phallus throbbed with priapism, distended and gibbous with more blood than was natural, more blood than was healthy, more blood than was logical, so much blood that his brain was being deprived of oxygen, leaving him lightheaded and disoriented. His mind rippled and contorted asNihilistika took his hand. She led him across the room, pulled him onto her bed and dragged him into her flesh. Her vaginal walls were as hot as the machinery of Gehenna, and the amniotic moisture of her womb clung to his flesh like the mists of Erebus.

After several minutes of copulation, Nihilistika showed no signs of climaxing. Harquebus' tantric abilities enabled him to delay ejaculation for several hours, but as the time began to pile up, he started to worry. The Necrohedron could only be triggered by simultaneous orgasms. If Harquebus reached orgasm first, and Nihilistika did not reciprocate, nothing but sperm would emerge from his phallus.

He wondered if she was afflicted with anhedonia, or a practitioner of tribadism. His every instinct screamed at him to withdraw, to withdraw from her flesh, her room, her palace and the bargain with the mysterious existentialist, and yet he remained hypnotically bound to all four.

A true tantramachy ensued, with Harquebus fighting to bring Nihilistika to orgasm while simultaneously attempting to negate his own. The undertow of her womb was calling him, beckoning. The tip of his phallus began to drip, and his flesh surrendered.

In the throes of a euphoric white orgasm, Harquebus threw his head back in ecstacy. As he turned his face toward the ceiling he suddenly noticed the bald existentialist from the cantina, standing on the balcony like a giant penis, peering over the pornographic railing with his one remaining eye. The twin, bulbous, testicular ubermensch were once again flanking the existentialist like Gog and Magog. The entire trio were observing the tantramachy with voyeuristic solemnity. Harquebus realized he had been deceived, that the existentialist was allied with Nihilistika and had lured him to her palace for some odious purpose, to be made into a sacrifice or a feast or a sex-slave or worse, to be tortured or raped or killed or all three. Harquebus attempted to escape the death-grip of Nihilistika's vaginal walls, but his euphoric orgasm chained him to her womb like a phallic fetter.

Harquebus' genitals began to itch and sting and vibrate with pain. He shuddered as the waves of pleasure turned into a series of excruciating red orgasms. Nihilistika's womb was churning like a vacuum, sucking all the blood from his body through his turgid penis. He could feel his veins and arteries being drained. His entire crotch roared with smashing agony as every drop of his blood passed through it. The rushing bloodstream abraded and eroded the inside of his penis. As his veins and arteries emptied, Harquebus could feel his consciousness and his life being drawn through his flesh as well, and then his very soul, ripped from its plane of existence and channeled through his physical body, to be ejaculated with the same unrelenting, excruciating, lethal orgasm.

Harquebus gazed into Nihilistika's eyes as she possessed him. The torment of his hemagogic orgasm, the painful clenching of his desiccated veins, the pangs of his hollow heart, the violent passage of his soul through his body, none were as horrifying as her succubus eyes, for those eyes were the most beautiful things he had ever beheld. But most horrifying of all was that he loved Nihilistika, loved her even as she sucked his soul into the black underworlds of her womb, into an abyss deeper and darker than Tartarus, into an afterlife more tortuous than Hell itself.

Metamorphtheism

"I," said the elf messiah, "seek only a good place to die."

Lying in the grass with his back against the trunk of the sapient Bodhi Tree, Asjarra watched his own mellifluous and mournful voice breeze through the Gardens of Enlightenment like a swarm of fireflies, illuminating the flowerbeds with its golden effulgence, opening sacred lotus petals as though it were the light of dawn, rustling through hedge-mazes like a stalking predator, floating along the cobblestone paths like a tribe of lost souls, and scattering the shadows cast by the Bodhi Tree's eight-mile canopy of heart-shaped leaves and sentient branches.

Above Asjarra's head, the Bodhi Tree was fashioning another cigar. Using its twigs like fingers, the Bodhi Tree rolled a small pile of its own fig leaves in a sheaf of brown paper gleaned from its own bark.

"Tell me something, Asjarra," said the Bodhi Tree, "how will you know when you have found this death-place?"

The Bodhi Tree lifted the cigar to its wide mouth with a prehensile branch and sealed it with the sap of its tongue. It used Asjarra's glowing soul to light it. The Bodhi Tree raised to the cigar to its mouth again, wrapped its wooden lips around it, and breathed in.

Several moments later, the Bodhi Tree exhaled a cloud of green smoke and handed the cigar to Asjarra. Asjarra placed the cigar between his lips and inhaled the sweet fumes of the psychedelic fig leaves. The sudden jolt of enlightenment caused his body to flash like a giant will-o'-the-wisp.

"The same way Buddha knew when he'd attained enlightenment," Asjarra responded, for a brief moment sensing the psychometric energies of his predecessor, Siddhartha Gautama, swirling and radiating in the ground beneath him. Asjarra was lying upon the exact spot where the Buddha had meditated for forty-nine days and attained enlightenment. "The same way one knows if they are falling, floating, or flying."

Asjarra handed the cigar back to the Bodhi Tree. The bark eyelids of the Bodhi Tree blinked open and shut as it breathed in another mouthful of fig smoke. The knotholes of its eyes glowed as it inhaled.

"The universe will not let you die until you've completed your mission, Asjarra."

Asjarra could feel the vibrations of the Bodhi Tree's voice in the wood against his back, ringing his vertebrae like bells and amphorae. His spine tingled and resonated, as if it were being tuned like a musical instrument, or harmonized like the chakras of an angel.

"Why does the universe need another messiah? Weren't Siddhartha, Jesus, and Demeter enough to save it?"

"You know how the universe works," said the Bodhi Tree. "You know the sacred number. Everything happens in fours."

A look of confusion crossed Asjarra's face. "I thought everything happened in threes. I thought three was the sacred number."

The Bodhi Tree took a long drag from the cigar.

"Not anymore."

The Bodhi Tree handed Asjarra the remaining stub of the cigar.

"Why did the sacred number change?"

"Asjarra, the only thing constant is change. The only thing infinite is change. The only thing eternal is change."

The elf messiah pondered this for several minutes. Questions were spinning in his head like zodiacs.

"Bodhi Tree, what is the true nature of God?" Asjarra asked as he smoked the last morsel of fig leaves.

"God is always omnipresent, sometimes omniscient, and never omnipotent."

"Why did He choose me? How can I save the universe when I can't even save my own soul?" Asjarra flicked the remaining bit of cigar into the gardens.

"God is a mysteriarch," was the Bodhi Tree's only response.

"God is the Monster," Asjarra replied.

*

The Bodhi Tree was but one part of Yggdrasil, the unfathomably large, interdimensional, trans-temporal World Tree whose bridge-like branches connected all of the planes in the universe and kept them safely suspended over the bottomless abyss of

Nethernirvana. Asjarra had descended from its cosmos-sized labyrinth the night before, taking a brief sojourn from his quest for a death-place to visit the Bodhi Tree, his ancient guru. Now, just after sunrise, Asjarra walked back along the branches of the Bodhi Tree, headed back into the arboreal maze of Yggdrasil, to resume his morbid pilgrimage and his jihad against both evil and himself.

Asjarra fit the tree like camouflage. Its deep brown branches were the color of his eyes and boots; its green leaves the color of his tunic and leggings. The springtime sun filtering through the treetops was golden and glowing, just like his aura and waist-length hair. Its heart-shaped fig-leaves were pointed like his elven ears. It was as though the fey messiah and the sessile yogi shared a singular, sylvan soul.

Three of the Bodhi Tree's hamadryads, Syke, Upeleva, and Moracea, had accompanied Asjarra into the treetops. Syke, the mistress of the Bodhi Tree's Hamadryad Harem, navigated the branches with an expertise acquired by centuries of experience and millennia of reincarnation. The tree-nymphs knew every twig and leaf of their beloved soulmate, and they knew where its interdimensional vortices lay hidden, as well.

From high in the treetops, Asjarra looked down upon the Gardens of Enlightenment and the Bodhi Tree one last time. He could still see the cerise illumination of the fig leaves burning in the pipe, the very fig leaves which had set his soul alight and caused him to evolve from human to elf, and shaman to messiah, on that halcyon day when he had come to the Tree to be enlightened by wisdom, and left the Gardens emburdened with knowledge.

Asjarra and the three hamadryads passed through an interdimensional portal and emerged in another part of Yggdrasil. Whispers of the Fourth Coming preceded and followed the elf messiah as tree-dwelling creatures glimpsed his luminous form. Asjarra paid them no heed, for he was looking around for a good place to die. Some of the chattering became malevolent. The sound of cloven hooves striking wood followed quickly thereafter.

Sensing danger, Asjarra pulled his thaumaturgical broadsword, the Godblade, from its scabbard with his right hand, and unhooked his incandescent morning star, Lucifer, from his belt with his left. An instant later, priapic satyrs began dropping from the treetops.

They were armed with nets and daggers, and each one fought like a retiarius.

The first satyr that landed in front of Asjarra charged like a taurean imp.Asjarra swung the Godblade. The ensorcelled sword tore into the satyr's chest and electrocuted him with a jolt of holy energy. Asjarra then spun to his left and struck the satyr in the skull with a backswing of his morning star. Lucifer's white-hot spikes melted the satyr's horned head from his shoulders. Molten brains dribbled around cloven hooves as the headless corpse toppled.

Within minutes, the entire branch was drenched with blood and entrails. Severed legs and goatlike heads were scattered everywhere. The corpses of electrocuted and half-melted satyrs were plummeting to the ground below. Soon, they would meet God. Soon, they would meet the Monster.

The sight of the satyrs' souls jumping to the afterlife, visible only to his enlightened eyes, brought Asjarra a strange and vicarious tranquility. He envied them their temporary respites, even though he knew that their longings, addictions, and desires would quickly return them to the world of flesh.

When he turned around, Asjarra saw that the satyrs had captured the hamadryads in their nets and were dragging them away, leaving smears of crimson upon the branches in their wake.

Asjarra threw the Godblade. It spun through the air, slicing through nets and satyr-flesh alike, then turned and flew back to Asjarra's open hand. The hamadryads tore themselves free from the remaining strands of rope as the satyrs died.

Asjarra walked over to the wounded hamadryads. He placed his palms upon Upeleva's lacerated torso. His hands glowed even brighter as he healed her. The wound sealed itself, with no trace of a scar. He touched Moracea's face, and the cut that had torn her cheek open instantly vanished. Lastly, he approached Syke, lay his hand upon her left breast, and closed the deep puncture wound which had penetrated her ribcage and nearly grazed her heart. The bloodstains upon the skin of all three hamadryads disappeared when Asjarra healed their wounds, leaving the tree-nymphs as clean and pure as if they had just bathed in a waterfall of hyaline.

A murder of crows were already devouring the corpses of the satyrs. Without looking back, Asjarra and the hamadryads continued their journey. An hour later, they arrived at another golden interdimensional portal.Upeleva and Moracea decided to return home, but Syke chose to remain with Asjarra for a while longer. The elf messiah exchanged kisses, embraces, and farewells with the other two hamadryads, then stepped into another dimension with Syke at his side.

*

Asjarra and Syke heard the distant call of a tree-nymph as they made love. They quickly disentangled themselves and rose from the center of the empty roc's nest as the cry grew nearer. Their hair was scattered and their naked bodies were streaked with sweat. Syke's face was flushed, and her breasts were heaving. Asjarra seemed more melancholy than usual. He quickly put on his green tunic and leggings.Syke likewise re-covered her lower parts with the scant leaves that served as her clothing.They turned their heads and peered through the treetops.

Another of the Bodhi Tree's hamadryads, Artio, was flying towards them on the back of her winged bear, Ursiad. She caught up to them a few seconds later. The flying bear halted and hovered in mid-air as she delivered her message.

"Lord Asjarra, Lady Syke" she said breathlessly, "the armies of the Anti-Buddha have invaded the garden."

*

Asjarra battled the hordes of Anti-Buddhists, slashing and smiting with Godblade and Lucifer. The Bodhi Tree's Hamadryad Harem descended from their hammocks and emerged from their knotholes to join the battle. As they did so, the Bodhi Tree closed its bark eyelids and drifted into a meditative trance.

The Hamadryad Harem fought with wooden spears and bo staffs fashioned from the Bodhi Tree's branches. The spearheads had been dipped in the psychedelic sap of the Bodhi Tree. The hamadryads wielded the spears with jousting and fencing techniques when forced into close-quarters combat. Whenever they had the chance, they launched the spears through the air with deadly aim. Once impaled or skewered from afar by the drug-tipped spears, the Anti-Buddhists crumpled to the ground, writhing with the enlightenment that was anathema to their dark and twisted souls.

The hamadryads wielding bo staffs used fighting techniques

involving constant movement. They flashed through the masses of warriors with sylvan speed, darting back and forth, repeatedly striking Anti-Buddhists in the face and skull. Artio fired arrows into the midst of the still-approaching army from atop Ursiad. The flying bear often dive-bombed the attackers and savaged them with its teeth and claws.

The Anti-Buddhists retaliated with whips and chains, entangling and strangling the hamadryads. Theywere obese and yet, despite their girth, they fought like berserkers, with an agility and celerity incongruous with their appearance. A thousand different kinds of jewelry adorned their bodies, stabbed and stuck through pierced ears, noses, tongues, nipples, and genitals. Gold rings encircled their fat and filthy fingers. They were led by the demon Mara, who rode a black elephant and fought with a javelin, sometimes throwing it like a spear and sometimes wielding it like a lance.

Asjarra fought like an angel of war. The Godblade crackled with white electricity as he sheared an Anti-Buddhist in half. He shot a bolt of lightning from the tip of the thaumaturgical broadsword at another Anti-Buddhist, who exploded even as Asjarra was bashing in the face of one of his brethren with Lucifer. The white-hot spikes of the incandescent morning star simultaneously melted flesh, skull, and brains.

An instant later, somewhere in the universe, the souls of all three Anti-Buddhists reincarnated, each one immediately rechanneling its consciousness into a random womb. They completed their metempsychosis before their former bodies even hit the ground. Thus had it always been, and thus would it always be, for the samsaric cycle of every Anti-Buddhist was an ouroboros, a never-ending circle which they had no ambitions of breaking. They refused to reflect upon past incarnations, or orchestrate future ones in accordance with accrued karma and experience. The Anti-Buddhists never spent any time in the afterlife whatsoever.

The battle lasted for nearly an hour. Gradually, the Anti-Buddhists were beaten back and destroyed. The remaining survivors retreated at the bellowing command of Mara and followed in the wake of his black elephant steed,back through the Gardens of Enlightenment and into the interdimensional portal from which they had come.

The Bodhi Tree continued to meditate. As Asjarra was delivering a deathblow to one final Anti-Buddhist, a humongous shadow obscured the sun. The elf messiah looked up to see a one hundred foot tall apparition looming over the garden like a black hole god. It had the form of a muscular demon and a head shaped like a tilted spade. Its body was the color of an abyss, and it held an equally dark Sawscythe in its clawed hands. It was the Anti-Buddha himself, dark brother of the Anti-Christ, and he had come to slay the Bodhi Tree.

A flurry of spears flew through the air. The Anti-Buddha raised one hand and the spears all halted in mid-flight, reversed direction, and impaled the hamadryads who had flung them. Asjarra used the Godblade to fire bolts of lightning at the Anti-Buddha, which were deflected as well, but Asjarra reabsorbed them into his glowing sword before they struck his flesh. He aimed the Godblade again and fired a concatenation of corposants, stunning the Anti-Buddha and driving him backwards. Asjarra charged across the gardens while the Anti-Buddha staggered, swinging Lucifer over his head, faster and faster, until it seemed as though the elf messiah possessed a white halo spinning at the speed of light. He released the morning star and it flew through the air, striking the Anti-Buddha in the face. It returned to Asjarra's hand with black blood sizzling on the tips of its heated spikes.

The Anti-Buddha halted briefly, then continued his silent approach. Despite his immensity, his footsteps made no sound as he walked. As he drew closer, Asjarra could see that he cast a shadow in every direction at once, regardless of the angles of light which fell upon him. He seemed to absorb that light, as well, like a sapient incarnation of night.

Asjarra ran at the Anti-Buddha and slashed at his knees. The Anti-Buddha raised his foot and kicked Asjarra squarely in the sternum. The elf messiah flew backwards through the air, flipping over repeatedly, until finally landing in a tangle of the Bodhi Tree's branches, high above the garden.

The Anti-Buddha raised his Sawscythe. The serrated blades began to cycle and the entire device vibrated, yet, just like its master, it made no sound whatsoever. Pacing forward with the silent Sawscythe, the Anti-Buddha approached the Bodhi Tree and began severing its thick branches. Hamadryads beat him about the legs with fists, spears, and bo staffs, but he was oblivious to their attack. Humongous branches fell from the treetops, crushing bushes and flowerbeds beneath them, and sometimes crushing hamadryads, as well.

Perched high within the Bodhi Tree, Asjarra bided his time. When the Anti-Buddha aimed his Sawscythe at the branch he was crouching on, Asjarra leapt into the air and parried the churning weapon with Lucifer. The spikes of the morning star clogged the serrations of the Sawscythe, and its gears ground to a halt. The Sawscythe began to melt, trapping Lucifer like adamantium candlewax. Asjarra pulled upon its handle but could not free it from the viscous mass. He abandoned Lucifer, leapt onto the Anti-Buddha's right shoulder, and attempted to sever his jugular vein and carotid artery with the Godblade. Black blood spurted, but the Anti-Buddha only turned his head and blew a foul wind from his mouth,sending Asjarra through the air once again. The elf messiah's spine cracked against a large branch. He struck his head upon another branch as he ricocheted downwards, then landed heavily on the ground, gasping with pain.

Throughout the entire battle,the struggles and deaths of its hamadryad soulmates, the valiant efforts of the elven messiah, and its own dismemberment by the Sawscythe of the Anti-Buddha, the Bodhi Tree had remained in a meditative trance. Finally, after more than anhour, its knothole eyes opened. The Bodhi Tree exhaled a green cloud of smoke the size of a castle and stronger than ten hurricanes. The cloud of smoke caught the Anti-Buddha in its verdant winds and lifted him bodily from the ground. A green tornado formed around the Anti-Buddha, wrapping him up like a chrysalis and lifting him into the skies.

The bruised and bloodied Asjarra watched the Anti-Buddha rise. Lucifer was still welded to the Sawscythe. Asjarra held out his left hand and called the weapon home. Instead, Asjarra found himself soaring through the air, hurtling towards the Anti-Buddha. An instant later Lucifer was once again in his grasp, but not in the way he had intended.

The cyclone of leaf-colored smoke swirled and spiraled and lifted through the skies, higher and higher, until finally the breath of the Bodhi Tree had been completely expended. Meanwhile, Asjarra had clambered atop the Sawscythe and was hacking at the Anti-Buddha's shoulder. The Anti-Buddha's arm loosened as the Godblade grew more and more powerful with every strike. The Anti-Buddha continued to hang, suspended from the stratosphere, silently coughing, poisoned by enlightenment. The Anti-Buddha snarled, turned, and, with Asjarra still flailing away at its upper arm, began to float back down to Nethernirvana, its home at the bottom of the universe.

At the last instant, the Anti-Buddha's right arm finally came loose. Severed appendage, Sawscythe, Lucifer, Godblade,and Asjarra all tumbled from the sky and landed in a pile in front of the Bodhi Tree.

The Bodhi Tree did not notice, for it was fast asleep.

*

Asjarra wiped the last remnants of black residue from his morning star. The giant Sawscythe still lay at his feet, with a vast, sticky hole like a tar pit in the spot where Lucifer had been lodged.Right next to it lay the severed arm of the Anti-Buddha.

Once Lucifer had been cleaned, Asjarra hung the weapon from his belt, then sat down and leaned against the trunk of the Bodhi Tree.The Bodhi Tree had just reawakened and was pulling a long, sigmoid hookah from the knothole of its right eye. The hookah had been made from the wood of the crucifix upon which Jesus Christ had died, which itself had been made from the wood of the Bodhi Tree. The hookah was filled with Holy Water. A few moments later it was full of fig leaves, as well.

They traded the water-pipe back and forth. The restorative powers of the psychedelic fig-leaves healed Asjarra's wounds and regenerated the Bodhi Tree's severed branches. Both elf messiah and sentient tree were nearly asleep when the garden erupted.

Dirt rained down like a meteor shower as the left arm of the Anti-Buddha emerged from the ground. An instant later the gargantuan apparition climbed through the dimensions separating Nethernirvana from the Gardens of Enlightenment. He emerged from the bottom of the universe and, through the earthquake he had wrought, covered the entire garden with his shadow. Only the unquenchable light of Asjarra's soul, the glow of the Godblade and Lucifer on the grass, and the tiny cherry flame in the Bodhi Tree's hookah were visible in the darkness. Asjarra's eyes snapped open. He grabbed his weapons and sprang to his feet. The Bodhi Tree did not waken.

The Anti-Buddha reached down and retrieved his Sawscythe.With his single arm, he used it like a machete, hacking away at the branches of the Bodhi Tree. Obsessed with dismembering the Bodhi Tree, the Anti-Buddha seemed not to notice Asjarra's presence. The glowing elf messiah was but a firefly in comparison to the pitch-black monstrosity.

Asjarra held his left hand over his eyes to protect his face and head from the falling debris. As leaves, shards of wood, and entire branches fell around him, he raised the Godblade and aimed it at the severed arm of the Anti-Buddha on the ground. The amputated limb levitated from the bloody grass. Asjarra swung the Godblade as though delivering a deathblow, and the hovering appendage flew through the air, following the trajectory of the ensorcelled sword. The Anti-Buddha's severed arm crashed through his chest like a trebuchet through a battlement, then emerged from his back with his own black heart beating in his clenched fist.

As the Anti-Buddha toppled, the Sawscythe fell from his lifeless grip and dropped through the interdimensional chasm he had torn in the ground. The corpse of the Anti-Buddha struck the earth without a sound, but the impact created a seismic disturbance which could be felt by every creature and plant for miles around.

The Anti-Buddha's corpse began to bloat in the heat of Asjarra's aura. A murder of crows descended from the skies, to feast upon the fresh carrion.

The Bodhi Tree was already smoking fig leaves again, this time from a calumet carved from one of its own roots.Asjarra joined him. Together, they watched the crows reduce the Anti-Buddha's corpse to nothingness. It had not possessed a skeleton.

Mesmerized by the fig leaves, Asjarra and the Bodhi Tree watched the cascades of dirt falling through the interplanal sinkhole which the Anti-Buddha had wrought. Ashes and sparks from the calumet floated through the air. A few drifted into the small pit and disappeared into the bottomless abyss below. Asjarra and the Bodhi Tree gazed upon these with equal fascination.

"Asjarra," said the Bodhi Tree, some indeterminate amount of time later, "you do realize that the Anti-Buddha returned to the garden for the same reason you severed his arm."

"Which is?" Asjarra asked skeptically.

"Possessiveness. You could not bear to part with your morning star, Lucifer. The Anti-Buddha lost his arm and his Sawscythe because of this. He returned for both, because he could not bear to part with his physical possessions any more than you could. Desire and materialism, Asjarra, are the causes of all the suffering in the universe."

"Maybe I just don't like change," Asjarra replied as he rose to his feet. He expelled four wreaths of green smoke, forming a mandala of concentric circles in the air, then said goodbye to the Bodhi Tree. The Bodhi Tree summoned six of his hamadryads, including Syke, to accompany Asjarra into the branches. They climbed into the treetops and made their way to an interdimensional portal.

Before exiting the Gardens of Enlightenment, Asjarra thanked the hamadryads for their assistance. He kissed Syke upon the lips, then stepped into the shimmering tunnel and disappeared into another plane.

Syke turned around with a worried expression upon her face, and told the other hamadryads to start for home without her. When she was positive they were out of sight, she pulled her tunic of fig-leaves away from her torso and glanced down.

There was a growing shadow in her stomach.

*

Nidhug's reptilian eyes grew wide as he watched the Sawscythe plummet through the chthonic skies of Nethernirvana. The Sawscythe was heading directly for the bottomless abyss surrounding the little dragon's island. Nidhug scrambled to the edge of his tiny realm. His tongue uncoiled from his mouth like a serpent, shot across the vacuum, retrieved the weapon, and placed it on the ground before him.

The small dragon laughed with glee as he pondered the Sawscythe. He raised it in his paws, but it wouldn't start. He noticed the hot, oozing pit in the side of the weapon and began glancing around his island, his eyes darting left and right, sometimes independent of one another. He scurried back and forth, looking for anything which might repair and re-start the Sawscythe. He scrabbled through the various piles of treasure he had accumulated over the eons, all the fascinating trinkets and debris that had fallen from the planes above to the bottom of the universe. Looking around once more he spied a small, cherry-red gleam of light that had just fallen from the skies in a cloud of ashes. It smelled of burning figs. He giggled and chattered to himself.

Nidhug gathered up the still-kindled fragment of fig leaf from the pile of fresh ashes. Holding it in both palms, he stood on his hind legs andsprinted back to the Sawscythe. He placed the glowing ember inside the Sawscythe's viscous wound. The bitumen-like slag sizzled and sparked, flowing together like healing flesh beneath the revivifying heat of the sacred, smoldering fig leaf. The damage to the Sawscythe had been reversed. It was ready to carve and dismember once more.

A moment later, the serrated edges of the Sawscythe were churning again. Nidhug laughed uncontrollably, his eyes bright and his eager mouth smiling. He hefted the Sawscythe into the air and staggered like a drunken basilisk lizard to the center of his island, where the half-gnawed, tooth-marked Root of Yggdrasil formed the base of the World Tree that supported the entire universe.

*

Asjarra journeyed through the pathlike branches, searching once more for a good place to die. Whispers of the Fourth Coming rustled through the treetops, from the beaks of meditating owls and soothsaying doves to the mouths ofdevoted squirrels and tale-telling lemurs.One bold fairy princess dropped through the branches to flutter like a hummingbird before him, excitedly asking, "Are you the Fourth Coming?"

"I am," replied Asjarra, "but I am also the coming of death."

"For who?" she chirped.

"For myself, and for everything evil in my path, until I find a good place to die."

Asjarra continued to stoically travel from branch to branch. The fairy princess hovered in mid-air for a few moments, then followed him.

"I am called Dream Berry," the fairy princess said.

"And I Asjarra."

"Would you like to visit my enchanted forest? Perhaps you'll find your death-place there?"

"Perhaps," Asjarra laconically replied.

Dream Berry hesitated for a moment, but the elf messiah gave no further answer. She flew to him again and tugged upon the sleeve of his tunic, pulling him in another direction. She flew ahead of him in dizzying patterns, speeding through the air, dodging twigs and leaves like a dragonfly. After several minutes she flitted back to Asjarra and perched upon his right shoulder. When they came to the interdimensional portal leading to her enchanted forest, she had already flown back into mid-air again. She pulled Asjarra along by the front of his tunic, smiling upwards into his glowing eyes all the while. She fluttered into the golden portal, and the elf messiah followed.

*

Springtime hung warm as a body in the enchanted forest. It was a time of rebirth. It was not a time of death. Asjarra was disheartened by this.

"Do you believe in God?" Dream Berry asked, smoking strawberry leaves from a golden flute that played music as she inhaled. Pink smoke swirled through the air and drifted from between her lips.

"I believe in the Monster," Asjarra replied, drinking blueberry absinthe from a golden chalice.

"Why do you hate Him so?" she inquired, her eyes the eyes of a child. They traded flute and chalice. Dream Berry sipped upon the intoxicating indigo absinthe as Asjarra inhaled the sweet, tranquilizing fumes of the strawberry leaves.

"I don't hate Him," Asjarra said, "but he chose the wrong soul. I love God and I love the universe, and it is my weaknesses and sins which are going to bring about the destruction of both."

The leafbed they shared began to stir. Asjarra looked around concernedly.

"Tis' the wind," said Dream Berry.

"That's no wind," Asjarra replied.

The trees in the enchanted forest began to shake. Leaves, twigs, fruit, and nuts plummeted from the vibrating branches.

"Tis' an earthquake," Dream Berry said.

"That's no earthquake, either."

Asjarra stood, his eyes heavy with doom, as the entire universe shuddered. He quickly spoke an elven mantra and transformed into a small sphere of light, hovering like a corposant or a will-o'-the-wisp. The glowing orb hummed, then flew off in a flash of quanta.

Asjarra traveled through the dimensions at the speed of light. He hurtled like an unstable sunbeam towards the axis mundi of the universe, passing directly through trees and slingshotting through interplanal portals. Within seconds, he arrived at the hollow Omphalos Tree which formed the nexus of Yggdrasil.

Still maintaining the form of a miniscule sun, Asjarra flew through a tiny knothole in the hollow trunk of the Omphalos Tree. Glancing downward, he saw nothing but bottomless darkness. He returned to his normal form.

The descent began.

*

Asjarra slid down the smooth, curving, twisting chutes of the Omphalos Tree. It was a diagonal and vertical labyrinth of downward slopes, often veering into forked entrances where the right decision was a matter of life or death. Some of the corridors led straight to the bottomless abyss of Nethernirvana. Others led to dead ends that lived up to their names, either because they ended in spiked pits, or because they contained heat-activated avalanches of betel nuts. At best, one might starve to death in an empty oubliette with walls so sheer and slippery no species of lizard or spider could ever climb them.

Using the glow of Lucifer to light his way through the vertical labyrinth, Asjarra hurtled through downward spirals and endless free-falls. He passed through thousands of planes as he fell. When he finally burst through the interdimensional portal linking the Omphalos Tree to the bottom of the universe, he twisted onto his stomach and formed a cross with the Godblade and Lucifer. He held both weapons out in front of him, like a shield, as he slid. The light at the end of the tunnel shined beneath him. It was like having an upside-down near-death experience. Asjarra saw the black Sawscythe tearing through the Root of Yggdrasil. He saw chips of wood flying and dragon eyes gleaming. He saw the thin strand of wood upon which the entire universe was teetering. He saw true death.

Asjarra shot to the tip of Yggdrasil's root like a comet. The crux of Godblade and Lucifer caught Nidhug's Sawscythe, snagging its serrated edges on their hot, ensorcelled steel. Some of the Sawscythe's teeth broke off, but it continued to vibrate and churn.

With the Sawscythe still trapped between Godblade and Lucifer, Asjarra emerged from the tunnel-sized root and rose to one knee. Elf and dragon engaged in a test of strength, which Asjarra slowly won, first battling his way to his feet, then driving the Sawscythe backwards until it cut into Nidhug's forehead and snout. Chips of skull flew, just as chips of wood had flown a moment before. The Sawscythe tore through Nidhug's face and began to separate the hemispheres of his brain. In the meantime, Nidhug had been forced backwards, step by step, and teetered now on the precipice of his island. As the serrated blades began grinding through his corpus callosum, Nidhug fell backwards into the void. He plummeted through the bottomless abyss with the Sawscythe still gnawing away at his bloody head.

Asjarra walked back to the Root of Yggdrasil. He placed his healing hands upon the torn and sundered wood. An instant later, it the Root of Yggdrasil was whole for the first time since Genesis. The worlds above stopped shaking. Order had been restored.

The bottom of the universe seemed, logically, like a good place to die. Asjarra walked around, intensely scrutinizing every square foot of grass. After an hour of searching, he gave up and walked to the edge of the island. He knew there was nothing down here but Nethernirvana, so he whistled into the vacuum and waited to see who or what would come to his rescue. Perhaps it would be Garuda. Perhaps Pegasus. Perhaps Gabriel. He didn't know, and he didn't care.

The ba of the Virgin Mary appeared, winging through empty space. She flew to the edge of the island and hovered before Asjarra. Her body and spirit had taken on the shape of a giant dove. Her face and hair were the same as her human form. Asjarra climbed onto her back and they soared away.

"Do you believe in God?" asked the ba of the Virgin Mary as they flew.

"I am an agnostic," Asjarra replied.

*

Syke writhed in agony upon the bed of leaves inside the Bodhi Tree. The shadow in her stomach had grown to encompass her entire body. Her flesh was completelyblack, as though every inch of it had been bruised. Her skin was starting to tear itself apart. A clawed hand ripped out of her chest, stretching her skin between its fingers as it held her flesh open for the rest of its body to climb through. An instant later, the reincarnation of the Anti-Buddha emerged, shedding Syke's flesh as though it had been nothing more than a caul.

Reborn inside the Bodhi Tree, the Anti-Buddha spread like a gigantic black cancer, filling its every crevice like pouring pitch, squatting inside its hollow trunk like a Stygian parasite, possessing the Bodhi Tree's soul like a dybbuk would possess the soul of a human.

The Bodhi Tree, like so many great trees before it, invincible on the outside,was dying from the inside. The Anti-Buddha gradually twisted the Bodhi Tree into a mutation of its former self.Leaves withered and fell, branches contorted and rotted, wood transformed into solid ebony. Where once the Bodhi Tree had stood, so strong and full of wisdom, there was now only a massive, deformed, hideous, black baobab. The Anti-Buddha nestled into his new lair and christened it Chaitan.

Hamadryads flew in swarms from the Bodhi Tree's knotholes to escape the Anti-Buddha, like birds fleeing a forest fire. The Garden of Enlightenment had been transformed into a lethal gauntlet of belladonna and nightshade, Venus flytraps and strigefleurs, Nezerai flowers and gigantic asphodels.The Bodhi Tree had been transformed into the Devil Tree, and the Gardens of Enlightenment were dead.

One last ember of kindled fig-leaf was all that remained of the Bodhi Tree. It burned with a tiny, inch-high flame for over an hour, flickering in the breeze, before a gust of wind finally blew through the gardens and extinguished it forever.

*

The ba of the Virgin Mary landed upon the edge of the cliff. Asjarra dismounted and bade her spirit farewell. She flew into the skies and disappeared. Asjarra turned and began walking down a dirt path leading into the Forest of Suicide.

As he walked, his elven footsteps crushed tangled masses of lascivious woodsprites. Enraptured by their ritual springtime orgies, the woodsprites were oblivious to his approach until they heard the screams of their kin, and the crackle of their splintering bones.Asjarra paid them little heed as he trampled their prone and prostrate forms, smashing their miniature bodies, subconsciously weeding the evil woodsprites from the good. Crushing the woodsprites to death brought Asjarra a sadomasochistic pleasure, the kind a messiah such as he should not have experienced.

Whispers of the Fourth Coming preceded and followed the elf messiah. He felt no need to respond.

When he came to the queen of the woodsprites in a bed of roses, he paused. She shrieked and drew back, her naked flesh exposed to the sole of his leather boot. Asjarra stared into her tree-brown eyes and was overcome by a magnetic surge that could mean only one thing.

She was a soulmate.

Asjarra reached down and picked her up. His touch healed her fear, and her flesh began to glow like his. Her smile was like an upside-down sunrise.

"Are you the Fourth Coming?" she asked.

"I am,"

"I am called Valhanii."

"And I Asjarra."

"I can guide you through the Forest of Suicide. Perhaps your death-place lies within, your path to enlightenment and heaven."

"Perhaps."

Without accepting or declining her offer, Asjarra set the queen of the woodsprites back on the ground, then began walking down the path once more. Valhanii hesitated, then decided to travel with him.

At times, Asjarra would pause, look around, and feel the earth. He used his psychic powers to study ley lines, seek out power spots, and tap into geomantic vibrations. When he became satisfied that he had not yet found his death-place he would sigh, rise again, and continue his journey.

*

The first thing Asjarra noticed when he entered the Forest of Suicide was that the Bodhi Tree's hamadryads were hanging from the branches on freshly-made nooses.He closed his eyes, for he knew exactly what their deaths meant. Tears streamed from the corners of his shut eyelids. For an hour he stood unmoving, paralyzed by grief, before he was finally able to re-open his eyes and once again look for a good place to die.

Ursiad, Artio's flying bear, was wandering about the forest, lost in its own mourning. Asjarra called it to his side and pressed his glowing hands upon its muzzle. The flying bear nuzzled against Asjarra's chest. Once healed, it licked the side of Asjarra's face, then flew off in the direction of the cliff.

Asjarra gazed upon the dangling corpses of the Hamadryad Harem again. Each had chosen an individual tree from which to hang themselves. Asjarra began to weep once more as he walked through the Forest of Suicide.

All around them, Asjarra and Valhanii could hear the moans ofthe tormented spirits trapped inside the trees. Broken twigs and branches, and patches of peeled bark, dripped blood instead of sap. The Forest of Suicide was the antithesis of the Bodhi Tree.

A harpy rose from a nest of bones and another emerged from a nest of entrails. They flew at Asjarra like twin raptors.Asjarra killed them both instantaneously, impaling the one to his right with the Godblade and caving in the skull of the other with Lucifer.

Dark elves emerged from burrows and hollow logs, brandishing torches and black scimitars. Asjarra swung the Godblade in a circle of death around his body as they attacked. The thaumaturgical broadsword crackled as it electrocuted its victims. The incandescent morning star glowed as its spikes melted eyeballs and entrails. Like sciamachy was the battle, each dark elf the shadow of some facet of Asjarra's soul.

Valhanii, perched upon his shoulder, pulled a handful of pixie dust from her pouch and blew it into the eyes of one of the dark elves. The dust ate his eyeballs alive. Blinded, he was easy prey for the Godblade, and his severed, eyeless head was soon rolling through the forest.. Several other dark elves perished in a similar manner. When she was out of pixie dust, Valhanii withdrew a tiny blow-gun from her belt and placed it between her lips.She fired curare-tipped arrows with the precision of Eros: through the heart, every single time.

The forest floor was soon covered with corpses. All about them lay dark elves with punctured chests, melted skulls, liquefied entrails, smoldering lacerations, and dismembered body parts that belched smoke from their sizzling wounds.

After the battle with the dark elves, Asjarra and Valhanii walked unmolested through the Forest of Suicide.

"Do you believe in God?" Valhanii asked Asjarra, some time later, as they traveled.

"I am an atheist," Asjarra replied.

Eventually, they came to the ring of four trees that marked the nexus of the forest. Each contained the soul of a famous suicide, trapped in an arboreal prison reflecting their chosen method of death. The knotholed Tree of Dido teemed with giant termites, grubs, and serpents. The poisonous Tree of Phaedre was blooming with nightshade and belladonna, and surrounded by the corpses of dead bats and eagles. The water-logged Tree of Aegeus loomed like a giant piece of driftwood, a sweating wooden effigy, with mold and fungi visibly crawling across its branches and up its trunk. The Tree of Elissa was surrounded by the stench of burning leaves, and dropped ashes from its blackened branches to the ground below.

The four trees encircled the towering, eight-mile tall Yaxche Tree, from which Ixtab, goddess of suicide, ruled the forest.Hanging high overhead from a rope and gallows intertwined with the treetops,Ixtab's eyes remained closed as Asjarra and Valhanii approached.She smelled of peyote and rot, and her flesh was in a perpetual, yet eternal, state of decomposition

Asjarra climbed into the Yaxche Tree and Valhanii fluttered behind. The elf messiah sought to exit the Forest of Suicide, and find a different part of Yggdrasil to wander. He quickly scaled the gargantuan tree, then carefully walked along the branch which served as Ixtab's gallows pole. When he stepped upon the piece of wood directly above the crown of her skull, Ixtab's eyes flashed open, and the goddess of suicide immediately began climbing her own noose.Asjarra reacted simultaneously, severing the rope from which she hung with the Godblade. The goddess fell, but as she did so she removed the noose from around her neck and threw it into the air like a lasso, encircling Valhanii's waist and torso. The slipknot immediately tightened, squeezing the air from her lungs. Ixtab struck the ground eight miles below and died. Valhanii did the same a second later. The vicious force of the fall shattered all of the hollow bones in the tiny woodsprite's body, and she died before Asjarra's healing hands could reach her.

The death of Ixtab immediately freed all the souls trapped inside the trees. Ixtab's death was their life, just as her life had been their suicides. She was a parasite whose existence had been dependent upon despair, tragedy, and demise. Now, she had only her own pain, suffering, and death to feed upon.

Released from their private purgatories, all the spirits that had ever committed suicide were finally able to resume their samsaric cycles. Their salvation had come at a price, though, and that price had been the life of Valhanii.

Looking off into the far distance, Asjarra was saddened to see that the hanging hamadryads were not among the freed souls. The elf messiah knelt down and quietly buried the queen of the woodsprites. He tested the ground with his right hand, but Valhanii's deathbed was not his. Asjarra rose and scaled the Yaxche Tree once again. At its very top he found a violet interdimensional portal, hovering in the air just above him like a seventh chakra might hover above the crown of a behemoth monk. Asjarra gripped its vibrating edge with both hands and pulled himself inside.

*

Asjarra climbed down the Tree of Good and Evil and entered the Garden of Eden. The instant his feet touched the grass, he felt the long-awaited jolt in his body, mind, and soul, the vertiginous deja vu, the brand-new yet somehow familiar emotion that meant his death-place was near.

The sweet magnetic pull, the psychic gravity, drew him down a cobbled path which ended in a catafalque. Atop the catafalque lay a coffin, glowing as bright as his soul. The light beckoned him with a call that could only be perceived with a synesthesia of all six senses. As he approached the funeral platform he saw Satan lying in the casket. An angel and a demoness, both with butterfly wings, were slowly closing the coffin.

Asjarra flung the Godblade. It flew through the air, end over end, and jammed the lid of the casket. Satan roared with rage and exploded from his intended deathbed. The butterfly-winged angel and demoness faded into the background.

Asjarra calmly caught the Godblade as it returned to his open hand. He unhooked Lucifer with the other. Satan charged like a taurean behemoth. Asjarra somehow felt tranquil as the Devil bore down upon him.

Asjarra swung Lucifer into Satan's gut as the two adversaries collided. Satan rammed Asjarra and knocked him halfway across the garden.

Asjarra rose to one knee as Satan leapt several feet into the air and dropped from the sky. With a single blow, he knocked Asjarra back onto the ground, then knelt over him and cuffed him about the face and head with his huge paws. From his supine position, Asjarra impaled Satan through the solar plexus. The Godblade crackled and Satan's solar plexus exploded, knocking him backwards.

Asjarra sprang to his feet, raised Lucifer over his head, and charged. He struck Satan in the forehead, burning flesh, bone and soul alike, all the way down to the third eye. Satan's third eye was crimson like his other two. It blinked at Asjarra in response, then Satan breathed a fireball from his lungs, burning the tunic from Asjarra's body and scorching his chest. Asjarra raised the Godblade and shot a stream of quanta at Satan's third eye, but Satan closed his third eyelid and the particles of light fell uselessly to the grass in a shower of sparks.

Asjarra swung the Godblade in a rainbow arch, and a blast of sheet lightning rose a hundred feet in the air, blinding Satan's trio of eyes. Asjarra moved in quickly, swinging Lucifer over his head in a rapid succession of concentric circles. The chain of the morning star spun like a whirling dervish. The air vibrated with a ringing sound, like that of weapons being forged upon an anvil. Asjarra unleashed Lucifer in one mighty blow, smashing Satan in the face and knocking four fangs from his mouth. He swung the Godblade again and severed Satan's left horn.

Satan roared and spun, impaling Asjarra's side on his forked tail. Using the tail like an arm, he bashed Asjarra against the ground repeatedly, until Asjarra finally managed to roll over and sever Satan's tail with the Godblade.

He flung his morning star at Satan and it lodged in his skull. Asjarra called the morning star back to his hand, but it flew right past him and began to circle the Garden of Eden in an erratic orbit. It flew around both Asjarra and Satan alike, until finally Satan raised his right hand and Lucifer flew into his palm, settling in his fist like a fugitive serpent returning to its long-lost lair.

Asjarra went numb. He had been betrayed by his own weapon. The very weapon whose retrieval had led to the death of the Bodhi Tree. The very possession he had desired so greatly that he had unwittingly sacrificed his guru to save it.

The morning star burst into flames, rousing Asjarra from his cold trance of betrayal, guilt, and melancholia.Lucifer burned with Hellfire, and Satan attacked its former master with it. Tongues of fire rose from the red-hot spikes, scorching the air and scalding Asjarra's skin. The flaming morning star tore smoking puncture wounds in Asjarra's flesh. He parried it with the Godblade and opened his own series of crackling lacerations across Satan's body. Asjarra feinted, then swung the Godblade again. Satan swung Lucifer at the same moment. Broadsword and morning star collided in mid-air with a pyrotechnic explosion. A mushroom cloud blotted out the sun, bursting with multi-colored sparks. The shock and impact of the blow knocked Asjarra and Satan flat on their backs. Showers of scintilla rained down all around them.

Asjarra rose to his feet. His right arm was burned black, all the way to the elbow. Satan was already standing, his right hand consumed by fire. He switched Lucifer to his left hand and used the flaming fist of his right to pummel Asjarra about the face and head. With one final, brutal punch, he knocked Asjarra into the air and sent him sprawling across the grass.

Satan spat a fireball at his head. Asjarra ducked and began crawling towards the Tree of Good and Evil. Satan followed him like a rabid predator. Asjarra stumbled to the across the garden, dodging fireballs all the while.

When he reached the Tree of Good and Evil, he used one of its branches to pull himself to his feet. As he leaned against its trunk to keep from collapsing, he secretly slipped his right hand around the back of the tree and began sawing it with the Godblade.

Satan moved in for the kill. Asjarra spun and backslashed the Tree of Good and Evil with the Godblade. The thaumaturgical sword sheared through the trunk.Satan started to back-pedal, then tried to dodge to the side, but it to no avail. The tree dropped as heavily as the Anti-Buddha had, crushing Satan and pinning him to the ground.

Satan struggled to lift the tree from his shattered ribs, but both of his arms had been broken when he had flung them into the air to protect his face from the falling tree. He wriggled like a serpent and managed to slide his face and head from underneath, but his body would not follow. He tried breathing fire, but the jagged ends of broken ribs were stuck in his lungs. After a few minutes of trying to wrestle with the Tree of Good and Evil, the only part of his body he could move were his eyelids. They blinked as he stared up at the form of Asjarra, looming over him like white death.

Asjarra swung the Godblade in a colossal arch. The broadsword hurtled through the air at the speed of light, sweeping over the crux of his shoulder and the crown of his skull in a blinding fury of brilliance and ripping through Satan's throat. The impact of sword meeting ground caused Satan's head to ricochet into the air. The severed head shot into the skies and hurtled high over the Garden of Eden, flying on a slowly curving trajectory that carried it beyond the horizon.

It took Asjarra several hours to heal all the wounds from the cataclysmic battle. When his glowing hands and luminous soul had finally made his flesh like new, he stood up and pulled the Godblade out of the ground. Asjarra slowly made his way across the Garden of Eden until he came to the cobbled pathway. Solemnly, Asjarra approached the catafalque, the coffin, and his long-awaited death-place.

He lay down in the open casket. Gripping the Godblade with both hands, he slowly dragged it across his neck, severing both jugular veins and carotid arteries. The angel and demoness returned, fluttering on butterfly wings, and lowered the lid of the casket. Asjarra closed his eyes and dreamed.

The faces of his previous incarnations orbited around him like severed heads. Buddha, the First Coming, the Enlightened One, who had meditated beneath the Bodhi Tree and transformed into a messiah. Jesus, the Second Coming, the Son of God, who had been crucified on a cross made from the Bodhi Tree's wood. Demeter, the Third Coming, the Psychedelic Nature Goddess, first wife of the Bodhi Tree and mother of the elven race.

A fourth head slowly materialized and began to circle along with the other three. It was a replica of his own. Asjarra, the Fourth Coming, who had smoked the fig-leaves of the Bodhi Tree and evolved from a human shaman into an elven messiah, who had saved Yggdrasil and thus the entire universe from Nidhug the dragon, who had prevented Satan from sealing himself in the coffin/cocoon of Eden and evolving into God, but whose sins had almost destroyed the universe as well, and had led to the deaths offriend and foe alike.

Asjarra's soul looked down upon its physical body.Its breathing was shallow, its heartbeat faint. The angel and demoness with butterfly wings continued to attend to the coffin. They seemed to be spinning some type of substance around it.

Asjarra snapped back into his body. He opened his eyes to the darkness of the casket, faintly lit by his flickering life. His skin was detaching and spinning around him. He could feel himself growing, stretching, changing. Outside the casket, the butterfly-winged angel and demoness were spinning a cocoon. He thought he heard them call each other by the names of Eve and Lilith. His body was rearranging itself. His own flesh was betraying him. He was mutating, transforming, evolving. He was metamorphosing.

A year later, the coffin/cocoon began to break apart in pieces. There was a hole like a star in the wall, and Asjarra peered through. The entire universe was arrayed beneath him. The coffin/cocoon crumbled and left him floating in space, rising gently against the top of the cosmos. He could see every branch of Yggdrasil, every plane in existence, every sentient being, be they living or dead.

"I don't want to be God," he screamed,but his voice was too loud, too large, too mighty to be heard by anyone else.He could feel all the suffering in the universe, but he knew not how to assuage it, and there was no one he could pray to but himself. The words of the Bodhi Tree resonated in his impossibly vast brain, over and over again.

"God is always omnipresent, sometimes omniscient, and never omnipotent."

His soul became heaven and shined light upon Yggdrasil from above, feeding it with the warmth of a googolplex of suns. His energy, his very consciousness,filled all of Yggdrasil, every tree, branch, and leaf of the World Tree, from the Omphalos Tree to the

Forest of Suicide, from the Garden of Eden to the Garden of Enlightenment. Yggdrasil became Asjarra's body; Asjarra became Yggdrasil.

Asjarra's holy light burned the Anti-Buddha as it crouched inside Chaitan, the Devil Tree, expelling it from its lair. The Anti-Buddha flowed like a sluggish Styx down the abyss it had torn open in its previous incarnation. It floated back down the interdimensional tunnel to Nethernirvana. The pit closed itself like a constricting pupil and existed no more.Chaitan began to glow and heal, and the Gardens of Enlightenment began to grow and bloom once more. The Hamadryads Harem spontaneously reincarnated and fluttered about their master.

The words of the Bodhi Tree echoed in the breeze. "The only thing constant is change. The only thing infinite is change. The only thing eternal is change."

As the winds began to hum, a synesthetic permutation of the Bodhi Tree's wisdom swirled through the Gardens of Enlightenment. "Change is omnipresent. Change is omniscient. Change is omnipotent. Change is God."

The Bodhi Tree slowly returned to life, its branches stretching like arms, its twigs twitching like fingers. It held a lit cigar in one branch; a bubbling hookah in another. Rugose bark turned to wrinkles around its knothole eyes. A face stretched in the wood, but it was not the face of the original Bodhi Tree. It was the face of a glowing elf. It was the face of Asjarra. He was smoking his own fig leaves, and awaiting the First Coming.

The Rhabdomancer of Spacetime

In the Kaleidoscope Nebula at the Nexus of Infinity dwells the Rhabdomancer of Spacetime. He has been known by many names, for he possesses an infinite number of souls and seven times as many chakras, and his legends are myriad, for his Wand of Synesthesia is a symbol for several things.

It is the dawn of a new kalpa. The Rhabdomancer of Spacetime opens his eyes. Twin mirrorballs they are, illuminating his wizened face with pellucid shadows. His hair and beard are the color of rock and stone, and rugose like a brain, as though they were a crown and veil of cerelites. He is so ancient that his robe has petrified and become one with his hair and beard, a hooded cloak of brilliant grays and bright browns, stratified with petroglyph-like sigils, decorated with labyrinthine yantras, and embroidered with musical superstrings. Just as his robe is a part of his body, so too is the prismatic, mellifluous, orgasmic, incensed, ambrosial, psychedelic, enlightening Wand of Synesthesia in his gnarled hands.

Sitting in the lotus position, with his hands raised and folded in the uttarabodhi mudra, and his wand trembling and crackling with energy like a multi-colored thunderbolt between the pyramid of his forefingers, the Rhabdomancer watches a black orb the size of an atom float upon the spectrums, music, emotions, perfumes, nectars, dreams, and samadhis of the Kaleidoscope Nebula.

He rises from the Disc of Tao upon which he meditates. Spiral rainbows swirl from the tip of his wand, like a kundalini serpent. He raises the Wand of Synesthesia and strikes the microscopic sphere like a gong. The sempiternal note of Om resonates through the ether as yet another Big Bang explodes from the Nexus of Infinity.

The Disc of Tao levitates to the zenith of the Kaleidoscope Nebula and the Rhabdomancer beholds the birth of another cosmos. As the new universe expands, the Rhabdomancer strums its one-dimensional superstrings with his wand, playing them like a harp and creating the vibrations from which reality springs. Space and time reincarnate as the Rhabdomancer tunes the cosmos. With his wand he weaves them into an eleven-dimensional tapestry, tessellating the neoverse with branes, creating the maze of quiddity that stretches from genesis to armageddon and back again.

As the Rhabdomancer creates the space/time continuum, the evolution of the neoverse begins. Swirling nebulae coalesce into galaxies. Stars marry and give birth to planets. Planets give birth to moons, the grandchildren of suns. As the creator of the neoverse, the Rhabdomancer knows that he will inevitably be its saviour or a martyr, for he possesses more karma than any entity that has ever existed, and his Akashic records, if written and drawn in physical tomes, would fill the entire newborn cosmos.

He waves his Wand of Synesthesia and conjures black holes and white holes alike. New samsaric cycles commence as the first collapsars and supernovae channel death into the neoverse. The Rhabdomancer watches the invisible implosions and listens to the silent explosions with solemn eyes and wary ears, for the resurrection of death signals the reincarnation of the Rhabdomancer's eternal adversaries. He pauses. He waits.

Of demonic sonica and sonic demonica the Hellifluous come.

The Rhabdomancer's mirrorball eyes narrowed into shards of glass as the gigantic silhouette of a hundred-armed Titan beshadowed the rainbow arete of the Kaleidoscope Nebula. Every kalpa, the six demonic soulmates of the Rhabdomancer take on different forms and battle him for possession of the cosmos. Sometimes it is the Rhabdomancer who knows the ephemeral ananda of victory, and the eternal treasure which comes with it. Sometimes it is the Hellifluous. This kalpa, the first demon has taken on the form of the hecatoncheire Briareus.

Holding a giant bone in each of his hundred hands, Briareus hammered a concatenation of anti-Oms upon a multi-tiered congeries of drums as he crossed the reverse event horizon of the Nexus of Infinity. The faces of past incarnations of the Rhabdomancer, dried out and stretched into dead skin masks, were Briareus' drumskins. Their open mouths and empty eyeholes moaned like amphorae, adding their own whistling threnodies to Briareus' frenetic dirge. Two trickles of blood runneled from the Rhabdomancer's ears as the cacophany grew louder and closer.

Briareus glared at the Rhabdomancer as he approached. His eyes were binary pulsars, blasting the Rhabdomancer's brain with radioactive waves. Briareus bashed the hymn of the Rhabdomancer's own biorhythms upon his drums of death, faster and faster, until the Rhabdomancer fell to his knees in agony, the drumbeats cracking his souls.

The Rhabdomancer twirled the Wand of Synesthesia, wielding it with a supersonic, supraluminal legerdemain. He fired corkscrews of colored quanta into Briareus' chest that synchronized the Titan's heartbeat with the little Big Bangs of his drums. Briareus' heart pounded at the speed of sound and thundered with sonic booms, spurring his blood to rush through his veins and arteries at the speed of light. Briareus roared as his heart bludgeoned itself to a bloody pulp. The Rhabdomancer pointed his wand and sent two streams of hypnotic mantras into Briareus' ears, possessing his brain and nervous system. An instant later, the Titan found his arms paralyzed. His song mutated into a mephitic crescendo and died.

The Rhabdomancer fired a hundred-forked bolt of violet lightning at the drums, and every undead face, every voodoo drumskin, shriveled into smoke. As the drumskins disintegrated, the Rhabdomancer spun his wand in concentric circles, wrapping coils of light around Briareus' every inner organ and then ripping them out, one by one, to orbit his bleeding body like a zodiac of mutilation.

The tip of the Wand of Synesthesia murmured an incantation, and the gargantuan organs of Briareus slowly replaced the drumskins, flying into the drums and nestling inside them like newfound bodily orifices and cavities. Within the drums the organs continued to beat and pulse and quiver. The Rhabdomancer continued to wave his wand, sucking out Briareus' glands and nerve clusters, then tearing his chakras from his soul. Each gland, nerve cluster, and chakra settled into one of the empty drums. When ninety-eight of the drums had been filled with Briareus' vitals, the Rhabdomancer extended his wand-bearing arm to its full length, then abruptly pulled it back towards his body. As he did so, Briareus' heart flew out of his chest. The Rhabdomancer directed it into one of the two remaining drums, where it landed with a wet noise and continued to beat.

The Rhabdomancer ended the battle by flinging a crescent-shaped, boomerang-like guillotine blade from the wand, decapitating Briareus. The Titan's head slowly toppled from his neck into the last empty drum, and then his hundred arms began moving again, beating upon his organs and severed head with the drumsticks of bone.

Briareus could still feel his every body part. His severed head screamed a hundred screams every second as his decapitated and vivisected body hammered a bruising requiem upon its own excised organs. The brutal timpani was like rapid-fire water torture with trillion-pound droplets of liquefied neutron stars.

The headless hecatoncheire marched about like a circumambulist, then wandered around like a somnambulist, then walked along the reverse event horizon like a funambulist until he toppled back into the void from which he had come, to float deathlessly through eons of space and parsecs of time.

The Rhabdomancer watched the fall of Briareus, then left the Kaleidoscope Nebula himself, soaring atop his Disc of Tao into the nascent cosmos beyond. The Disc of Tao, painted with the symbol of yin and yang, the two halves of which changed color every second, bore the Rhabdomancer to the expanding edge of the neoverse. He rode the temporal crest of the Big Bang to the Ocean of Milk.

Just as the Rhabdomancer must battle the six demons every kalpa, so too must he perform six sacred tasks. The first two-the initiation of the Big Bang and the weaving of the cosmos-he had already accomplished. Now, hovering over the Ocean of Milk on his flying discus, the Rhabdomancer held his wand out with both hands and prepared to perfrom the third. The Wand of Synesthesia elongated to the size of a quarterstaff, and the Rhabdomancer began churning the Ocean of Milk.

The sounds of tantric sexrose from beneath the tranquil, pure-white surface as the Rhabdomancer stirred the marmoreal seas. As he toiled, he could smell the susurrus and hear the miasma of the black wings of Azrael, the Angel of Death. He glanced into the innocent skies. Azrael was circling him like a predator and strummingan ebony harp with his clawed hand, riding the hideous notes and eldritch octaves of his own dark fantasia. Strung with the hair of shorn seraphim, the harp smelled like murder and rape, like assassinated beauty and freshly-stolen virginity. The Rhabdomancer tasted necrophilia on his tongue as Azrael swooped down upon him.

The Rhabdomancer drew a heptagram of white light with his wand and directed it towards Azrael. Azrael played a black pentagram upon his harp to block it. The two sigils interlaced and interlocked and rose into space, forming a black and white star that would spin for many an epoch, then separate into a binary system of black hole and white hole and spin for many an epoch more.

Azrael descended through the air and stroked a song of crepitus. The Rhabdomancer's ribs and spine began to tremble like the harpstrings, faster and faster, to the point of breaking, and then his entire skeleton began to rattle, the tips of jagged bones scraping together in his bloody joints, his marrow turned to bubbling sludge.

The Rhabdomancer shot a concatenation of Chinvat bridges into Azrael's harp, transforming the harpstrings into razorwire. As Azrael continued to play, the sharpened harpstrings sliced his fingers off. The severed digits fell, one by one, into the Ocean of Milk, forming a roseate ocean-within-an-ocean that tasted like attar and sounded like menses.

The Rhabdomancer's bones resettled. With an undulating wave of his hand he conjured a cloud of pure psychedelia. Rainbow smoke fumed from the tip of the Wand of Synesthesia, as though the wand were the pipe of Morpheus. The shimmering cloud engulfed the Angel of Death. Azrael inhaled, and the rainbow smoke possessed the Angel of Death like a drug. Unable to control his body, the Angel of Death continued playing his black harp, severing his own hand and then chopping off his own wrist, forearm, elbow, and upper arm. The amputated stump dangling from his shoulder dripped blood into the ocean and the pool of attar grew larger. Azrael lurched and continued to pass through the Chinvat harpstrings, swinging the harp like a gate with his right hand, shredding his own skull and then grating his entire body to pieces.

As the mutilated remnants of the Angel of Death floated upon the serene Ocean of Milk, the song of his blood and the taste of his dismemberment summoned Charon to collect his body. Upon a piano built into the wood of the ship did Charon play, his fingers delicately passing over keys made from the teeth and bones of dead demiurges, stolen from their corpses while he ferried their souls across the Styx of Space and into the Big Crunches of bygone eras. One of the keys had been made from the teeth and bones of Briareus, who lay comatose inside the piano.

The music of Charon's piano powered the ferry across the Ocean of Milk. The psychopomp gathered Azrael's still-living body parts with a trawl. The pieces of the Angel of Death took their place beside Briareus in the purgatorial piano.

After collecting his grisly cargo, Charon turned his attention to the Rhabdomancer. The Rhabdomancer himself was dreaming of Charon's approach. As the ferry drew closer, the song of Charon stabbed the Rhabdomancer as though with tiny needles, each note opening a puncture wound upon his flesh. Blood began to trickle from a thousand tiny wounds, and then the tinkling of the piano keys began to machicolate his bones until hot marrow poured from the tiny holes. The song perforated his skull, widened the bodily cavities in his innards, and created new bodily orifices in his flesh.

The Rhabdomancer turned and shot a flurry of spears from his wand. They landed atop the piano and disappeared. An instant later, a spike arose from each and every piano key, puncturing Charon's fingers. As Charon tried to pull his fingers free, another spike grew from the bench upon which he sat,ascending through his body and emerging from the crown of his skull, impaling him upon his bench.

The Rhabdomancer cast ten helices of neurological energy into Charon's fingers, possessing them and forcing him to continue playing the spiked piano keys. Puncture wounds became impaled fingertips, bloody perforated fingernails, and crimson chiaroscuro fingerprints. Charon howled and played a beautiful song of lamentation upon the blood-drenched piano keys. The ferry levitated and flew away, as musically and aesthetically as if it were a chariot drawn by muses in pink silk-and-leather harnesses.

The Rhabdomancer continued to churn the Ocean of Milk, healing his wounds as he stirred the liquid ylem, until the Earth arose from the soft white depths. His wand thenreturned to its normal size, and the Rhabdomancer flew across the curving plains and forests of the new world, eventually landing in the Garden of Eden. In a fountain at the center of the garden a primordial ooze bubbled and murmured.The Rhabdomancer shot a lightning bolt of sentience into the amorphous mass, bringing life to Earth, completing the fourth task.

The fourth task also summoned the fourth demon, for the first entity to emerge from the primordial ooze was the succubus Lilith. Playing a violin strung with the guts of alternate Adams and parallel Eves, Lilith attacked. She screamed the siren song of a phantasmagoric epithalamion, and every time she drew her bow across the strings of the violin, one of the Rhabdomancer's veins or arteries was sawed in two. She played furiously, disconnecting the Rhabdomancer's circulatory system. The Rhabdomancer raised his wand and pointed it at Lilith's violin. The violin exploded in a pyrotechnic cloud that, for the briefest of moments, was an exact replica of the Kaleidoscope Nebula.

Lilith continued sweeping her bow back and forth, unaware that she had nought to play upon but the smoking void left by the immolated violin. The Rhabdomancer shot seven hundred and seventy-seven Zen riddles into her brain. An instant later, besieged with mind-numbing confusion and mind-blowing enlightenment, Lilith found that she could not stop playing her musical epithalamion. The bow slowly lifted her arm with a will of its own, dragging itself to the crown of her head. The bow drew closer and closer, then bit into the flesh of her scalp. It continued to move back and forth, playing music all the while, sawing through hair and skin and skull and corpus callosum, separating the two hemispheres of her brain, then dividing her face and continuing downwards through her neck. Through torso and trunk the bow did cleave, separating esophagus from trachea, estranging her lungs, bursting her stomach, and untying her intestines. Still standing, even though her entire upper body had been separated into diagonal slabs of bloody meat, Lilith continued to sunder her own flesh, at last cutting her own womb and vagina in half and toppling to the garden grass in two pieces.

Cursed with the same quasi-immortality as Briareus and Azrael, the gory halves of Lilith retained full sentience and awareness. As Charon returned to gather Lilith's quasi-dead body, Adam and Eve emerged from the primordial ooze. Within a blink of the Rhabdomancer's mirrorball eyes, the entire human race and trillions of animal species covered the entire planet with life. Simultaneously, on a septillion other planets, did the cortege of evolution commence, as well.

The Rhabdomancer ascended back into space, where the Earth

had been joined by eight brothers and sisters and a myriad of child-moons. He soared through the newborn planets and their satellites, waving his Wand of Synesthesia in intricate patterns, conducting the Music of the Spheres, his fifth task, while mankind conquered the Earth.

With four blinks of the Rhabdomancer's mirrorball eyes, the four yugas came and went. As the sun began to broil and bloat, cooking the Earth with its solar flares, the fifth demon, Kali, ascended from the nadir of the neoverse, using the corpse of her husband, Shiva, to glide through space in a dark perversion of the Rhabdomancer and his Disc of Tao. Singing her hideous song of laughter, mating calls, and battle-cries, Kali hastened the demise of the Earth. The Rhabdomancer observed all, but did not interfere with the sacred cycle of life and death.

After the human race was extinct, and the Earth had been swallowed by the sun, did the Rhabdomancer and Kali begin their battle. Kali played upon a sitar whose strings were living veins and arteries. The magnetic pull of her music sucked the Rhabdomancer's blood to the surface of his skin. She used her necklace of skulls like amphorae, her breath whistling through the empty eye sockets as she danced her danse macabre upon the flying cadaver of Shiva.

Kali's hemagogic cacophanies continued to draw the Rhabdomancer's blood through his flesh, soaking his body in scarlet sweat. Her song quickened. Blood began to drip from the Rhabdomancer's every bodily orifice. Two fountains of infrared holy water poured from his mirrorball eyes. The vermilion cries of sacred cows and sacrificial lambs leaked from his ears with every heartbeat. His phallus began to menstruate, as did the twin stigmata which suddenly appeared upon his palms. The morning mists of Aceldama drifted about his face. Apple soma poured from the ruby chalice of his lips. A wet tilaka of blood stained his forehead. From the crown of his skull burst a flaming kundalini salamander.

The Rhabdomancer twirled his wand as he bled, over and over, faster and faster, until the veins and arteries with which Kali's sitar was strung began to unravel. The blood vessels tore themselves free and wrapped themselves around the Wand of Synesthesia. As the Rhabdomancer continued to spin his wand, the strings of Kali's sitar began to yank at her own veins and arteries, for they were connected to her circulatory system as surely as her circulatory system was connected to her black heart.

The wind of Kali's foul gasps turned her song into an orchestra of dying breaths. The Rhabdomancer continued pulling Kali's circulatory system through the sitar, inch by bloody inch, yanking her carotid arteries and jugular veins through her fingertips, winding her blood vessels around his wand as though it were a spool. The skein of veins and arteries pulsed like choking naginas. As the battle ended, Kali's still-beating heart burst through the palm of her hand, her aorta trailing behind it. With Kali's entire circulatory system in his grasp, the Rhabdomancer's own bleeding ceased. The flow of combat reversed, then returned a thousandfold upon the goddess of death and destruction.

As the Rhabdomancer began to spin his wand in the opposite direction, all the veins and arteries heliced around it began to unwind. He aimed the wand at Kali and the blood vessels shot through the air like a living matrix, wrapping themselves like cerements around her body, tighter and tighter, cocooning her in her own blood vessels, mummifying her in her own circulatory system.

The sixth task and the sixth nemesis were one and the same. Hovering upon his Disc of Tao in the middle of outer space, the Rhabdomancer could feel the four wings of Israfel, the evil twin of Gabriel, beating a lament at the zenith of the cosmos. Tasting the apocalypse, the Rhabdomancer flew to the edge of space and time.

In the Erebus Nebula at the event horizon of the universe, with the Horn of Chronocide surgically fused to his lips, did Israfel sound the black clarion call of armageddon, playing the dirge of the universe and killing time itself. If Israfel were to murder time, time's twin, space, would die along with it, and the entire neoverse would unravel into Chaos and Hell.

The Rhabdomancer soared through the swirling, black gases of the Erebus Nebula. He could hear the dying screams of seraphim in Israfel's song, for the golden Horn of Chronicide had been forged from molten haloes, melted from the heads of angels in gamma ray-filled gas chambers. Israfel was like a manifestation of spacetime itself, for he possessed four of every body part, except for his mouth and tongue, of which he possessed only one.

Israfel tightened the grip of his clawed hands upon his horn. He glared at the Rhabdomancer with his four infrared eyes and listened to the Rhabdomancer's biorhythms with his four pointed ears. His four hearts beat faster, his four lungs breathed deeper, his four stomachs growled, and his four brains radiated pure atomic death.

As the Disc of Tao drew level with Israfel and his horn, the Rhabdomancer began spinning his wand in a giant circle, like a Rainbow Serpent ouroboros. Multi-colored keys spiraled from the circle, unlocking tesseracts that vacuumed pieces of Israfel into random eons of the past, ripping an eye and an ear from his head, tearing a brain through his skull, excising a heart and a lung and a stomach and a liver and a kidney and an intestine from his insides, severing an arm and a leg and a wing and a phallus, and sucking them all up like Tartarean time machines, scattering them to various points of the neoverse's past, to be discovered and sometimes worshipped by the denizens of bygone eras.

Israfel blew a blast of neutron starlight from his horn, opening a black hole that began to pull the Rhabdomancer into its abyss. The Rhabdomancer fired a quasar from his wand, opening a wormhole that engulfed the black hole and shot it through a white hole at the other end of the universe. The wormhole wrapped a web of event horizons around Israfel, then tore another set of organs from his body. An eyeball flew out of a socket like a comet, its corona the coma, its bloody optic nerve the tail. His brain was a pink asteroid, his heart a red giant, his kidney a brown dwarf, his liver a neutron star, his intestines a spiral galaxy, his glands a constellation. The wormhole digested Israfel's innards and bore them into its labyrinth, then released each one from a different white hole, dispersing them throughout the universe to drift like rogue planets in Abaddon vacuums.

Israfel blew his horn again, blasting a stream of dark matter into the Rhabdomancer's eyes. Blinded, the Rhabdomancer fell to his knees. Israfel moved in for the kill. The Rhabdomancer drew a series of Calabi-Yau formations in the air, opening the portals to the seven curled-up dimensions that existed between space and time. The tiny dimensions devoured a third feast of Israfel's limbs and vitals, siphoning the organs through the air with their interplanal undertow and hiding them away.

Nearing death, Israfel desperately blew a Hellmouth from his horn. The Hellmouth broiled and dilated as it flew towards the Rhabdomancer. The Rhabdomancer sweated rainbows as the fiery abyss bore down upon him. At the last moment, the Rhabdomancer raised his Wand of Synesthesia to his lips and blew a pneuma of white light into the Hellmouth. The pneuma was filled with glowing hadrons, each bursting with all six types of quarks, as well as the mysterious seventh quark known only by saints, messiahs, Bodhisattvas, and the Rhabdomancer himself. The pneuma shot from the wand, detonated the Hellmouth with an explosion like a supernova, and flew directly into the Horn of Chronicide, stifling its lethal music.

Israfel staggered as the pneuma of quarks flew down his throat and into his body, turning his nervous system inside-out and upside-down. When Israfel blew his horn again, not music, but blood, flowed from its golden entrance. The blood floated and separated, forming crimson nebulae in the black void. Israfel tried to breathe in, then tried to hold his breath, but he could do neither, for the quarks had rearranged his nerves and filled his neurotransmitters with liquid chaos. As he continued to blow his horn, more blood sprayed forth, followed by his tongue and teeth, and then all of his remaining organs, beginning with his esophagus and followed immediately by his stomach, then his liver, his intestines, his kidneys, and every other vital organ except for his last lung, which could not stop exhaling. Through the Horn of Chronicide Israfel blew his insides into space, expectorating his own organs in supernovas of blood and gore. Finally, when there were no more organs left to vomit, Israfel exhaled his very soul in a single white mantra of torture.

The Rhabdomancer's mirrorball eyes cast pellucid shadows across his face as he observed Israfel's torment. As he listened to the wet trumpet dirge of Israfel blasting his own innards across the galaxies, the Rhabdomancer tasted eschatology and caught the scent of the Big Crunch on the neutrinos passing through his flesh.

Charon and his ferry emerged from one of the Rhabdomancer's conjured wormholes to collect the empty hull of Israfel's body. The Rhabdomancer raised his wand and blasted the hull of the ferry apart, freeing all of the souls trapped inside it. For the briefest of moments the white supernova of spirits lit up the entire cosmos with their combined auras, then formed a living spiral galaxy devoid of gravity.

The music of Charon's piano transformed into a glowing black hand, lifting the empty husk of Israfel up and then laying him down upon the bloody deck of the ferry, forming a pentagram with the bodies of Lilith, who had been sewn back together with serpents; Azrael, who had been stitched back together with the strings of his black harp; Briareus, who had been glued back together with coagulated blood; and Kali, who remained cocooned in her own veins and arteries.

Of sonic demonica and demonic sonica the Hellifluous die.

With his destiny complete and his thanatos unleashed, Charon heads straight for the supermassive black hole at the center of the neoverse. Deep in thanatopsis, the whiteshifting Rhabdomancer watches the blueshifting music of Charon's piano as the redshifting ferry sails into the blackshifting abyss. In a state of synesthetic ashubha he contemplates the decomposing corpses of the Hellifluous with all seven of his senses, gazing upon the decay creeping through their flesh, listening to their bones fossilize, feeling the paralysis of their rigor mortis, smelling the raw meat of their carcasses, tasting the miasma of their rictus grins, dreaming of their damnations, and knowing that the souls of the Hellifluous will be forever bound to the torture wheels of their samsaric cycles.

Just as the necrosonic demons have died, so too dies the neoverse. Another war has come and gone. This time, it is the Rhabdomancer who has known victory, and it is he who adds yet another universe to his collection. The neoverse has been saved, and will exist in in its own personal heaven for all eternity, in a single spacetimestream stretching from genesis to armageddon that can be entered, exited, and re-entered at any point.

Weary from combat and dreaming of samadhi, the Rhabdomancer returns to the Kaleidoscope Nebula. He seats himself in the lotus position, folds his hands into the uttarabodhi mudra, and meditates upon his war with the Hellifluous. In a simultaneous trance of pnemensis and prescience, he remembers every triumph and every defeat that have passed before, and dreams of all the battles yet to come. Thus has it always been, and thus shall it always be, for stars are the Rhabdomancer's neurons, constellations his dendrites, and zodiacs his nerve clusters. The cosmos itself is the very gestalt of his brain, and the Hellifluous are the drugs that fuel it. Reality is a form of synesthesia, and so too is the Rhabdomancer of Spacetime.

It is the end of a kalpa. The Rhabdomancer of Spacetime closes his eyes.

Quasar D'Arete and the Centauri Strangler

"I'm telling you, Quasar," said Hercules, "there are two Centauri Stranglers. If it isn't lung-harvesting squid cyborgs, then maybe it's time-traveling lesbian nurses."

Quasar D'Arete glanced up from the autopsy table in annoyance. A tiny curl of black, greased hair fell across the crosspiece of his dark spectacles as he raised his head and looked at his partner. Through his omniscopic sunglasses, Quasar could see Hercules Moonsmasher's bare chest and bulging muscles in eleven dimensions, as well as the holographic hydra tattoo that covered his entire back.

"Hercules," said Quasar, removing the black cigarette from his mouth and blowing a dark nebula of smoke into the air, "I didn't haul your ass off of Jupiter to solve murder mysteries. All you have to do is carry that gun around for me."

Quasar turned his attention back to the autopsy table while Hercules fixed his blue-eyed gaze upon the gigantic, nine-thousand pound X-Gun lying next to the cadavers. The progeny of the recently discovered formula for solidifying space/time, the X-Gun had been invented by the six-brained Merzaquii of the Hourglass Nebula and immediately stolen by the two rogues.

With a gargantuan biceps forged in the heavy gravity of Jupiter, Hercules lifted the four-and-a-half ton weapon into the air with one massive arm.

Quasar glared at his partner through his sunglasses. "Damn it, Hercules, put that thing down. I don't know what it's capable of yet."

Hercules placed the X-Gun back on the table, his veins bulging like living serpents, the cords of tensile neutronium reinforcing his muscles, tendons, and ligaments visibly stretching and contractingbeneath his skin.

"What the hell'd you even bring it in here for?"

Hercules shrugged. He'd been carrying it everywhere since the day they'd stolen it, like a child with a doll. He seemed to be developing an emotional attachment to it.

Quasar leaned over and playfully slapped Hercules on the side of the head.

"Fucking brute."

Hercules rubbed his velvety brown hair as Quasar refocused upon the cadavers. The Centauri Strangler always murdered in fours. The serial killer's latest quartet of victims-two males, one female, and a hermaphrodite-had been anonymously teleported into the morgue of Quasar's spaceship while they were still warm. Three identical finger-holes perforated each side of the corpses' necks. Their eye sockets were empty, and their larynxes, esophagi, tracheae, and lungs had all been violently extracted through the cavernous wounds in their throats. None of the organs were present.

"I'm serious about the time-traveling, co-dependent lesbian nurses,Quasar. Didn't you ever hear that old legend from ancient Earth? There were these two nurses who worked in a convalescent home. They took turns suffocating their patients. It turned into this big sexual thing. Every time they murdered someone, they went into a closet and made love. If they had somehow happened upon a time machine, it's entirely possible that..."

Quasar cut him off. "I'm pretty sure it isn't lesbian nurses, Herc. There's sperm in the throat wounds."

Quasar pulled a handheld necrometer from the right pocket of his red-and-black designer spacesuit. As he scrutinized the data readings on the eleven-dimensional screen of the all-in-one autopsy, forensics, and necromancy device, he leaned back in his chair and rested his boots on the autopsy table.

"There's two of them." Hercules' veins and muscles looked as though they might burst from his mega-calcium strengthened skeleton as he placed his hands on the edge of the table and leaned forward. His seven-foot frame loomed over the bodies like a colossus.

"There are not two of them." Quasar was becoming exasperated. Swarms of nanobot bacteriophages were flying around the corpses like microscopic flies. Quasar could see them with his sunglasses, and swatted at a few trillion that were hovering too close to his face.

"What about evil twins? You know how they say everyone has an evil twin."

"Hercules, the handprints, finger-holes, cell scrapings, pressure readings, biorhythms, psychic residue, psychometry statistics, motive equations, and DNA samples are always the same. All four victims perished with shared death experiences and similar brain chemistries, along with matching impressions in their optic lobes and pineal glands. And they died within seconds and inches of one another. Every report the Xenarchy sent me on the other four-thousand, two-hundred and twelve victims coincides with the analysis of the necrometer and my sunglasses. The Centauri Strangler works alone."

Quasar casually tossed the necrometer to his partner.

"Here. Read the data yourself."

Hercules glanced at the necrometer readings for all of three seconds before placing it back on the table.

"It doesn't make any sense," Hercules said as he poured a vial of steroids from the Rutilician and Kornephorian systems into a large syringe. "If the victims always die at the same place and the same time, then there has to be two of them."

"Herc, have you ever heard of quadlings?"

"You mean things with four arms?"

"Yep."

"Oh." Hercules jabbed the needle into his arm and emptied the syringe into his veins.

Quasar reached into the left breast pocket of his designer spacesuit, pulled out another cigarette, and placed it between his lips. As he leaned back in his chair and put his feet up again, the tip of the self-lighting cigarette blazed to life and started fuming.

"You're going to piss a lung one day, the way you smoke that stuff all the time," Hercules said, removing the needle from his arm.

"It's Aesculapian weed, Herc. The plant they cured cancer with. That's why it's named after the god of healing. They named the whole planet they found it on after him. It's completely harmless."

Quasar reached into his right breast pocket and pulled out a large joint.

"This, though," he said, lighting it with the tip of the black cigarette, "this will kill you."

The room immediately filled with the scent of gamma lotus, a cross-breed of cannabis, opium, nightshade, and quarkvine grown in the ultraviolet rays of dying suns and dried in the glow of nuclear reactors. Quasar inhaled a lungful of acrid smoke and instantly relaxed. His eyelids began to flutter shut behind his sunglasses.

"What now, Quasar?"

Quasar didn't look at Hercules, didn't even open his eyes. "The ship's already on course for Alpha Centauri," he said, dreamily. "The necrometer says the next four victims die on the planet Chiron within the next twenty hours. We sneak in, kick ass, sneak out, and collect. Simple as that."

*

"There are not two of them."

Quasar and Hercules stepped into the central elevator of the spaceship. The door irised shut behind them.

"What about doppelgangers? Simulacra? Homunculi?"

"Homunculi? If it's homunculi I'll sign my ship's papers over to you and retire." Quasar pushed the down button, then finished tightening the utility belt around his waist. He had his usual black cigarette in his mouth, and Hercules, as usual, had the X-Gun hoisted over his massive shoulder.

"I thought the Black Seraph was stolen." Hercules readjusted his grip on the X-Gun.

"I stole the papers, too. I'm a professional, not an amateur."

The elevator began to descend. Halfway down, Quasar looked back to find Hercules playing with the X-Gun's switches.

"Leave it on the first setting, Herc," Quasar said, even as he set his own Chroma Blaster to black. "None of those symbols have been deciphered yet."

Hercules flicked the switch back to its original position.

"And don't fire it unless you absolutely have to."

The elevator dropped through the nexus of the opulent, seven-story spaceship, emerged from the center of its plastron-like hull, and lowered itself to the surface of the planet Chiron. The rest of the landing gear touched down along with it, four thick rods that resembled the legs of triple-jointed spiders and combined with the elevator to balance the large vessel ten feet above the ground. Along with the two guns jutting from the front of the ship, the Black Seraph resembled a gargantuan cross-breed of Scorpio and Arachne.

The elevator door slid open and the two mercenaries stepped out into the night. Quasar pulled a remote control from his utility belt and tapped a code on its keyboard. The Black Seraph became invisible a moment later.

Of the fifteen planets and fifty-two moons spinning through the triple star system of Alpha Centauri, twenty-one had reported murders by the Centauri Strangler. The majority of the slayings had been on the four capital planets of Chiron, Nessus, Eurytion, and Bienor. The necrometer's various analyses, which ranged from the probabilistic to the esoteric to the psychic and beyond, had identified the city of Chiropolis as the probable location of the serial killer's next slaughter. With the assistance of radar jammers, cloaking devices, and the natural camouflage of the Black Seraph's night-hued and space-colored exterior, they had secretly landed on Chiron in an empty field, a mile away from its neon-lit capital.

As they were walking, Hercules glanced back in the direction of the invisible space vessel. "Have you ever lost your ship?" he asked.

Quasar removed his omniscopic sunglasses and handed them to his partner. Hercules slid them over his eyes and glanced over his shoulder again. The Black Seraph was clearly visible through the lenses. "Right," he said, then handed them back.

Quasar's sunglasses seemed even darker at night, while the holographic tattoo on Hercules' back, a three-dimensional masterpiece of the Lernaean Hydra native to the Alphardian system, seemed even more colorful, and sometimes flickered like stained glass beneath the starlight, its nine heads seeming to writhe and strike.

Across the terraformed meadows of Chiron, where genetically-engineered centaurs grazed upon grass, drank drugged wine, and openly copulated, Quasar and Hercules followed a sixteen-lane highway into the streets of Chiropolis. Quasar used the necrometer like a navigation device to thread the mazes of glowing sidewalks and neutronium-paved streets

"Rogue sexbots," Hercules suddenly exclaimed. "The Centauri Stranglers are rogue sexbots. I can feel it in my bones. You search downtown. I'll scan the perimeter of the city for sexbot spoor."

"You can look for all the sexbot spoor you want, Hercules, but you do it at my side. We stay together, no matter what."

Dodging the humans and genetically-engineered centaurs that

populated the city, Quasar and Hercules made their way to the centerpoint of a ten square-mile area which the death-computer had designated as the vicinity of the imminent slayings. Quasar spied a skyscraper with a panoramic view of the city that would serve as a perfect vantage point.

As the two mercenaries strode for the tower, a purple, drug-crazed centaur careened around a street corner and came racing towards them, an electric spear crackling in its right hand. The loaded centaur aimed it directly at Hercules' solar plexus and charged. Hercules sidestepped the thrust of the spear, and then, using one of his old professional wrestling maneuvers, grabbed the centaur by the throat with one hand, hoisted it into mid-air, held it up for several seconds, and then smashed the beast into the sidewalk. The centaur's vertebrae exploded with a concatenation of tiny popping noises, like defective fireworks.

Quasar glanced down, admiring his partner's handiwork. "Which move was that?"

"Mount Olympus Choke Slam," said the former Jovian World Heavyweight Champion.

"Very nice," Quasar said, taking a drag off his cigarette and watching the puddle of blood and brains ooze across the sidewalk. "Very efficient. You'll have to teach me that one."

"It's not efficient when small people use it."

"So I'll only use it on red dwarves and Pleiadean prostitutes, then. And six-foot one isn't small, Hercules. You're just a fucking leviathan."

The two mercenaries came to the skyscraper and rode an escaladder to the rooftop, then watched patiently, like two snipers, for any sign of the Centauri Strangler in the streets below.

They spent the next hour gazing over the Chiropolitan cityscape. The planets and moons of Alpha Centauri's three stars had been the first extrasolar systems to be conquered, colonized, and terraformed by mankind. Thus, Chiropolis was an anachronism, an ancient amalgamation of anthropocentric utilities, archaic architecture, and obsolete technologies. Primitive monorails were interwoven in symmetrical patterns through the tiny, mile-high skyscrapers. Antique biodomes abounded, and television screens on the sides of buildings flickered and flashed in a mere five dimensions. As he gazed upon the senescent megalopolis, Quasar felt as though he were peering through a wormhole to the distant past.

Hercules began to point out all the gaudy, neon-lit statues of centaurs adorning the city. The garish sculptures were as ubiquitous as traffic lights.He seemed fascinated by them. Quasar was less impressed.

"Fucking Mythophiles," Quasar said, as much to himself as his partner, then flicked his cigarette stub over the side of the skyscraper and watched it fall in a slow arc of crimson before shattering on the street in an explosion of tiny sparks. "Half a god-damn galaxy, christened, designed, terraformed and decorated by Mythophiles."

Quasar inserted another cigarette in his mouth. The Aesculapian weed and the black paper it was rolled in instantaneously flamed to life.

"What are Mythophiles?" Hercules asked.

Before Quasar had a chance to answer the necrometer began to vibrate in his pocket. "Hold on," he told Hercules as he pulled out the device and read the alert on the pulsing screen. "The necrometer says something's going to die nine hundred and fifty five feet from here, sixty-eight degrees to the south, in the next twenty to thirty minutes. It's bounty huntin' time."

Quasar and Hercules rode another escaladder from the roof of the skyscraper to the ground below. Following the lead of the necrometer, they sprinted through the streets and rounded a corner just in time to see a drunken blue centaur gallop into the path of a quintuple-decker bus.

"Shit!" Quasar turned and threw his cigarette onto the sidewalk in disgust. He glared at the corpse of the centaur for a few seconds, then pulled out his Chroma Blaster and spitefully opened fire. The Chroma Blaster was capable of shooting lasers in sixty-three different colors, each with its own destructive properties. As a result of certain high-tech and illegal modifications, the gun was also capable of combining omega rays and dark matter into the seemingly paradoxical black laser beams that were unceremoniously cremating the centaur in the middle of the street.

"The necrometer didn't know it would just be roadkill?" Hercules was incredulous.

"It can only predict when and where something's going to die, not what or who." Quasar removed his finger from the trigger of the Chroma Blaster, then placed the gun back in its holster.

Hercules started to reply, but Quasar halted him by placing a hand on his chest. "Wait, Herc. I'm getting another reading." Quasar studied the screen of the necrometer for a few seconds, then started to run down the glowing sidewalk.

"This has to be it. C'mon."

Hercules followed right behind him. They raced through a mile and a half of twisted streets and shadowed alleys, emerged in a vacant lot, and came to a halt as suddenly as if they had been shot with paralyzer rifles.

There it was.

The Centauri Strangler.

Or rather, Centauri Stranglers.

All four of them.

They were like giant, eyeless, blood-red snakes, wet and glistening as though they had been freshly skinned, and it looked as though they were choking four prostitutes to death with their tongues. Upon closer inspection, however, the tongues were really telescoping concatenations of arms. The primary ones were rooted in their mouths and had smaller arms growing out of their palms. The secondary arms extended outwards, and from the palms of their hands grew the third and final set, the six fingers of which were squeezing the throats of their prey to a purple pulp. One of the serpentine serial killers had its prey suspended in mid-air. Another had forced its victim onto her back and was choking her against the ground.

The four creatures turned their heads as Quasar and Hercules emerged from the shadows. Dropping their prey, they hissed and then lunged like giant cobras, abandoning the half-dead prostitutes and springing through the air with an uncanny and terrifying celerity.

Quasar ripped the Chroma Blaster from its holster and fired a stream of black laser beams. He was the fastest draw in the universe, but he was only able to shoot two of the creatures in mid-flight before the other two were within inches of him and his partner. The creatures' arms were sticking out of their mouths, ready to wrap their fingers around Quasar and Hercules' throats.

Then the universe exploded.

Quasar found himself sitting on the ground several seconds later. The entire sky was glowing white, and there was a completely straight, horizontal line of demarcation a few feet in front of him. Everything beyond it was gone. The Centauri Stranglers. The four prostitutes. Half of Chiropolis. Everything within the scope of his vision. There was nothing but a perfectly flat plane of soil reaching all the way to the horizon.

"I thought I told you to leave that thing on the first setting!" Quasar screamed from his seated position.

Hercules turned his head and carefully scrutinized the X-Gun. "I did!" he yelled back.

Smoothing his grease-slicked pompadour back into place, Quasar rose to his feet and, with a worried expression on his face, looked behind him. Everything on the other side of the line was completely unharmed.

"Jesus Fucking Christ! If we'd been facing the other direction my ship would've been destroyed."

"No, it wouldn't. It's invisible. Remember?"

"Hercules, shut the fuck up." Quasar lunged at his huge partner and swatted at his head. Hercules leaned back and laughed as he avoided Quasar's gloved hand. Quasar scowled at him, then looked at the still-smoking gun and shook his head in disbelief.

"We're going to have to experiment with that thing on an uncharted planet."

"Sounds like fun."

Quasar's mood suddenly changed. "It will be," he said, grinning. "We'll get loaded and blow shit up until we pass out."

"Nice!" Hercules exclaimed enthusiastically, then abruptly stopped smiling.

"Um, Quasar? I think I destroyed all the evidence. We won't be able to collect the bounty."

Quasar looked at him and tapped the frame of his spectacles with his right forefinger. "It's all in the sunglasses, Herc. They record everything like a camera. It can all be played back on a monitor."

"But what about everything I just killed? What about the buildings I destroyed? What's the Xenarchy going to say about that?"

"Nothing. I'm going to edit all that shit out."

A wail of sirens from the city tore through the air as red lights flashed over the horizon. The sound of helicopter blades began rattling the skies. Hercules looked over in the direction of the invisible Black Seraph.

"Uh, Quasar? I know I'm new at this, but I think we should probably blast off now."

"You're a quick learner, Herc," Quasar said, pulling the Black Seraph's remote control from his utility belt. "Let's get the fuck out of here."

*

With space streaming past and music blaring through the cockpit, Quasar D'Arete lit a gamma lotus joint and Hercules Moonsmasher opened a can of protein-beer.

"See?" Quasar said, leaning back in his pilot's chair. "I told you there weren't two of them."

Both mercenaries burst out laughing, and continued to laugh even harder when Hercules sprayed protein-beer all over the control console and Quasar started choking on his own smoke.

Six gamma lotus joints and one-hundred twenty-seven cans of protein-beer later they were jolted from their victory celebration by a roar from the cockpit's antechamber.

"What the fuck was that?" Quasar turned the music down.

Another bestial scream followed, even louder than the first. The necrometer in Quasar's right pocket began to vibrate. There was a stowaway aboard the Black Seraph, and it had brought death along with it.

Quasar hit a compartment over his head and a tiny door popped open. Two small wafers fell into his hand. He put one in his mouth and flipped the other to Hercules.

"Eat that."

"What is it?"

"Panacea. Eat it." Quasar threw a half-smoked joint onto the floor, rose out of his chair, and drew the Chroma Blaster.

Hercules ate the panacea wafer and found himself completely sober in a matter of seconds. He placed his one-hundred twenty-eighth can of protein-beer on the control console, hoisted the X-Gun over his shoulder, and followed Quasar out of the cockpit.

As the door slid shut behind them Quasar and Hercules beheld a ten-foot tall, light purple, horned monstrosity with eight arms, roaring and laughing at the same time. A pair of arms grew out of its shoulders, and from the elbows of those arms grew two more. Identical double-appendages extended from its midsection. The creature's elbow joints were such that the outer arms could move independently of the inner ones.

With the six-fingered hands of its upper arms the monster held four live victims, two male and two female, upside-down by the ankles. The fingers of its lower arms were wrapped around their throats. The victims' heads were already bruise-colored and bulging with burst blood vessels, brain damage and internal injuries.

The beast's chiseled physique rivaled Hercules' own. Each of its eight biceps had a black rumel wrapped around it like an armband, making its already huge muscles swell even more. It wore a spiked choke-collar around its neck, from which a black cord of tensile adamantium was stretched tautly to a slipknot fastened around its erect penis, forming some sort of autoerotic asphyxiation device. The horn in the middle of its forehead was encircled by a garrote; the two horns on each side of its skull by ligatures. The shriveled corpses of strangled infants hung from the nooses it wore as earrings, and ten tiny chains with desiccated lungs at their ends dangled from the piercings in its nipples. Large, triangular scales ran down the back of its head and spine to the tip of its tail, which had a lasso of Silvanian hemp tied to the end of it.

Through his sunglasses Quasar could clearly see that the palms of the creature's hands had hands of their own, extending outwards on short arms like baby hydras emerging from blossoming lotus flowers . Each of these, in turn, bore a third arm and hand. All of the hands were completely identical in size, shape, and texture. The tertiary ones were dug deep into the throats and upside-down chests of the victims. Quasar watched as the creature suddenly squeezed the necks of its victims with its outer hands, then just as suddenly released its grip. Its inner hands simultaneously shoveled their respiratory systems from their chests through the gaping throat wounds. Vertebrae shattered, eyeballs shot across the room and bounced off the wall, and four avalanches of lungs, esophagi, tracheae, and larynxes hit the floor.

The monster shimmered. It hissed at Quasar with a flickering, triplicate, prehensile tongue, just like the ones the serpentine stranglers back on Chiron had possessed. Quasar flashed back to the vacant lot and the four snakelike things springing into the air and hurtling towards his throat. He fired the Chroma Blaster as the creature faded and disappeared, with the corpses still in its grasp, laughing and roaring all the while. The black laser beams passed through its vanishing image and burned two holes in the wall behind it, leaving a pair of jagged portals to the adjacent weapons gallery in their wake.

"Shit!" Quasar cursed the damage to the interior of the Black Seraph.

"Quasar, what the hell was that?"

Quasar reholstered the Chroma Blaster. "The Centauri Strangler."

A look of utter confusion came over Hercules' face.

"Then what were those things we smoked back on Chiron?"

"Its offspring, probably. Decoys, maybe. Or copycat killers. Maybe all three."

"But why didn't it attack us? Why sneak on board just to teleport out when it saw us?"

"I have no idea what breed of alien that was, Herc, let alone how its brain works, but a lot of serial killers are megalomaniacal exhibitionists, regardless of species. They love to fuck with the minds of law enforcement."

Hercules was bemused again. "We're law enforcement?"

"Yep. Just not the legal kind."

Quasar glowered at the sizzling holes in the wall of his spaceship for several seconds, then glanced down at the four piles of lungs, esophagi, tracheae and larynxes, and then the eight eyeballs still rolling around the room. As he surveyed the carnage he recalled that the four corpses in the Black Seraph's autopsy room were missing the very same organs that littered the floor in front of him. He had intended to sell the cadavers to some necrophiliacs in the Cerberus system, but now realized he would be able to refurbish them and negotiate a higher price elsewhere. Quasar's scowl turned into a smirk as he pulled a tachyphone from the left pants-pocket of his designer spacesuit and hit a quick combination on its keyboard.

"Doc...It's Quasar..." Bonded to audible tachyons, the cumulative sound of his voice was carried through space at supraluminal speeds. "I've got four bodies for sale...Dead...They're not intact, but I have all their organs...Human...Two males, one female, and a hermaphrodite...The hermaphrodite costs double, for obvious reasons...Yeah...I'll be in your system in two days...Aesculapius days...See you then, Doc."

He put the tachyphone back in his pocket. "That'll pay for the repairs to the wall, and then some."

Hercules turned and looked directly into Quasar's sunglasses. "What do we do now, Quasar?"

"We give the footage from Chiron to the Xenarchy and collect, same as before." Quasar turned, reopened the door to the cockpit, and stepped through. Hercules followed right behind him.

"But what happens when that thing starts slaughtering people again?"

"They rehire us," Quasar said, easing into his chair with a freshly-lit black cigarette between his lips. "For twice the price."

Season of Blood

The crimson ichor rained down in torrents. The Season of Blood was upon us, and all that it portended. Every year, for seven days, the angels go to war, fighting each other across the terrains of Heaven, and every year, for seven days, their cascading tsunamis of blood flood the entire city, submerging the streets in crimson rivers more than ten-feet deep. There must be googolplexes of the haloed bitches and winged bastards up there, dying at a rate of one million per second.

None of us know very much about the geography of Heaven, but the one thing we do know is that it has a lot of holes. The occasional fallen angel with life left in its brain is usually taken to the Tower downtown, to visit the Interrogatrix. While being tortured they speak of things like vertical labyrinths, floating mountain ranges, and societies of cliff dwellers whose habitats lie face-to-face with one another over valleys which serve as mass graves. They say the entire realm is honeycombed with bottomless abysses for the blood to drain through. Bottomless to them, that is. Down here we know the truth. We're the bottom.

None of us know why they do it. Some of the fallen angels, while being tortured by the Interrogatrix, tell her it's a ritual.Others say it's a form of sacrifice. One motherfucker

said it's God's personal form of entertainment.

In retrospect,it probably wasn't wise to build a city beneath Heaven.

I was perched in the eyrie of a bell tower, surveying the city below in much the same way that its founders had envisioned God would, guarding and protecting the metropolis of Chosen Ones with His omnipotence and His omniscience. Problem is, I'm not omnipotent. I have my superpowers, to be sure, but they have their limitations. Legally speaking, I'm not supposed to use them anymore anyways, but that's another story.

I looked out across our beloved city, with its looming lighthouses and tenebrous alleyways, its skyscraper churches and crippled sewers, its grand palaces and eroded tenements, its vertical labyrinths of ladders and stairways and elevators and balconies, its broken bridges and rusted monorails, its cantilevered bazaars where the blessed walk side by side with the damned, and the unfinished, mile-high Tower which serves as the nexus of the entire megalopolis.

New Babel.

Population: over seventeen billion.

Population Status: declining.

Rapidly-the Season of Blood is also the Season of Crime, and New Babel's superhero team, the Avatars, are overworked and undermanned. You can literally get away with murder.

I watched the streets metamorphose into canals of gore. You can swim short distances in it, but it's a big city, and unless you've got the lung capacity of a demigod or a hooker you can't get very far. If you're rich, you own a yacht. If you're bourgeois, you own a ferry or a canoe. If you're poor, you're fucked. Some folks are a little more creative than others. One guy walks around on stilts. Another guy imported a submarine and scuba diving gear from Atlantis. Another crazy motherfucker uses the electrical wires like his own personal monorail. Walks 'em like tightropes; rides 'em like pulleys. Uses 'em for catapults. Has the most uncanny sense of balance in the universe. He's got this aerodynamic cape and these jumping superpowers that let him glide from wire to wire, building to building, street to street. Wears a black rubber costume so he won't get electrocuted, and a double-tubed breathing mask to keep the blood out of his face. Runs the wires like a fuckin' monkey all year long, whether it's raining blood or not.

That crazy motherfucker's me.

I made my way to the outer perimeter of the city and climbed to the top of the wall that encircled the entire metropolis. The wall had been conceived with a twofold purpose. The first was to keep the world out. The second was to keep the citizens in. The objective was isolation for mystical and spiritual purposes, and the wall was an extremely efficient tool in this regard. Of course, there were always ways to get out, if you had the money, the connections, and the balls to face the devil-haunted Wilds that surrounded the rest of the planet, or the...inclinations...to pack up and move to New Sodom or New Gomorrah. Most of the people that try their luck in the outside world are dead within a week.

I slipped between a pair of dueling searchlights and crouched down in the shadows of the nearest watchtower. I was immediately knee-deep in blood. My supersaviour senses detected a potential crisis in an alleyway to my left.I flipped the dark, mirrored lenses in my giant goggles to a higher magnification, turned the wipers up two levels, and zeroed in on the alley. Stupid kids trying to surfin this shit again. Fuck 'em. I ain't no superhero.I ain't no Avatar. Not anymore.

 I clicked my normal lenses back into place and turned around. I needed a fix, and I needed it soon. Gotta find an apothecary.

I adjusted my rubber cape and prepared to glide to a window on the other side of the street. I turned around instinctively to check on the kids. Old habits are hard to break. Sure enough, one of them was drowning. Predictable. Everything becomes predictable after a while. Whoever said history repeats itself was a genius. That's why I believe in reincarnation. I just wish I could believe in redemption.

As I watched the kid struggling against the vermilion tide I reminded myselfI wasn't a superhero anymore. I was an ex-superhero. As in ex-communicated. Ex-iled. Ex-tinct. And one who needed a fix, at that.Still, my conscience was gnawing a hole in my fuckin' brain. A moment later I was tightroping the electrical wires to the alleyway where the kid was drowning.

Another word for tightrope walking is funambulation. It's not very fun when the wiresare dripping with blood, though.Still, I've had plenty of practice, and I haven't slipped yet, drunk, stoned or otherwise.

I used the tensile strength of the electric wire to catapult myself over two buildings, let the wind and my aerodynamic cape do the rest, and landed on a far-off rooftop. Two leaps and two window sills later and I was almost down to street-level. The blood was rushing through the street like redwater rapids, carrying the kid along like a piece of detritus. I reined him in with my lasso, pulled him onto the window sill beside me and removed the mouthpiece from my mask. A couple of minutes of mouth-to-mouth resuscitation, maybe a little CPR and a touch of my healing superpowers, and the kid would be fine.

The thing about mouth-to-mouth during the Season ofBloodis that it's a little gory. Whereas under normal circumstances the kid would be coughing up water, now he was coughing up blood. He was literally drowning in blood. The blood of angels. Anyways, it makes for a pretty grotesque scene. With the blood shooting out of their mouths like a jetstream, it looks like they're vomiting up the contents of their entire circulatory system. Half the time I expect to see a vein or an artery floating in there like a fluke. This time was no different than usual. I saved the kid, a feat which wasn't any different than usual either. It's just that I don't have superhero status anymore.

The kid kept coughing for a couple more minutes, shaking the blood out of his hair and eyes. He mumbled his thanks for saving his life, peering at me apprehensively. I returned his gaze for a long while before speaking. When I did, it was short and succinct. "The next time you pull a stunt like that, I won't save you. Even if I'm on a balcony right above you, I'll spark a joint and watch your ass fuckin drown."

"Thanks man", he said again, uncertainly now, then followed with the oldest cliche in history, superhero history at least. "How can I ever repay you?"

"You can't." It was cold, but it was the truth.

"Hey, aren't you...." he started.

"No. Not anymore."

The kid's friends sailed by in their canoe and dropped anchor. They were all looking at me like I was some kind of deity. Like I was an Avatar. He thanked me again and began making his way back to them.

"Hey kid," I said. He stopped and looked back.

"You got any heroin?"

*

I laid back on my bed as the smack hit my veins. The syringe clattered to the floor. I closed the hidden patch in the left sleeve of my costume, then reached up and clicked my darkest lenses over my constricted eyes, sunglasses so black they made you blind. Most people would think this a pointless accessory. It actually has several uses, most of which have to do with heightening your other senses.Good for fighting ghosts and other invisible enemies. Good for escaping labyrinths. And, when combined with negasonic earplugs and a black rubber costume that provides insulation, not just from electricity but from pain and other stimuli as well, it makes for a pretty damned effective sensory deprivation chamber.

I slowly relaxed as the heroin coursed through my veins. The opium-visions started coming fast and hard, and I welcomed the hallucinations like they were old friends. I had a lot of shit to sort out, and all night to do it. So what if there was a robbery, an assault, a murder somewhere in the city? That wasn't my problem anymore. Let someone else handle it. My ass is retired.

I drifted into peaceful, dreamless, pleasant sleep. It was the most pleasant sleep I've ever had in my entire life.

I woke up in a hospital bed.

*

As I awakened from my coma, the first thing I noticed was that the blood was still raining outside. I just lay there for several minutes before I even opened my eyes, listening to the hypnotic tympani. The blood was coming down pretty hard this year, harder than I could ever remember. It had started on Sunday, the 7th. I'd O.D.ed on Wednesday the 10th, so the week-long Season of Blood should be just about over now. Too bad I missed most of it this year. Finally, curiosity got the better of me and I pried my eyelids apart. I immediately looked around for a digital calendar, found one on the wall to my right, read it.

It was the 16th.

What the fuck?

*

Thankfully, the doctors had allowed me to retain what shred of dignity I have left and "neglected" to remove my mask and costume. Superhero status-even ex-superhero status-has its advantages. The med-charts next to the hospital bed showed that I had been declared clinically dead on two separate occasions during my coma. Coming back from the dead is one of my superpowers. I don't have to play possum. I can do the real thing.

After detaching myself from the various tubes stuck in my arms and down my throat, I used my superpowers of echolocation to find the hospital's pharmaceutical level, my superpowers of mass hypnosis to distract the guards and nurses, my superpowers of stealth to steal a shitload of morphine, my superpowers of burden-bearing to carry that shitload of morphine on my back, and my superpowers of ricochet to bounce around the windowless storage rooms until I broke through one of the solid steel walls.

I landed on a balcony, climbed a telephone pole, and navigated the electric wires to my tenement in the slums. It's a far cry from the fifteen-thousand square foot luxury suite I had in the Tower, but you gotta sleep somewhere. After a brief conversation with my landlord, during the course of which I learned it was him who had taken me to the hospital in his canoe, I headed straight for bed and shot up again. Some people never learn.

I kept feeding my vein every few hours until the 21st. It had been fourteen days now since the Season of Blood began, and still the vermilion rainfall had not ceased. In fact, it was intensifying. Even in my near-catatonic state of stoned bliss and opium-visions, I was starting to get concerned. My own conscience pussy-whipped me again, like the bitch it was, and I eventually sobered up and emerged from my opium den to try and find out what the fuck was going on.

A few hours later, as I was walking the wires, my supersaviour senses started going crazy. I followed a stream of psychic vibrations to a vacant lot, or, more accurately, a lake of blood that had been a vacant lot, and spied a strange, golden glow in the air. I slid my telescopic lenses over my eyes and zeroed in. It was a blonde man in a tattered white robe, stuck to the gargantuan, crimson web of a Morae Spider.

If you're thinking the spiderweb caught him like a safety net, think again. It caught him like a trawl of barbed wire. He was a bloody, broken-boned mess. His golden halo was still circling his head though, which meant he was still alive. I immediately recognized him as a fallen angel, but there was something different about him. Something familiar. I'd seen his face before, in some long out-of-print book called The Bible. I remember reading it once. The authors were complete hacks, but the pictures were pretty cool. One of them even reminded me of myself. I wondered if there'd ever be a sequel...

I sifted through my memories, trying to figure out who this busted-up motherfucker was. It took a couple of minutes, but when it hit me, it hit me like a sack of rocks.

Gabriel. The angel in the crimson spiderweb was Gabriel. And not just an angel. An archangel. No one had ever seen one of them before, and this one was still breathing.

I dropped into one of the balconies overlooking the lake of blood.

A family of blood-red, skull-sized Morae Spiders had spun their crimson webs all across the vacant lot, from building to building, and a pair of Morae Spiders were converging upon Gabriel from either side. I couldn't use my jumping superpowers to rescue him, because I'd get caught in the vermilion spiderwebs if I tried. I did, however, possess another superpower that would do the trick.

Just as I was about to make my heroic rescue of the archangel, I heard a hiss from the corner of the balcony.In my exuberance I had failed to notice the Morae Spider right before me, lurking in the shadows. It was squatting on the face of a still-living woman and pulling her jugular vein from her throat, inch by bloody inch, like a scarlet thread. In a matter of seconds it had completely unraveled her circulatory system like a tapestry and swallowed the single, lengthy, continuous cord of blood vessels into its stomach and spinneret.

I heard another hiss and turned my head just in time to catch a Morae Spider with my face. It wrapped its legs around my head while I tried to pull it off. I could feel its fangs puncturing my rubber suit and trying to pierce my jugular vein, trying to get a firm grip on it so it could yank my circulatory system out through my neck.

I channeled the electricity stored in my suit through my hands and electrocuted the Morae Spider. It fell from my face to the floor of the balcony, sizzling like a freshly cooked steak. The other Morae Spider was already weaving a web from the veins and arteries it had pulled from the woman's body. I turned and spat a bolt of lightning from my mouth.The Morae Spider exploded like a bladder that had been hit with a sledgehammer.

I refocused on the dying angel, suspended cruciform in the spiderweb of veins and arteries that reached across the vacant lot. The other two Morae Spiders were within a few feet of him now, and fixing to have themselves some dinner.

My superpowers of funambulation and equilibrium give me the ability to skim the surfaces of small bodies of water for short distances, like a basilisk lizard. I used these superpowers now, and damn near glided across the lake of blood like a flying fish. Damn near got myself tangled up in the web of veins and arteries when I came to a halt, too. The Morae Spiders were pulling Gabriel's blood vessels from his neck, preparing to cocoon him in his own circulatory system.

I grabbed Gabriel by the feet and pulled him from the spiderweb. His wings chose not to accompany him. The Morae Spiders smelled blood and converged upon his reflexively beating pinions, oblivious to the fact that the rest of their meal had been stolen.I skimmed back to the balcony and lowered Gabriel to the floor.

I looked down upon the unconscious form of the archangel, lying supine atop the gaping wounds where his wings had been torn from his back. Most people would have seen a tragedy of cosmic proportions. All I saw was a ticket back into the Avatars. I did my little mouth-to-mouth and CPR routine, then gathered his limp body in my arms, looked to the skies, and began mapping my route through the electric wires above. After nine long months, I prepared to make my triumphant return to the Tower.

*

"He's a fucking archangel, and I killed eighty Morae Spiders to save his life," I shouted into the portable phone. I exaggerated a bit, but I'd do anything to get back into the Avatars. "How does this not redeem my ass? We have to get him into the Interrogatrix so she can make him sing before he dies. He knows why the blood isn't stopping; I can smell it. He knows everything, all the answers to all the mysteries, and he's ready to sing. I'm tellin' you, Pete, the bastard is ready to God-damn sing, and when he does they'll have no choice but to reinstate me."

"Leave him on the steps of the Tower-anonymously-and go home. You've got twenty-eight charges of vigilantism against you. If you go back to the Tower, they might not let you out again. You know the policy on vigilantism."

"What the fuck do I care about policies anymore?"

"Because you're going to find yourself imprisoned if you don't stop."

"My ass is already imprisoned."

I slammed the phone against the wall of the bell tower I was perched in. It shattered into a million pieces. Just like my heart, I thought.Just like my soul.

I took his advice and, from an eyrie at a safe distance, attached the fallen angel to eight swinging grapnels, then lowered and maneuvered his limp body through the streets to the stairs in front of the Tower. I started walking home, paused, then pivoted on the

151

electric wire.

"Fuck it."

I jumped down to the steps of the Tower and picked Gabriel back up. I climbed the walls of the Tower,kicked in a bulletproof window, marched down the hallway, and burst into the room of the Interrogatrix.

My ex-wife looked up from the naked man she was grilling. She hadn't changed a bit. Same steely eyes, same imperious lips, same austere face. Same skin-tight leather, same whip, and same chains, as well.

"Messiah Man," she gasped. I thought I saw pain in her eyes, but the scars on my mind, body and soul told me otherwise. Besides which, she only liked inflicting pain. She didn't go both ways.

"Mistress Magdalene," I replied coldly. I gazed over the familiar torture chamber. Some of the bloodstains on the floor, walls, ceiling and torture devices were my own. The man in the chair was one of my ex-partners, a renowned superhero in his own right: Red Judas. I wondered what he was suspected of.Looked like I was going to have a brother in excommunication soon. Maybe we could form an antihero team.

The eyelids of the Interrogatrix narrowed as she spied the unconscious native of Heaven in my arms.

"It's an archangel," I told her. "Gabriel. He's almost dead. We need to grill him now."

An instant later the Interrogatrix freed Red Judas from the torture chair. After readorning his mask, cape and costume he was escorted from the room by four guards. Based on the handcuffs and fetters, I assumed he was headed for the penitentiary level. I'd probably be joining him shortly. Poor bastard was probably as innocent as I was. Probably got framed by the same son of a bitch, too, whoever that was. Maybe our first mission as an antihero team would be to find out who the traitor was, cut off his genitals, and shove them up his ass.

I carried the limp body of Gabriel across the room to take Red Judas' place. The Interrogatrix stripped the angel naked, strapped him to the torture chair and switched on the electricity. Gabriel's eyes fluttered open.

As I was being led from the room in handcuffs there was a loud explosion down the hall, in the direction which Red Judas had been taken. There were blood and guts everywhere. The motherfucker had used his pyrokinetic powers to blow himself up, like a suicide bomber. He'd taken a couple of guards along with him.

After the medics had swarmed to the scene and the commotion died down, the Interrogatrix began questioning the archangel, using her superpowers of persuasion to coax the truth from his bloody mouth. It had to be the shortest inquisition ever.

"When is it going to end?" the Interrogatrix demanded.Her sonic and hypnotic superpowers echoed and ricocheted from the sound-proof walls. She was a siren dominatrix, and she could shatter glass, eardrums and bones with her voice.

"Never," Gabriel answered.

"Don't fuck with me," the Interrogatrix shouted, cracking her whip and placing her stiletto heel between his legs.The room was rapidly filling with the perfumes of her Delphic pheromones, subtle truth-drugs which she emitted from her glands during interrogations. "Tell me when it's going to end."

"Never," Gabriel said again, flinching in anticipation of another lashing and adding, "It's not just the blood of angels now.It's flowing from an infinite source. It's going to rain blood for all eternity."

"Why?"

Gabriel didn't respond

"Why?"

The guards that were leading me from the room paused in the doorway. With a mixture of dread and morbid curiosity they all looked back into the torture chamber. I managed to jerk my head around and look back with them. I knew that what I saw and heard next would haunt me for the rest of my life. Or life-sentence, as the case might be.

"Because," the fallen angel cried, sobbing as golden tears ran down his face and his halo went cold and slowed to a stop.

"God committed suicide."

*

So, on account of the fact that the Season of Blood is now an eternity, and the blood of God is going to rain down on New Babel until the end of time, we need all the superheroes we can get to enforce justice and maintain the peace. The Tower is literally hiring people off the streets. Needless to say, considering the circumstances, I've been reinstated as an Avatar and exonerated of all charges, false, bullshit, or otherwise. I've got my old luxury suite back, and all the opium I can eat. It's a grotesque irony, but it took the death of God for my prayers to be answered. I'm Messiah Man again, and it's the dawn of a new age for the Avatars. The Era of Blood is upon is, and all that it portends.

The Stygimancer and the Squid Muse
A Tale From Between The Sinistral Earth and the Widdershins Moon

The cyclopean eye of the Squid Muse dilated as the Stygimancer poured a vial of blue fear-toxins into a syringe of black glass. Peering through the eyelet of the studded executioner's mask tied around its head, the Squid Muse tried to recoil as the Stygimancer approached, but the chains and flechettes binding it to the walls of the giant prison-tank would not allow it. Dangling cruciform in the ebullient fluids, the colossal cephalopod strained its two upper tentacles against the crosspiece around which they were heliced, pulling at the nails driven through its suckers. With four of its tendrils trapped against its body by a black leather straitjacket, and its remaining four tendrils bound in pairs by large iron cuffs and shackled to the walls, the struggles of the Squid Muse were futile and excruciating. The silver buckles and metal clasps on the straitjacket clattered as the Squid Muse squirmed, and the transparent walls of the prison-tank rattled as the Squid Muse shook its chains.

The Stygimancer pushed back the sleeves of his black robe, whose embroidered designs and symbols declared his High Priesthood in the Church of Charon, and climbed a wheeled staircase positioned behind the tank. His long, cobalt-colored fingernails audibly scraped the adamantium lid of the torture chamber-like aquarium as he slid it to one side. He paused to screw a hollow drill into the syringe, then plunged his hand into the waters. With a push of his thumb the corkscrew needle of the drill-syringe began to whir and spin. The Stygimancer lowered the gyrating needle through a jagged tear in the top of the Squid Muse's hood and jabbed it into an open wound in the dome of its head. With another push of his thumb, he injected a swirling stream of the blue fear-toxins into the brain of the Squid Muse.

As the familiar phobigens saturated the Squid Muse's nervous system, its three hearts began to race and palpitate. Its gills quickened and pulsed, like the lungs of a hyperventilating Prometheus. The rings and pieces of brain coral and quartz crystal piercing its penis, vagina, and swollen nidamental glands vibrated and hummed, and the sacks of liquefied fish connected to its stomach by feeding tubes rippled and sloshed. The Squid Muse gnashed upon its ball gag and thrashed even harder, throttling the walls of the tank.

As the fear toxins coursed through its nervous system, the Squid Muse descended into a realm of pnemensis and phantasmagoria. All types of memories-recent, ancient, forgotten, repressed, confabulated, archetypal, shared, communal, genetic, evolutionary, atavistic, anemnesic, akashic-replayed themselves before its mind's eye. The Squid Muse recalled all of the past experiments that had been performed upon it by philosophers, all the studies in thigmotaxis, every detail of the underwater labyrinths specially constructed by Daedalus to test its immense memory capacity. It relived every corridor and corner of those mazes, every dead end and shortcut, every trap and exit, every delectable fish-tailed Ariadne and menacing aquatic Minotaur.

Its statocyst seemed to spin and lurch, like a galley tossed on the tides of a storm, spreading concentric circles of vertigo through the Squid Muse's brain. Hallucinations ensued. Coils of color arose from the bottom of the tank, like the entrails of Ungud the Rainbow God being unwound on a disembowelment crank. Like the kundalini of a thousand meditating Morpheuses the colors ascended in spirals, serpentine and dreamlike and spinning and shimmering with a thousand glowing hues. The Squid Muse's flesh began to bubble before its eye, its suckers transforming into painful waterspouts and hurricanes. Abaia the leviathan eel and a tribe of rabid bunyips emerged from the eyes of the storms in the Squid Muse's tentacles. Abaia simultaneously electrocuted and strangled the Squid Muse while the bunyips chewed off pieces of the Squid Muse's flesh. Plesiosaurs rammed the prison-tank while a priapic Dagon tried to force its way through the walls. The tank exploded into a million tiny seashells. Megaladons swarmed and swam around the Squid Muse's head in predatory ellipses, drawn by the perfume of blood and the musk of fear. A retiarius whaleman stabbed the Squid Muse in the eye with a trident, then entangled the Squid Muse's tentacles in a battle-trawl and dragged the Squid Muse through an interdimensional whirlpool to a Hades of pink and purple fire.

The visions continued, unrelenting, until, with a single paroxysm of terror, the Squid Muse released a torrent of pitchlike ink into the machine attached to its siphon. The ink runnelled through a series of metal pipes before pooling in a small chamber in the wall of the tank, just above an open compartment containing an empty vial and a round faucet wheel.

Looking on with the whiteless eyes of a lotophagos, the Stygimancer slowly turned the faucet wheel and watched the ink pour from a trapdoor at the top of the compartment. He collected every drop in an inkwell, then turned the faucet wheel again and closed the trapdoor.

Smiling to himself, his cobalt-colored teeth gleaming behind his blue-stained lips, the Stygimancer picked up the inkwell. He carried it to a desk made of petrified wood and seated himself in a chair made of ebony. He placed the inkwell down, dipped his pen, with its quill of harpy feathers and its shaft made from the bronze beaks of man-eating Stymphalian birds, into the fresh ink, and began scribing more spells and sigils in the siren-vellum pages betwixt the green fishscale covers of his half-finished tome.

Simultaneously necromancer and hydromancer, the Stygimancer's powers were a mixture of death and water, just like the river Styx whose ferryman he worshipped. With these powers the Stygimancer could sense the memories of the Squid Muse in its ink, and all the genetic memories and oral histories of its ancestors, including its evolutionary forefathers, the mighty krakens. The ink of the Squid Muse provided the High Stygimancer with boundless inspiration, energizing his imagination, enchanting his quill, and powering his hand as he penned the Hydronecronomicon. It was for these reasons that the Stygimancer referred to his gargantuan familiar as the Squid Muse.

The Stygimancer chewed upon petals of blue lotus and leaves of black water lilies as he chronicled his hydronecromantic knowledge. He paused to smoke the combined exsiccatae of both plants through a hookah that bubbled with the dusky, phosphorous, deadly waters of Lake Avernus. Filled with psychotropic chemicals, the blue lotus sounded, felt, smelled, and tasted blue as well. The black lilies created similar synesthesias of shadow, darkness, and gloom. The synergistic effect of the combined drugs was like eating the sky and drinking the night and inhaling the horizon like a line of black cocaine.

Watching all the time was the Squid Muse, peering through the opening in its mask with its single front eye like a Fomorian voyeur, a peeping Balor, an Arimaspian spy. Though able to see its surroundings with its front eye, the leather hood confined its rear eye to blindness, and an animal collar with a variety of buckles and straps prevented the Squid Muse from shifting or loosening the mask. With a baleful glare, it observed its captor for several minutes, then swept its gaze across the musty room.

The hollowed-out manor was tenebrously lit by black candles of mermaid tallow and incense sticks of powdered zeuglodon ambergris. A frighteningly lifelike painting of Charon hung over the doorway, presiding over the chamber.

A collector of death and a master of bio-alchemy was the Stygimancer, and his lair was like a pleasure chamber of necrobestiality and a torture chamber of chemical diablery, equal parts menagerie, mausoleum, museum, and laboratory. Taxidermied animals lined the shelves and dangled from the crossbeams in the high, vaulted ceiling. The stuffed heads of chimeras, griffins, basilisks, and manticores were mounted on the walls. Propped up in one corner was the carcass of a hydra; in another, that of a kraken. The corpses of naiades, hippocampuses, and cockodrills floated in aquariums of formaldehyde. A sphinxskin rug lay before the door in acouchant deathpose. It seemed to guard the entranceway, although the likelihood of visitors in the Archipelagoes of Acheron was nearly nonexistent.

In a dusty chair next to the doorway sat the cadaver of the philosopher who had sold the Squid Muse to the Stygimancer. Beside him sat the cadaver of the pirate who had imported the Squid Muse from southwestern Lemuria and bartered it to the philosopher. Beside him sat the cadavers of the oneirochrononaut shaman from southwestern Lemuria and the boreal angekok cryomancer from the Archipelagoes of Cocytus who were the Squid Muse's original keepers and had been kidnapped by the pirate when he pilfered the

Squid Muse.

Staring at the quartet of preserved and stuffed bodies, it was as though the Squid Muse's history were written before it in a language of death, where corpses served as words and pictograms alike, a necrophasia of morbiglyphics. Reading the carcasses like a grimoire the Squid Muse relived its journey from the depths of the Antarctic Ocean to the reefs of Lemuria, from the acropolises of Greece to the mountain of Helicon, and finally to the Archipelagoes of Acheron. It had been captured for its karma and ambisexuality, stolen for its size and hermaphroditism, bartered for its intelligence and curiosa, and sold for its memories and enlightenment.

The shelves along the walls were filled with grimoires and tomes (including attempted forgeries of the ancient and hideous Necro-Sutras and Yama-Yana, and inchoate versions of the Popol Vuh and the Cimiamatl), surgical instruments and prosthetic body parts, torture devices and sexual paraphernalia, potions and philtres, and large canopic jars containing still-living organs that pulsed and gurgled while floating in embalming fluid. An alembic filled with blue lotus petals and Stygian water lilies perched inconspicuously amongst the shelves, distilling the entheogens of the nigromantic flowers. The dark cerulean droplets extracted by the alembic fell into a boiling cauldron where the fear toxins were cooked, blending the blue lotus and black lilies with the cries of sodomized woodsprites, the screams of ravished Vestal virgins, the wails of molested cherubs, the repressed memories of Moloch's offspring, the nightmares of comatose pixies, the nightsweats of narcoleptic elves, the adrenaline of sacrificial unicorns, and the smoke of immolated suttees. Every few minutes the volatile concoction erupted with a gout of blue flame.

Unbeknownst to the Stygimancer, the psychotropic chemicals of the blue lotus and the Stygian water lilies were strengthening the Squid Muse's brain. Every dosage of fear toxin increased its memory capacity and raised its consciousness to new levels. As the weeks passed, the Squid Muse evolved an almost humanlike intelligence, and with it, an extremely humanlike lust for revenge upon its keeper.

*

"Tonight, my Squid Muse," said the Stygimancer, chewing upon a mushroom, "we are going upon a journey."

The Stygimancer climbed the staircase behind the prison-tank. He removed the lid, withdrew the drill-syringe from his pocket, and injected a stream of liquid psilocybin, distilled from the same genus of mushroom his cobalt teeth were mashing, into the Squid Muse's brain.

"You see, my pet, there are certain sigils whose form I knoweth not, sigils which have been drawn but once in all of history. Alas, they lie beyond my ken, for they exist only in the palace of the Mersibyl, at the nadir of Charybdis' womb, wherefrom no mortal man nor beast nor ship can ever return, and so we must project through space and time, and view them from the astral plane...and you, my dear familiar, must accompany me, for I shall need your magic ink to tattoo the sigils on my soul."

The Stygimancer returned to his desk. As he scribed in his tome he devoured three more mushrooms. Soonafter, the psychedelic visions began...

The Stygimancer exhaled giant fungus balls which rose into the air like bubbles and burst in explosions of spores. His long, atramentous hair and pointed beard transformed into a verdant hedge-maze. He could feel an enchanted forest growing inside him. In his lungs blossomed a magical garden of aspergilloma where myciades fluttered and played. Gangrene and mildew coated his skin, and mounds of eumycetoma buried his feet all the way up to his ankles. Ergot grew in his armpits, behind his ears, between his fingers, and along his perineum. His pubic hair turned to moss, and his penis transformed into a toadstool wet with psychedelic smegma. Psychonaut dryades flocked into the chamber to partake of the Stygimancer's psychotropic fellacio. His sperm was etiolated ambrosia that caused spoiled milk to drip from their breasts. A mycophiliac succubus seated herself upon his lap and they made love in the yab-yum position until her womb grew gravid with yeast and agaric.

The chemicals pouring through the mind of the Squid Muse intensified as well. In its transcendental state the Squid Muse could see all of the Stygimancer's psychedelic visions. The Squid Muse sank into a deep reverie of its own, dreaming of bioluminescent lichen that changed color every second, of kaleidoscopic coral spinning in a breathing atoll, of poisonous algae transforming into severed tendrils transforming into singing anemones transforming into gardens of penises transforming into orgies of hydrastes, of pink seahorses and purple mollusks and seashells with entire universes inside them, and then suddenly the Squid Muse began to tingle and lost all sense of weight and mass. A moment later, the Squid Muse lifted out of its body and ascended to the astral plane.

The astrosome of the Stygimancer, with the spectral essence of his drill-syringe in one mistlike hand, was already waiting for the Squid Muse in the other dimension. The Stygimancer turned and bade the Squid Muse follow it from the manor. With an eleventh tentacle, a silver tentacle, connecting its astrosome to its physical body, the Squid Muse glided in the glowing wake of the Stygimancer like a remoral eidolon. They passed through the door of the chamber and down to the shore of the small island, where the Stygimancer's sentient ferry was docked.

Carved from the conscious wood of the lotus tree which the nymph, Lotis, had been transformed into by Zeus, the ferry possessed the intelligence and awareness of a human being. The astral bodies of lesbian hamadryads, imprisoned in the shards that the Stygimancer had whittledfrom their arboreal soulmate, could be seen twitching beneath the deck like butterflies crucified on torture racks.

As the Stygimancer and the Squid Muse floated into the ferry, twelve oars arose like arms from the sides of the boat. The Stygimancer grabbed two of them, and the Squid Muse instinctively wrapped its tentacles around the remaining ten. They began to paddle, and the living ferry astral projected, leaving its physical body of wood behind.

They levitated into the vibrating air above the astral waters, leaving their tiny black island and Gothic, Translvanianesque manor behind. Through the atramentous Mists of Erebus that enshrouded the Archipelagoes of Acheron they flew, then glided across the Aegean Sea, spanning hundreds of miles in mere moments, to the Straits of Messina. In the distance they could see the sea-beast Scylla, brooding inside her giant rock.

As they drew closer the form of the sea-nymph which Scylla had been, before Zeus had transformed her into a tentacled leviathan, could be seen deep inside her monstrous astrosome. Like a living caul it lay, trapped in Scylla's very soul like a drowned or miscarried cherub, a naiad trapped in amber, the amber of its own mutation.

The six wolfheads ringing Scylla's waist could smell the astral bodies of the Stygimancer and the Squid Muse, and began to growl. Scylla scanned the seas, looking for the source of the wolves' agitation, but failed to notice the spectral invaders.

The Stygimancer veered the ferry towards Charybdis, the leviathan, batrachican, gorgops-like phagimancer whose flesh was bound to the very sea beside Scylla's rock. Just as Charybdis' physical body swallowed water like a sapient maelstrom and vomited it back out in waterspouts thrice daily, so too did her astral body breathe ether and exhale geists. The mouth of Charybdis opened like the maw of Tauret the Hippopotamus Goddess and bulged like the pouch of Heket the Frog God as the Stygimancer's ferry drew closer. The Stygimancer had timed his astral trip to coincide with her midnight breath. As she spewed waterspouts and ectoplasm, the Stygimancer bided his time, then flew the ferry down her throat in the ephemeral instant between storm and whirlpool.

Just ahead of a crashing cataract of air and water they flew, diving through the eyes of hurricanes and through the tornado of Charybdis' esophagus, driven by the gale-force winds of her breath. They rode a coriolis wave into Charybdis' gravid stomach, where squalls of bile sprayed their souls and a mass grave of half-digested corpses lay. They descended through her golgotha gizzard and then maneuvered through her duodenum, which had been surgically and permanently grafted to the bottom of the sea.

Her miles of intestines emptied into a subterranean, suboceanic womb the size of a city. It was lined with a thousand layers of impenetrable placentas, but devoid of any vaginal egress. They sank through the warm, bubbling saltwater to the bottom of Charybdis' abyss, where Shipwreck Castle lay. Comprised of all the boats and vessels Charybdis had swallowed over the millennia, Shipwreck Castle was sheer chaos made architecture, a crooked congeries of Persian biremes, Greek triremes, Babylonian pleasure-barges, Indian subjuggernauts, Viking longships, Lemurian warships, Atlantean battle-yachts, Lemurian fishing schooners, and the sunken ships of a hundred other realms, all interlocked and balanced precariously atop one another in the shape of a palace.

Pieces of boats and vessels protruded from Shipwreck Castle in odd and seemingly impossible angles, as if the entire edifice had been designed by the lunatic scion of Daedalus and a psychotic maenad. Prows emerged from the roof like slanted minarets, and broken, jagged masts stuck out everywhere like twisted turrets and giant corbels. Crenellated and machicolated by erosion and time, the fortress of sunken ships seemed as though it might collapse at any moment.

The Stygimancer docked the ferry a short distance from Shipwreck Castle, next to a fossilized sea serpent. To be surrounded by water and yet completely dry created strange, dreamlike sensations in Squid Muse and Stygimancer alike. They levitated from the ferry and floated to the palace. The ghosts of drowned sailors were drifting about the outer walls like boneless corpses in the winds of a simoom. The Stygimancer and the Squid Muse slid through the shattered hull of an Egyptian decareme and entered Shipwreck Castle.

Through mazes of undead wood they drifted, searching for the inner sanctum of the Mersibyl. Sometimes swimming through jagged holes, sometimes projecting through walls of detritus, sometimes flying over corpse-strewn, bloodstained decks, they wandered through the palace. Nearly an hour later, they discovered a giant ark that somehow seemed half-created rather than half-destroyed. The ark housed a cabin the size of a temple. They floated through the locked door of the cabin and beheld the Mersibyl.

A hybrid of Scylla and Charybdis she was, with the face and body of a human, the shimmering scales of a piscean temptress, and ten-foot long, prehensile octopus tentacles for hair. Half-covered by a veil of seaweed and algae, the Mersibyl's face bore the rugose scales of a reptile, yet the slant of her eyes and the curve of her cheekbones possessed the delicate features and soft expressions of a virgin princess. Two large, dark green conchshells, curled like the horns of a ram, covered the gills on either side of her head. Each shell was a cornucopia filled with a neverending supply of Delphic water, fueling her soothsaying trances. Her breasts were retractable wolfheads, with jaws powerful enough to break bones and mouths large enough to swallow severed heads. Her inner thighs and vaginal walls were covered with suckers capable of skinning a phallus, plucking a testicle, or ripping off sets of male genitalia in their entirety. Her clitoris and pubic hair were tiny tendrils that waved and undulated like an anemone. Beyond the tendrils her womb was a poison-filled gas chamber that, like a miniature Charybdis, was capable of vacuuming a man into its depths.

A pictomancer, part conduit and part artist, the Mersibyl spent her endless time painting secret sigils in her adytum, summoning symbols from beyond into her oracular palette, forever inventing white magic spells which blended hydromancy with soothsaying, prophecy, and prescience, and parallel black magic spells which blended hydromancy with storms, floods, and mass destruction.

The Mersibyl was the daughter of Scylla and Charybdis, who for a single hour in a bygone century, had been freed by Poseidon and Eros (whose motives were mysterious and clandestine, but unknown to any but themselves) and doused in hormones and sea foam. Eros had perforated their flesh with hundreds of arrows, each dipped in philtres and aphrodisiacs, like some erotic or fertility-enhancing form of acupuncture. Scylla had grown a single, spermiferous tentacle and then, using it like a phallus, copulated with the vagina-like Charybdis, impregnating her with a single egg. As their egg incubated, Charybdis used her phagimantic sorceries to construct Shipwreck Castle. Months later, the Mersibyl hatched inside the palace, and has dwelled therein ever since.

The spellmaking abilities of the Mersibyl were so prolific, and the incantations she invented so powerful, that at one time they had threatened the existence and reign of many aquatic realms, races, and royalties. Dakuwaqa the Shark God had invaded Shipwreck Castle one night (some legends say he was hired by Charybdis herself) and devoured the Mersibyl's larynx from her throat to keep her from speaking her neomancies aloud. A sharktooth still remained in the side of her neck, embedded in her jugular vein, a permanent reminder of her battle with Dakuwaqa.

The wolfhead teats of the Mersibyl snarled as the Stygimancer and the Squid Muse floated into the chamber, but, like Scylla, the Mersibyl could not perceive the presence of the invaders. As the Mersibyl painted, the Stygimancer inserted the drill-syringe in the Squid Muse's siphon. When he removed it, the hollow needle was dripping with ink, and the Stygimancer began tattooing the sigils of the Mersibyl upon his astral body.

The Stygimancer slowly circumnavigated the adytum of the Mersibyl, copying all the designs and mandalas depicted in her paintings. He cursed upon finding an empty space in a gallery of transportation sigils, where a painting had obviously been hung at one time, then removed or destroyed for reasons beyond his divination. He tattooed the remaining transportation sigils on his astral body, then resumed his tour of the chamber. Throughout the night and beyond the dawn, the Stygimancer continued to copy the magiglyphs of the Mersibyl.

Two hours after sunrise, the Stygimancer and the Squid Muse returned to their ferry . As Charybdis took her morning breath, they ascended through her digestive system and spewed like flotsam from her whirlpool mouth.

Scylla looked on from her rock as the Stygimancer and the Squid Muse erupted from the maw of Charybdis. The sextet of wolfheads around her waist barked as they floated past, like a living chastity belt made from the heads of the Siamese twin offspring of Cerberus and a lycanthropess.

This time, Scylla perceived the presence of the Stygimancer and the Squid Muse, and her undulous tentacles were beckoning the Squid Muse. Hypnotized by the kraken-like monster that seemed to be both its matriarch and evolutionary cousin, the Squid Muse rose from the ferry and floated to the rock of Scylla. As the Squid Muse approached Scylla spread her tentacles wide, revealing the missing painting from the Mersibyl's gallery, lodged in the flesh between eight of her tendrils. The Squid Muse gazed upon the confiscated painting and the forbidden sigil. As the yantra-like artwork drew the Squid Muse forth, a teleportation portal opened like an interdimensional yoni in the nexus of the mind-bending designs. Scylla held the painting up, and the Squid Muse flew through the kaleidoscopic Telesigil upon it.

An instant later, the Squid Muse was projecting through the infinite skies of an eternalnight. Stars and entire constellations flashed past its bewildered eyes, too fast to comprehend. A palace of silver metal hovered in the cosmic firmament. Mysterious red lights gleamed in the various nooks and crannies of the flying fortress, and occasionally shot out like vermilion thunderbolts, but silently and without the serrations of lightning.

As the trajectories of the Squid Muse and the metallic castle intersected, a beam of ultraviolet light burst from the strange palace and vacuumed the Squid Muse into an underwater tunnel. Unlike the waters of the Aegean Sea or the amniotic fluids in Charybdis' womb, the astral body of the Squid Muse could sense this water as vividly as its physical body would have. It was the clearest water the Squid Muse had ever seen, heard, felt, smelled, or tasted. The hyaline currents swirled and sucked the Squid Muse through a maze of hallways and chambers, past brightly lit rooms with flashing lights where other squids performed incomprehensible tasks, and then suddenly it found itself in a throne room, prostrated before Kanaloa, the Squid God.

The myriad tentacles of Kanaloa cascaded in labyrinthine tiers, like an unfathomable hanging garden, terrace after terrace after terrace. The Squid Muse could sometimes see the souls of other squids swimming inside the tendrils. High above the cataract of tentacles, the front eye of the Squid God gazed over its dominion with the glare of the omniscient.

In another dimension, the Squid Muse saw that the peak of the Stygimancer's psilocybic trip had taken him to the zenith of a silver Mount Olympus, and that the Stygimancer now saw and communicated with Zeus in much the same way the Squid Muse saw and communicated with Kanaloa. There was a certain symmetry to their deisthesias, like an empathic experience or a synergy of epiphany, but the Squid Muse could not quite comprehend what it was.

Kanaloa fixed his abyssal pupil upon the Squid Muse.'Five gifts,' the Squid God said telepathically. 'Five gifts I shall bestow upon thee. The first, an oracle stolen from Mnemosyne's bedchambers by my batrachian cousin, Heket. The second, a key dropped into the sea by Hermes and retrieved by my piscean cousin, Dagon. The third, a bag of magic dust bequeathed me by my draconian cousin, Lung Wang. The fourth, a blast of wind tortured from Aeolus by my ophidian cousin, Utachet. The fifth, the excised larynx of the Mersibyl, ripped from her throat by my selachian cousin, Dakuwaqa.'

Five winged squid angels emerged from the twisted hallways of Kanaloa's tentacles. One by one, they approached the Squid Muse and bestowed the presents of Kanaloa upon it. The first gift came in the form of a small mirror. The Squid Muse held it up to its eye. The mirror began to vibrate in the tip of the Squid Muse's tendril, then flew through the Squid Muse's pupil and disappeared into its brain. The second gift took the form of a book. The Squid Muse raised it to its mouth. With a volition all its own, the book placed itself inside the beak of the Squid Muse, and the Squid Muse swallowed it whole. The third gift was contained in a vial of jade. The vial shattered, and a cloud of metallic dust flew into the Squid Muse's siphon like a dust devil of black sand. The fourth gift was contained in a surging, rippling sack. The sack opened, and two small tornadoes spun through the air and into the twin gills at either side of the Squid Muse's siphon. The fifth gift was hand-fed to the Squid Muse by the tentacles of one of the Squid Angels. She placed it in the beak of the Squid Muse like a piece of raw meat. The Squid Muse chewed up the extracted larynx of the Mersibyl and swallowed.

'Use these gifts well, my child, and vengeance shall be thine,' said Kanaloa as the Squid Muse felt itself shimmering and vanishing and descending back to the physical plane. 'Go now, return to Earth, exact thy vengeance upon the human...and repay me by spawning a race of teuthid warriors...'

*

As the effects of the fear toxins and the psilocybin dissipated, the Squid Muse felt as though its mind, body, and soul had been thoroughly cleansed and purified. It blinked its front eye and reacquainted itself with the physical dimension, the prison-tank, and the lair of the Stygimancer.

The Squid Muse watched as the Stygimancer wheeled the Catroptastralis from an alcove to his writing table. The golden frame of the ensorcelled mirror gleamed and glittered as the Stygimancer positioned it to the right of his chair. Within the silver glass, a reflection of the astral plane shimmered and vibrated. Wraiths and ghosts and phantoms could be seen in the Catroptastralis, as well as the hideous Genius Loci of the Stygimancer's manor, a gigantic, pitch black, squatting, batrachian, two-penised incubus from the interdimensional confluence of Styx and Acheron, gurgling and slobbering and masturbating in a far corner of the room.

The Stygimancer backed away from the Catroptastralis and gazed upon the reflection of his astral body in the silver mirror. He could see his seven blue-stained chakras spinning in his soul, and the new colors they had evolved into-purple at the base of his spine, magenta above his phallus, green inside his solar plexus, turquoise upon his chest, midnight blue within his larynx, damson across his third eye, and azure at the crown of his skull. He could see the black tattoos of the Mersibyl's sigils as well, indelibly etched upon his astrosome.

Still standing, the Stygimancer used the reflection of his astral body to copy the magiglyphs into the Hydronecronomicon. After several minutes he sat down in his chair and continued to scribe, rising every now and again to gaze into the Catroptastralis and memorize yet another design.

As the Squid Muse observed its environment, it recalled its meeting with the Squid God, and the mirror which it had been given. It found that, like a hall of mirrors, its mind was absorbing everything it saw, and saving each vision like an eternal painting in the labyrinth of its brain. The first gift of Kanaloa had been the gift of eidetic memory.

It shifted its gaze to the Stygimancer as he wrote in his tome. The Squid Muse focused upon the words the Stygimancer was writing, and the magiglyphs suddenly sprang to life before his eye. They had encrypted meanings. They were symbols, and the Squid Muse knew what the symbols represented. It could decode the Stygimancer's every inscription. The second gift of Kanaloa had been the gift of language.

Continuing to read the Stygimancer's furious scribing, the Squid Muse absorbed every letter, every word, every sentence, every inflection. As the hours passed, the Stygimancer wrote another dozen incantations, which the Squid Muse read while simultaneously leafing through all the other pages of the grimoire embedded in its brain.

Eventually, the Stygimancer's inkwell ran dry. He pulled the drill-syringe from his robe, filled it with a dosage of fear toxins, and climbed the stairway to the tank. As the Squid Muse reflexively recoiled in terror, it realized its siphon was dry and completely drained of ink. The siphon, however, was not empty. It was filled with the magic dust of the dragon Lung Wang, given to the Squid Muse by Kanaloa.

As the fear toxins descended through the Squid Muse's flesh, the dust in its siphon began to stir. Collectively, every granule began to glow, gathering heat and intensity, growinghotter and heavier and more and more unstable and then, suddenly, there was an explosion at the bottom of the tank and the Squid Muse rocketed into the air, breaking free of its every restraint with the assistance of the magic dust, the volatile chemicals in the fear toxins, and its own powers of jet propulsion. A second later, the Squid Muse found itself perched atop the tank which had been its prison for so long, its waters now black with smoke and soot. The third gift of Kanaloa had been the gift of gunpowder.

The force of the explosion sent the Stygimancer tumbling down the staircase and onto the floor. Perched atop the tank, its entire body turned black by the explosion, the Squid Muse tore off its hood and straitjacket and inhaled the musty air of the chamber. As the air flowed into its beak, through its maw, down its throat, and then back through its rostrum once more, the sacred oxygen/carbon dioxide continuum formed, and two lungs sprouted deep inside the flesh of the Squid Muse. The fourth gift of Kanaloa had been the gift of breath.

The Squid Muse focused its dilated pupil upon the Stygimancer. The Stygimancer gazed up at it with wide eyes, quaking in terror as he beheld the uncaged black leviathan overhead. Holding the iron crosspiece like a quarterstaff and shaking the chains still linked to its bottom tentacles, the Squid Muse loomed over the entire room. Its shadow fell across the Stygimancer, over his desk of petrified wood, and into his tome like a tsunami of the Squid Muse's own ink.

The Stygimancer's eyes grew even wider as the Squid Muse leapt into the air and descended in a fusillade of black tentacles and silver chains, flailing and squirming and swinging and lashing. It landed atop the Stygimancer, bombarding him and pinning him to the floor. It flogged his body with its chains, bashed him in the head with the iron bar, perforated his flesh with its suckers, and raked his face with its radula.

The Stygimancer uttered a spell from his blue lips. A moment later, the Squid Muse found itself covered in viscous sludge from the shores of the river Styx. The black slime dried rapidly, and the Squid Muse could already feel it trapping him like a tar pit. As the Stygimancer ran for the door, the Squid Muse struggled against the Stygian plasm. The Squid Muse searched through the pages of hydronecromantic spells stored in its memory. When it found a spell that would free it from the plasm, its mouth began to open and shut, and the words of the incantation clattered from its beak. The fifth gift of Kanaloa had been the gift of speech.

The Squid Muse cast the spell and an interdimensional portal connected to Kanaloa's lair opened in mid-air. An instant deluge of hyaline flowed through the shimmering portal, washing the bituminous morass from the Squid Muse's body. The blackness covering its flesh, however, remained, for the Squid Muse had been blackened by something more powerful than fire, smoke and ashes; something sinister and sempiternal, something permanent and wicked.

Even after the Squid Muse had been cleansed and freed, the hyaline did not cease to flow until the entire room was flooded in three feet of water. Wading through the shallow lake of hyaline and destruction, the Stygimancer floundered and slipped as he ran, then began crawling for the door. The Squid Muse pounced and enwrapped the Stygimancer in its tentacles. Its suckers leeched on to his skin, and then it dragged the Stygimancer through the waters like prey, across the room, to the empty prison-tank.

With one tendril the Squid Muse pulled the lever which opened the doors of the prison tank. Gallons of soot-filled water came rushing out in a blackwater torrent. The Squid Muse stripped the Stygimancer's robe from his body. The Stygimancer's flesh was covered with the tale of its battle with the Squid Muse, lacerated by the flagellations of chains and tentacles alike.

The Squid Muse tore a long piece of cloth from the Stygimancer's robe. It used the cloth to tie the Stygimancer's wrists together, hang him from the ceiling of the prison-tank, and bind his feet like those of an Oriental odalisque. The Squid Muse disentangled its tentacles from the Stygimancer's limbs and pulled its suckers out from his skin, tearing gobbets of flesh from his bones and perforating his body with round, bleeding wounds.

While the Stygimancer struggled against his bonds, the Squid Muse slithered across the room and removed the portrait of Charon from the entranceway. With its suckers, it pulled the frame to shreds, then turned the painting around. The backside of the painting was nothing more than a blank canvas of white Elysian hemp. Using the slime of its suckers as an unguent, it mounted the portrait, facedown, upon the Catroptastralis.

Half-slithering, half-crawling through the shallow water flooding the chamber, the Squid Muse spent the next several minutes gathering vials, prosthetics, surgical instruments, sexual paraphernalia, and torture devices from around the room. It placed them all upon the Stygimancer's ebony desk. After pondering the array of sadistica for several moments, it grasped a different item with nine of its tentacles. With the tenth it unscrewed the lid of a large canopic jar containing the preserved fetus of a centaur. It turned the lid upside-down, holding it like the discus of Apollo, and returned to the prison-tank.

Just as it had once been bound by the Stygimancer, the Squid Muse now hooked the malefic sorceror to a variety of pipes, prosthetics, bondage instruments, and torture devices. The Squid Muse stapled a breathing apparatus of black iron and silver-studded demon leather across his nose and mouth. The pores and slits in the demon leather pumped the tepid air of the laboratory down the Stygimancer's throat. The latticework of iron covering the leather was like a portcullis upon his face. A proliferation of breathing tubes hung in coils from the bottom of the mask, and were attached to four oxygen tanks, shaped like giant human lungs, that fit directly over the Stygimancer's shoulders, two in front and two behind.

The Squid Muse filled the surgically extracted womb of a Stygiade with blue lotus and attached it to the Stygimancer's belly, then threaded a prosthetic umbilical cord through his naval. An IV drip it hooked up to his cervix, a quasi-alembic which injected a single droplet of fear toxin into his spinal fluid every few seconds.

It then placed a spiked torture dildo around the Stygimancer's phallus. The hollow iron dildo was equipped with a number of metal screws and bolts, protruding like ampullangs and apodydoes from its spike-covered exterior. The Squid Muse used its tentacles to twist the screws and bolts into the flesh of the Stygimancer's penis. Dusted on the inside with crushed blister beetles, and lubricated with the aphrodisiacal royal jelly of Melissa the Bee Goddess, the torture dildo simultaneously irritated and stimulated the Stygimancer to painful priapism. The Squid Muse inserted a catheter in the tip of the dildo, shoved it several centimeters into the Stygimancer's urethra, and injected it with a stream of Dionysian wine. The Squid Muse held out the lid of the canopic jar, and the catheter dripped a pile of sperm onto it.

Because the Stygimancer's genitals were being utilized for semen, the Squid Muse inserted two prosthetic penises into his kidneys. The heads and glans of the synthetic members protruded from the flesh of his lower back. The Squid Muse attached two syringes to their urethras, then injected a diuretic made from the waters of the Oracle at Delphi into its kidneys. An instant later, a puddle of urine lay next to the blob of sperm.

Grabbing another nine tentacles' worth of tools and devices, the Squid Muse screwed three prosthetic devil's horns into the Stygimancer's skull, and then, in turn, inserted three straws into the horns, and three vacuum tubes into the straws. The vacuums sucked the blue-stained, lotus-laden, phobigen-saturated serotonin from the innards of his brain like the probosci of giant vampiric mosquitoes that fed on hormones instead of blood.

The Squid Muse slithered back to the table once more, then returned with another pile of torment. While the Stygimancer screamed, the Squid Muse attached an iron hemogogic device, with a wheel, a faucet, and a curving sewer-like pipe, to his heart. The pipe was a prosthetic blood vessel, and nestled into the soft spot between atria and ventricles like a cobra-sized heartworm.Once the hemagogic device had been implanted in the Stygimancer's left breast, the Squid Muse turned the wheel, opening the floodgate of the artificial vein and diverting the Stygimancer's blood into the pipe. The Squid Muse raised the canopic lid to catch the blood pouring from the faucet.

Its work finished at last, the Squid Muse buried the hooks of the prison-tank's flechettes in the Stygimancer's flesh, then closed the doors, locking the Stygimancer inside. It paused to pour the entire cauldron of blue fear-toxins through the top of the tank, then closed the lid, leaving the Stygimancer bound in metal torment and immersed in liquid terror, squirming like Melusina in a fisherman's trawl.

The Squid Muse made its way to the blank canvas mounted upon the Catroptastralis. Dipping the tips of its tentacles into the lid of the canopic jar, the Squid Muse blended the blue hormones, yellow urine, red blood, and white sperm together in a myriad of ways, creating greens and oranges and purples, pinks and violets and magentas, aquamarines and glaucouses and celadons, augmenting the palette with every color it desired, and then began to render a mosaic upon the canvas, using the bodily fluids of the Stygimancer as paint. The Squid Muse had evolved a cruel, calculating, more-than-humanlike sense of justice, retribution, sadism, and evil.

Using its tentacles as brushes and the lid of the jar as a palette, the Squid Muse imitated the Mersibyl for over an hour. Utilizing its imagination and its eidetic memory both, the Squid Muse painted a portrait of itself and the Stygimancer, trapped in two separate prison-tanks.

In between the renderings of the prison-tanks it used its suckers to create spherical objects, filling in the empty pieces of canvas with its own primitive sense of symbolism: night skies filled with eyeballs instead of stars; morning skies filled with rolling clouds of ink, presided over by a siphon instead of a sun; oceans with eyeballs instead of bubbles; krakens with phalluses for tentacles; leviathans with severed human heads for testicles.

The masterpiece of the Squid Muse was nearly complete. With the tip of its tendril, it mixed all of the blood, urine, serotonin, and sperm together, creating an alien hue which had never existed until that moment, a simultaneously ultraviolet and infrared congeries of mirror and prism and light and shadow and love and death and space and time. It dipped its tentacle into the newly invented color and then, in the center of the painting, it drew the forbidden sigil of the Mersibyl, the sigil revealed to it by the grace of Scylla, the psychedelic, mandalic Telesigil that bent the very geometries of the universe and reshaped them to its will.

As the painting of bodily fluids crusted over, the Squid Muse returned to the prison-tank and climbed the stairway beside it. It removed the lid, then reached down into the blue waters with a single tentacle. The tendril punctured the top of the Stygimancer's head, bore through his skull and crown chakra, and impaled him by the brain. The suckers of the Squid Muse vacuumed a concatenation of thoughts, memories, and dreams from the Stygimancer's mind. When the Squid Muse removed its tentacle, the tip was wet and dripping with the Stygimancer's black soul. As the Stygimancer spasmed with seizures, the Squid Muse descended the ladder and made its way to the Stygimancer's table. Using the semi-liquid fragment of the Stygimancer's atramentous spirit as ink, and its own tentacle as a pen, the Squid Muse began scribing in the Stygimancer's tome. It copied the thoughts, memories, and dreams that it had vacuumed from the brain of the Stygimancer with its suckers onto the empty pages.Like a vampire amanuensis, the Squid Muse completed the Hydronecronomicon and, simultaneously, completed its own evolution.

As the Squid Muse penned the final magiglyph on the last page of the Hydronecronomicon, the prison-tank began to bubble and grow murky. The rear eye of the Squid Muse watched as the Stygimancer channeled the river Styx. Droplets of pitch leaked from his every pore like black sweat, like the nigrothidrosis of Papa Two-Brain the Voodoo Messiah in the subterranean sweat lodge of his jungle catacombs. An instant later a lake's worth of the river Styx burst from the catheter, prosthetic penises, hemogogue, breathing tubes, and spinal tap of the Stygimancer, then from the crown of his head like a black mamba kundalini serpent, pouring out the top of the tank in a Stygian waterspout. As the prison-tank exploded, the gallons of fear-toxins inside it poured through the shattered glass in a bruise-colored torrent.

The sight of the fear-toxins triggered a grotesquery of flashbacks in the Squid Muse's brain, flashbacks which were intensified by the powers of its eidetic memory. Instinctively, the Squid Muse fled the flood of liquid terror. It crashed into its own painting and then dove into the Telesigil at its nexus, disappearing from the Stygimancer's manor entirely.

As the river Styx exploded from his every pore and orifice, the Stygimancer watched helplessly as the Squid Muse escaped through the Tele-sigil. Empowered by the Stygian waters, he freed himself from the strips of cloth binding his hands and dropped from the ceiling of the prison-tank. He stumbled through the raging waters, trying to catch up to the crest of the Stygian tsunami before it reached the Squid Muse's painting. He slipped and fell to the floor, and could only look on as the black currents washed the painting, and the Catroptastralis upon which it was mounted, out the door and into the sea.

The Stygimancer turned his head as the waters rose still higher, lifting the Hydronecronomicon free of the table and carrying it towards the door as well. The Stygimancer's eyes dilated with panic as the tome floated through the entranceway. Desperately, he chased it down the shore, wading into the river of Acheron as he pursued it, but the waves carried it away like the hands of a recumbent hecatoncheire casting a spell, leaving the Stygimancer screaming on the beach, for he kneweth not how his own magnum opus ended.

*

Like Charon himself, the Stygimancer stalked the waters in his sentient ferry, his drill-syringe in one hand, his quill in the other, chasing the Hydronecronomicon, the Tele-Sigil, and the Catroptastralis across the Aegean Sea. With its cover of fishscales, its pages of mermaid-vellum, and its indelible squid ink, the Hydronecronomicon was immune to the ravages of water. The Tele-Sigil at the center of the painting was indestructible as well, even though the pictures drawn with the bodily fluids of the Stygimancer had begun to fade and blur around it. For hundreds of miles the three objects spun and ricocheted on the waves before the Stygimancer, always within a few feet of his ferry, and yet he could never catch up to them. It were as though he were Tantalus, and the book, the painting, and the mirror were his fruit and drink, always just beyond his reach.

With his frightening breathing mask, his spiked iron penis, his prosthetic phalluses protruding from his back like the spines of an incubus echidna, the iron wheel and faucet protruding from his chest, and his three devil's horns, the Stygimancer's silhouette was that of a demon's, scaring off every ship for miles around. His raiment of wounds and scars and tattooed sigils, sometimes flickering in the moonlight beneath the ripped and tattered cape that had been his robe, likewise frightened any predator or sea creature which beheld him.

Like a wailing banshee he called for the Squid Muse, for without the memories the Squid Muse held in the suckers of its tentacles the Stygimancer could neither remember his spells nor scribe his sigils, nor rest or fulfill his destiny. He sailed in a cursed and cursing fugue, his incantations naught but schizophasias and glossolalias mumbled into his breathing mask.

Dreaming of the moment when he would regain the Hydronecronomicon and read its final pages, then pen the forgotten, eldritch sigil of its title upon the fishscale cover, the Stygimancer pursued the trio of ensorcelled artifacts across the Aegean Sea for days, eventually coming to the Straits of Messina. Scylla burst from her rock as he approached, lashing him with her tentacles as Charybdis greedily swallowed the Catroptastralis and the Tele-sigil. As the Hydronecronomicon drifted ever closer to the rim of Charybdis, the Stygimancer fought against the tendrils of Scylla, injecting her with a dose of fear-toxins from the drill-syringe to free himself. He veered towards the Hydronecronomicon, but the tome was already orbiting Charybdis in concentric circles, inexorably caught in the downward spiral of the sea-monstress. Without hesitation the Stygimancer steered his ferry into the living whirlpool, following his cathexis and life's obsession into the maw of the leviathan. As he disappeared from the surface world he wailed for his Squid Muse, crying for his lost familiar to return to his side.

*

The Squid Muse, however, is on the other side of the world, in the volcanic Archipelagoes of Phlegethon, off the coast of northeastern Lemuria, where the tribespeople worship Kanaloa and his minions. A harem of island princesses has been bequeathed to the Squid Muse, and already their first brood of squidmen have hatched in a submontane grotto. Amongst the newly spawned teuthids is an alpha male of purest Stygian black, the Chosen One of Kanaloa, who shall one day reign over squidmen and Archipelagoes of Phlegathon alike, and dwell beneath a gargantuan mountain temple sculpted in the likeness of his Squid God.

Quest for the Cimiamatl
The Syzygies of the Mayan Book of the Dead-Part One
A Tale From Between The Widdershins Earth and The Sinistral
Moon

Hell Jaguar perched atop a gargantuan Venus flytrap, spying upon the caravan of warriors and sorcerors navigating the jungle trails of Lemuria below. His black mane, sable fur, and obsidian claws blended with the shadows of the thick jungle canopy, camouflaging his muscular figure with darkness. With eyes that glowed like flaming hearts, he zeroed in on the group of Lemurians and inhaled, drawing their scent past his nose-ring and pierced septum, past his obsidian fangs and into his very core. He breathed in the chemical and psychic aromas of their brains; tasted the steaming energy of their thoughts on his tongue; read the wet pictographs engraved in the raw meat of their memories. Instinct and intuition combined to form an atavistic clairvoyance, telling Hell Jaguar that the Lemurians were questing towards the secret location of the Cimiamatl, the Mayan Book of the Dead. At last, he had found the means to repossess the sacred tome which had been stolen from his ancestors during the Cataclysm, several millenia ago. The mission of Hell Jaguar and the small pack of Mayan catmen who had accompanied him from Mesoamerica was a success.

Although he could smell and taste the content of the Lemurian's thoughts, the details of those thoughts were beyond his powers of telegustatory perception. He and his pack of felinids would have to bring a Lemurian to Aztlan, one of the capitals of the Mayan empire. There, he and the Overgorgon would interrogate the Lemurian and learn every nuance of the Cimiamatl's ancient theft.

He leapt onto the branch of a tree and then onto another Venus flytrap. The infernos of his eyes focused on Tuatara Man. The three-eyed Reptiliarch of Southern Lemuria was leading the group through the jungle, hacking at the colossal foliage with his battle-saw. In his left hand he bore a staff wrapped 'round with the excaudated tails of exotic lizardries, the tips of which still twitched and writhed like burning larvae.A glistening robe of excoriated scales adorned his body. His third eye was located in the center of his forehead, the crown jewel of his triangular face. Shifting his gaze, Hell Jaguar saw that Tuatara Man was seconded by Selachia, the Sharkwitch, she of the rock-hard hammerhead and razor-sharp fins, and a mouth and vagina like twin suction wells ringed 'round with nimbuses of scimitar-like fangs.

Hell Jaguar scouted the caravan of Lemurians behind Tuatara Man and Selachia, singling out the weakest of the herd with his feline senses and carnivore's cognition. His predatory analysis lasted a mere instant, for amongst their motley retinue of draconid, herpetid, and piscid predatoria, Tuatara Man and Selachia were also accompanied by three homo sapiens: a riparimancer, a lacustrimancer, and a speleomancer. The river wizard was accompanied by a giant otter familiar; the lake wizard by a regular-sized platypus familiar; the cave wizard by a small bear familiar.

Hell Jaguar nodded to his two warlords in the trees behind him. An instant later Fire Ocelot and War Cougar leapt to his side, and the rest of Hell Jaguar's felinid warriors began bounding and jumping through the jungles of Lemuria with the same grace and silence as their leader. Hell Jaguar could smell a watering hole ahead, and knew that the Lemurians would make respite at the oasis. Like all prey, they would be vulnerable as they drank and bathed.

With a growling command from Hell Jaguar, the Mayan catmen dispersed themselves throughout the trees rimming the pond. Hell Jaguar crouched behind a giant leaf. The jungle canopy shattered the sunbeams into a broken aurora astralis that made his silhouette ripple and flicker. The shards of obsidian piercing his nose, lower lip and penis glinted in the fractal sunlight. Fire Ocelot and War Cougar alighted beside him, their own piercings aglow with girasol and psammite.

"They possess the knowledge we seek," Hell Jaguar said, brushing aside a black butterfly that was fluttering around his face. "We'll capture one of the humans and take him to Aztlan. Leave the other two behind...and unharmed. They're slowing the entire group down."

Hell Jaguar unwound the ollinchord that was twined around his knuckles. The sentient ollinchord, a triple-helixed rope of still-living peccary hide, undead opossum guts, and bloodstained rubber gleaned from balls with which the sacred game of ullama had been played, squirmed in his hand like an interspecies menage a trois of serpent, eel, and tapeworm.

"The Overgorgon and I will torture the Cimiamatl's whereabouts from the river wizard's skull, then intercept the Lemurian's and reclaim the book." Hell Jaguar crouched down and tied the ollinchord to the branch.

"Shall we accompany you on that mission as well?" asked Fire Ocelot.

"No. T'will be a mission of stealth, best undertaken by none but myself and the Overgorgon."

Hell Jaguar gripped the ollinchord with his left hand. Directly beneath him, the riparimancer removed his pack, dropped to his knees, cupped his hands, and began drinking from the pond. The riparimancer's otter familiar lapped up the pondwater beside him.

Hell Jaguar stood and then dropped from the branch, free-falling towards the jungle soil, his black mane blowing around his face. The sentient ollincord instinctively lengthened itself, then suddenly stopped a few feet above the ground like a strappado device,jerking Hell Jaguar to a halt behind the riparimancer. Hell Jaguar wrapped his bulging biceps around the river wizard in a feline death-grip, piercing his throat with his incisors as though preparing to break his neck. The ollincord reflexively recoiled. An instant later, both jaguarman and riparimancer were hurtling toward the treetops.

Tuatara Man looked up from across the lake and fixed his trifold, bug-eyed stare upon Hell Jaguar. The Reptiliarch shot a beam of purple light from his third eye, severing the ollincord Hell Jaguar was riding. As Hell Jaguar dropped towards the ground, he hoisted the riparimancer over his head and threw him into the mouth of one of the Venus flytraps. The sessile predator seemed to smile as it swallowed its prey.Its treelike stem bulged as the riparimancer dropped into the green underworlds of its digestive system.

As Hell Jaguar landed, his obsidian claws burst into flame. Two lizardmen charged him and just as quickly fell to the ground with shredded, smoking faces. Tuatara Man fired another stream of purple energy. Hell Jaguar opened his mouth, revealing sabretooth fangs of obsidian that blazed with the same fire as his claws. He spat a fireball at the purple death-ray. A pyrotechnic explosion of orange and indigo lit up the jungle. Sparks rained like dying will-o'-the-wisps.

The rest of Hell Jaguar's catmen dropped from the trees and joined the battle. Fire Ocelot tied his ollinchord to a branch, gripped it with his feet, spread his arms cruciform, and fell backwards from the tree, to hang upside-down before Tuatara Man. Fire Ocelot brandished his girasol machetes. Tuatara Man parried the blades of fire opal with his staff of severed tails, then drew his battle-saw. The three-eyed Reptiliarch slashed at Fire Ocelot's jugular vein. The cat warrior curled-up, dodging the blow, then relaxed his body once again and lunged for Tuatara Man's solar plexus. Tuatara Man blocked the blow with his staff, then fired a stream of purple quanta from his third eye, knocking Fire Ocelot to the ground. Tuatara Man stepped on his tail. As Fire Ocelot tried desperately to escape from beneath Tuatara Man's taloned, draconian foot, Tuatara Man severed his tail with his battle-saw. Fire Ocelot yelled in agony and shot off into the jungle as though he had been fired from an arbalest.

War Cougar swung over the lake on an ollinchord, braining the fish-headed piscid warriors with his sandstone mace as they bathed. Selachia erupted from the middle of the pond and speared him in mid-air with her hammerhead skull. Her jaws sank into War Cougar's chest as they crashed into the lake. Selachia dragged War Cougar beneath the water and began mauling him like a rabid killer whale. A small cloud of blood rose like crimson effluvia to the surface of the lake, a vampire's oasis, a pool within a pool.

An instant later, Selachia burst from the rim of the pool and ran straight for Hell Jaguar. Hell Jaguar cuffed her with his right paw, knocking her backwards and opening four black, smoking, gelatinous lacerations upon her face. She snapped at him with her spike-nimbused mouth. Hell Jaguar struck her again, this time with his left paw. The blow was a mirror-image of the one he had struck with his right. Selachia staggered again, but this time spun and caught him across the chest with a backslash, her razor-sharp fins tearing through his flesh. Hell Jaguar kicked her in the solar plexus.

As Selachia stumbled, Fire Ocelot ran past like a shooting star, blood pouring from his severed tail. War Cougar followed behind.

Hell Jaguar vomited a stream of fire into the jungle, creating a gigantic wall of impenetrable flames between himself and the charging Sharkwitch, then chopped down the Venus flytrap with his obsidian claws, extricated the riparimancer from the morass of acidic chlorophyll and half-digested animals, and climbed back into the trees. Fire Ocelot gathered up the riparimancer's giant otter and followed on his leader's heels. War Cougar paused to pull a sharktooth out of his chest, then joined them.

The three catmen fled through the treetops, leaving the rest of their comrades behind. Miles away, with the sun setting behind them as they sprinted, leapt, and swung through the jungles of Lemuria, they could still hear the squeals of their brethren, screeching as their tails were severed by the battle-saw of Tuatara Man, then screaming as Selachia chewed their heads from their shoulders.

*

In her bedchamber at the zenith of her jade step pyramid, the Overgorgon reclined upon a jaguarskin blanket. The anacondas and bushmasters of her hair were splayed like the rays of a green and black sunacross her macaw-feather pillows. Beside the Overgorgon lay two homo serpens, former humans who had been surgically altered into incarnadine snakes and then trained as sex slaves. Like serpents, the homo serpens were devoid of limbs, breasts, ears, noses, and hair. Their backs and torsos were laced with diamondback patterns of keloids and scars. Their genitals had been altered to resemble those of serpents, as well. The male possessed a second penis, surgically grafted onto his groin beside his natural one, to simulate the twofold genitalia of male serpents. The crotch of the female had been cloven into a singular cloaca, a gaping, red, urogenital chasm formed by the mutilation and conjoinment of both vagina and anus.

The rattlesnakes and coral snakes of the Overgorgon's pubic hair clattered and writhed as she grabbed the serpentized male and pulled him closer. With reptilian hands and claws of jade, she inserted his original phallus in her vagina. An instant later, she guided his surgically attached phallus into her womb alongside it.

As the Overgorgon began to copulate with the two-penised homo serpens, her forked tongue uncoiled from her mouth, encircled the female, and dragged her across the bed. The Overgorgon positioned the scarlet pit of the female's groin over her face, then raped her with the forked-tongue cloacalingus of an ophidian succubus.

An hour later, the satiated Overgorgon laid back and gazed at the severed heads and black Nooses of Ixtab, Goddess of Suicide and mother of the Overgorgon, that dangled from the ceiling. Two reptilian guards in feathered raiment emerged from the elevator shaft at the center of the room. They stepped from the circular platform, retrieved the homo serpens, returned to the shaft, and disappeared back into the duct, with neither a word nor a glance from the Queen of the Mayan Empire.

The Overgorgon leaned onto her right side, stretching out upon the bed and glancing at the table beside it. Atop the table lay the six-foot tall Scales of Mictlan. One of the scales was weighed down by the sole extant copy of the Popol Vuh, the Mayan Book of Life. The ancient codex was comprised entirely of snakeskin, and had been penned in blood with the quills of Quetzalcoatl, the Plumed Serpent. A stark contrast to the thin, expurgated imitations scattered across the Earth as decoys in centuries past, the real Popol Vuh was several thousand pages long and several thousand years old, written by sages of ancient Mesoamerican empires that preceded even the Zapotecs, Olmecs and Toltecs. The tome had been handed down for generations, all the way from the antediluvian Balam and Coatl Dynasties to the conjugal reign of Hell Jaguar and the Overgorgon in the postapocalyptic age of the Widdershins Earth and the Sinistral Moon.

The scale opposite the Popol Vuh was empty, and hovered over the Overgorgon's head like a small mezzanine. She pondered it in post-coital languor, dreaming of the day when the Scales of Mictlan would be balanced by the Mayan Book of the Dead. When the scales were balanced, a cenote to Mictlan would open between them. Through that interdimensional, sacrificial well to the netherworld, the Overgorgon would be able to communicate with the dead, summon eidolons, cast burnt offerings and extracted hearts to gods and demons, and descend into the cold Mayan hell whenever she desired.

She turned to the other side of the bed and gazed longingly at her teleportation portal. The mystical gateway led to the Kajib Xalkat

B'e, a cosmic crossroads where eight interdimensional roads converged. From the Kajib Xalkat B'e, the journey to Hell Jaguar's obsidian ziggurat, hundreds of miles to the south,in the city of Tenochtitlan, could be made within seconds. The mind's eye of the Overgorgon filled with reveries and fantasies as she wished that her co-regent, her soulmate, her syzygy had returned from his mission and was resting in his bedchambers, waiting for her to emerge from the teleportation portal in his quarters and join him in a victory ceremony.

The Overgorgon stood up and walked to the east wing of her bedchamber, where an entire wall of tzompantli, wooden racks of skulls arranged in rows upon scaffolds and impaled through the temples with horizontal spikes, overlooked a stone altar laden with coca leaves, jimson weed, peyote buttons and goblets of pulque. The Overgorgon lifted one of the goblets to her mouth as the empty eye sockets of the dead looked on.The Overgorgon was a High Decapitress and a Counterdemon, and each severed head was a testament to her mastery of the arts of decollation, cephalomancy, gyromancy, and anti-taoism.

The bittersweet tang of aguave leaves filled the Overgorgon's throat. She could taste the pulque with her flesh, her organs, her brain and her very soul.As the intoxicating, psychedelic melange coursed through her mind and body, the Overgorgon climbed back into bed and leaned against the zoomorphic carvings that decorated her headboard. The wooden pictographs flowed seamlessly into the stone coatepantli, the wall of graven serpents which formed the southern end of the chamber. The sculpted snakes loomed over the bed like ithyphallic sentinels.

The Overgorgon gazed mesmerically at the giant aquarium which formed the north side of the room. Filled with yaxa, the green-blue water of life, the aquarium was home to swarms of candiru, stonefish, stingrays, and jellyfish. Behind the glass they darted, swimming in endless, kaleidoscopic patterns. The Overgorgon watched them for several minutes as she imbibed the pulque, then rose from her bed once again and replaced her empty chalice with a full one.

As the Overgorgon strode across the bedchamber, her anaconda and bushmaster hair trailed and writhed on the floor behind her. Her rattlesnake and coral snake pubic hair hung down to her knees like an arras, writhing like the serpent skirt of Coatlicue, mother of gods and grandmother of the Overgorgon.

The Overgorgon turned toward the west end of the room and the swinging gates to her balcony. To the left side of the doorway hung a calendar made from human skin that stretched all the way from the floor to the twenty-foot high ceiling. To the right of the gates was an astrological chart of the same composition and dimensions. The obsidian mantle over the entranceway was adorned with sculptures of gods and goddesses.

The Overgorgon emerged onto her balcony to watch the sunset. She made her way to the rail, which was like an upside-down portcullis, with spikes rising every four feet along its length, each adorned with a skull. A pterodactyl was soaring through the roseate crepuscula, circling the jade ziggurat. Overhead, the Overgorgon heard the sound of metal striking wood. She glanced up to the roof of her bedchamber, where the Toxisaur, a gigantic, sapient bufid, manned a blowgun the size of a cannon. The blowgun was so large that it had to be supported upon a base of stilts and wheels, which the Toxisaur controlled and maneuvered from a built-in seat.

The Toxisaur's throat expanded to the size of a Small Room. A moment later, he exhaled. A spear hurtled from the blowgun and spitted the pterodactyl against the sky. Having been wiped across the Toxisaur's poisonous scales, the spear was so saturated with venom that the pterodactyl died before it struck the ground.

The Overgorgon watched the pterodactyl plummet. A few of the Toxisaur's soldiers briefly paused to admire the handiwork of their warlord before once again resuming their perpetual patrol of the balcony. Between the Toxisaur and his artillery of toadmen, who carried eight-foot long blow-guns the same way sentinels carried halberds, the threat of invaders, spies, or assassins breaking into the Mayan queen's bedchambers wasnonexistent.

The Overgorgon gazed down upon her four-hundred story ziggurat, with its luxorious belvederes and built-in teocalli, and its shimmering moat of green-blue yaxa, where hydrastes and coral snakes slithered and swam. Comprised entirely of jade, the Overgorgon's gargantuan step pyramid stood at the nexus of Aztlan, the grand megalopolis which was the northern capital of the newly resurrected Mayan Empire. From the zenith of her eight-thousand foot tall palace, the Overgorgon observed her queendom, sweeping her stare across the malachite teocalli, buildings, and houses; the sapient lizards, serpents and dragons that inhabited them; the dinosaurs they kept and bred as familiars, steeds and beasts of burdens; and the lowly homo serpens which served as drones and sex slaves.

As a black butterfly alighted on the rail of the balcony, the Overgorgon watched a black-furred jaguarman, an orange-furred ocelotman, and a yellow-furred cougarman pass through Aztlan's city gates. The cougarman dragged a human, tied into a living ball, behind him on an ollinchord. The ocelotman was pulling a giant otter on a leash. The jaguarman led them down the main, jade-paved avenue of the megalopolis, past the Coatl Coliseum where the ullama games were played, bearing straight for the terraced palace of the Overgorgon. The Overgorgon smiled, for she knew that Hell Jaguar's expedition to Lemuria had been a success.

*

The King and Queen of the Mayan Empire simultaneously tortured the riparimancer. The Overgorgon lashed the river wizard with a whip of twelve serpents, decorating his back and chest with crimson, diamondback patterns while Hell Jaguar dragged his flaming claws of obsidian along the curve of the human's hairline. Blood dripped like scorched rain upon the jade floor of the torture chamber. As the Overgorgon continued to flog the river wizard, Hell Jaguar grasped the sorceror's long hair with his paw and pulled it back from his lacerated forehead, scalping him with a single, sinuous, feline motion. Suspended in mid-air, with his neck caught in a Noose of Ixtab and his wrists bound to the black rope that formed its slipknot, the sorceror could do nought but squirm and scream.

Hell Jaguar tossed the dripping scalp into the pit of caimans at the center of the chamber. The Overgorgon continued to torment the sorceror with her hypnotic susurrus of inquisition.

"Where is the Cimiamatl hidden," she asked, at once seductive and threatening, the ten-foot long bushmaster snakes of her hair writhing around her face, their mouths drooling venom, while their anaconda brethren beside them flexed like the muscles of nephilim warriors. The Overgorgon's jade fangs sank into the side of the sorceror's head and bit off his ear. The sorceror screamed as the Overgorgon swallowed. The Overgorgon swayed like a cobra to his other ear. A moment later, it had joined its counterpart in the sizzling acids of her stomach.

"Now you have the ears of a serpent, my pet." Her forked tongue slithered inside the crimson hole she had just gnawed in his skull, a red imitation of her own gash-like ear slits.

Hell Jaguar removed the obsidian shard from the piercing in his nose and used it to slice the skin around the sorceror's eyes. He then removed a drill from an alcove. With a single blast of his fiery breath, the drill simultaneously burst into flames and began spinning. Hell Jaguar pried the wizard's jaws apart and forced the fire-drill into his mouth. One by one, he simultaneously pulverized and incinerated the riparimancer's teeth. He completely emptied the riparimancer's gums of everything but his two incisors, creating a gruesome parody of cobra fangs.

The Overgorgon leaned forward and bit off the sorceror's nose. "And now," spake the Overgorgon, "the face of a serpent. Shall you speak, or must the serpentification continue?"

The sorceror spat a mouthful of blood and hot, powdered teeth into the Overgorgon's face. The Overgorgon pulled a pair of obsidian scissors from another alcove as Hell Jaguar gnawed off the sorceror's nipples and spat the bloody morsels into the caiman pit. The Overgorgon methodically amputated the sorceror's arms and legs as she interrogated him. Hell Jaguar followed in her wake, breathing fire upon the open wounds to cauterize them, then tossing the severed limbs to the caimans.

Limbless, chestless, noseless, earless, scalped, and dangling from the Noose of Ixtab, the riparimancer thrashed like an eel electrocuting itself in a suicide ritual.

The Overgorgon opened the sorceror's mouth with one hand and hooked a single jade claw through his frenulum. As she slowly closed the blades of the scissors upon the tip of his tongue, drawing a tiny droplet of blood, she hissed, "Once your tongue has been forked, you shall not be able to reveal the whereabouts of the Cimiamatl, nor shall you be able to speak your spells of healing. You shall be permanently transformed into a human serpent. I will make you my sex slave, my pet, my familiar, and then..." she whispered, glancing at his giant pet otter, collared and chained and in the corner, "I shall sacrifice your familiar to my father." The sorceror trembled, for he knew her father to be Quetzalcoatl, the plumed serpent whose worship entailed the extraction of living hearts and the casting of severed heads down the steps of teocalli.

The Overgorgon opened the scissors slightly so that he might speak.

"Tis in the Archipelagoes of Phlegethon," he relented. "Tis in the Temple of the Squid God, Kanaloa. Twas looted by the teuthids during the Cataclysm, the day after Lemuria sank beneath the ocean."

The Overgorgon smiled, closed the scissors upon his tongue, and turned away as blood poured down his chin and mutilated chest. Hell Jaguar unchained the otter and tossed it into the pit of caimans while its master wept.

"Take him to the Ophidiary." With a gesture from the Overgorgon, four guards removed the riparimancer from Hell Jaguar's clutches and carried him from the torture chamber. In the Ophidiary, hewould learn to slither like a crotalid, to crush like a constrictor, and to strike like a viper. He would be taught how to serve and pleasure his mistress. He would be schooled in the ways of the homo serpens.

As Hell Jaguar stood on the edge of the caiman pit, watching the grunting reptiles feast, the Overgorgon slid to his side and embraced him from behind.

"At last," she hissed, "the Cimiamatl is coming home."

*

The giant hummingbird soared over the jungles of Lemuria. Seated atop their brightly-feathered, sylph-swift steed, the Overgorgon and Hell Jaguar chewed on coca leaves and gazed down upon the recently resurrected continent. Pulled from the nadir of the Pacific Ocean by the forces of the Sinistral Moon, Lemuria once again thrived upon the Widdershins Earth.

The ancient wars between the Lemurians and the Mayans were legendary.Only when Lemuria had sunk into oblivion beneath the sea, several millennia ago, had the two empires been at peace. Now that Lemuria had arisen once more, the forced armistice had been terminated, for the legend of the Lemurians' theft of the Cimiamatl had been passed down through the ages, and the Mayans were not a forgiving culture. War was imminent, but it was crucial to the Mayan forces that the retrieval of the Cimiamatl precede it, so that its arcane nigromancies could be re-learned by the current regime. Only with the dark knowledge of the eldritch tome could the new Mayan armies reach their former levels of bellipotence, and only with the black magic detailed within its living pages could the Overgorgon exact the most terrible and hideous vengeances upon the Lemurians.

The Overgorgon raised her eyes and stared into the stelliferous firmament. Amongst the stars the tzitzimeme, the spaceships of the gods, were flickering, flashing and exploding as their pilots fought their eternal deimachies across the cosmos. The Overgorgon searched for the star-vessels of her father, Quetzalcoatl, and her mother, Ixtab. So too did Hell Jaguar attempt to espy the spaceships of his parents, Tlaloc and Chalchiuhtlicue. Somewhere amongst the celestial pyrotechnics the four deities were strafing and firing and dodging and soaring in their flying war-machines, fighting in the battles of the gods.

They soared along the northeastern coast of Lemuria, then veered toward the volcanic Archipelagoes of Phlegethon. The silhouette of the Temple of the Squid God soon crowned the horizon. A gargantuan sculpture ofKanaloa, it squatted atop a mountain, looming over the jungles below and watching all with its Cyclopean eye. Dozens of stone tentacles cascaded from the head of the sculpture, encircling the mountain. Its cavernous eye was the sole entrance, facing directly to the east as though staring at the rising moon. As Hell Jaguar and the Overgorgon approached, they spied Tuatara Man and Selachia leading their tiny army up a spiraling stairway and into the temple.

The hummingbird landed beneath a canopy of palm trees and weeping willows, a short distance from the mountain. The Overgorgon and Hell Jaguar dropped from its back and began their trek through the jungle. Behind them, a flock of black butterflies silently swarmed upon the hummingbird and devoured it, reducing it to a skeleton in minutes like a horde of flying piranhas.

Unaware of the demise of their avian steed, the Overgorgon and

Hell Jaguar stalked the jungle. The Overgorgon wore a loaded blowgun on a necklace of snake rattles, wielded a jade scimitar with her right hand, and carried a stone shield with her left. Her shield was a coatepantli, a wall engraved with pictographs of serpents, a miniature version of the one at the south end of her bedchamber. With the flip of a switch the shield could be transformed into a handheld tzompantli, a skull-rack like the one at the east end of her bedchamber, containing five rows with ten spikes apiece. It had the capacity to carry twenty-five severed heads simultaneously. The Overgorgon began every mission and battle with nought but rows of naked spikes and scaffolding in her left hand. When she returned home to Aztlan, the tzompantli was always full.

Hell Jaguar carried a large, wooden club studded with razor-sharp blades of obsidian in his right hand. He had twined an ollinchord around the knuckles of his left. A blowgun on a necklace of charred finger-bones dangled between his chiseled pectoral muscles. His septum, lower lip, and penis were pierced with long shards of obsidian that could be used as projectiles or weapons, and the tip of his phallus bore an obsidian ampullang with a small sculpture of the head of Tlaloc, the jaguar god of lightning, on one side and a small sculpture of the head of Tezcatlipoca, the jaguar god of mirrors and obsidian, growling at the other. The sacred ampullang possessed a myriad of sorcerous and deadly functions.

They came to the base of the mountain and Hell Jaguar jerked his ollinchord like a whip. The ollinchord sped through the air and adhered to the entrance of the temple. The Overgorgon embraced him, and they rappelled up the mountain. After an ascent of several hundred feet they alighted upon the entrance to the Eye of Kanaloa.

A flickering darkness obscured the moon as they prepared to enter the Temple of the Squid God. An instant later a horde of bats exploded from the night, ripping through the skies and heading straight for the mountain.

Hell Jaguar removed one of the shards of obsidian from his penis and placed it in his blowgun. He raised the blowgun to his lips and breathed a stream of fire. An instant later, a tiny, flaming javelin of obsidian arched through the night. It struck one of the bats in the chest, setting it aflame and then immolating it. A puffball of ashes hovered briefly in mid-air, then drifted lazily to the jungle floor below.

The Overgorgon simultaneously raised her blowgun to her lips and blew a caiman trichobezoar into the sky. The rock-hard concretion of hair, extracted from the stomach of a sacrificed caiman, struck one of the bats in the skull like a stone hurled from a slingshot, knocking its brains across the sky. Like tiny, incarnadine clouds the encerebrated pulp floated on the breeze for the merest of moments, then followed the corpse of the bat into the jungle below.

Hell Jaguar continued to pull pieces of obsidian from his various piercings, insert them in his blowgun, and skewer the bats on flaming spikes. Meanwhile, the Overgorgon kept lapidating the bats with caiman trichobezoars. The bats, however, were too numerous, and eventually converged upon the mountain in a frenetic swarm. The Overgorgon blocked their kamikaze dives with her tzompantli shield, rendering them unconscious. Dreaming bats ricocheted down the side of the mountain.

The Overgorgon's serpentine hair rose up to protect her. Its anacondas wrapped around the bats, squeezing them into broken masses of semiliquidity. Bat skeletons exploded with crackling sounds and sudden pops. Blood and innards dripped through the coils of the snakes and onto the floor. The bushmasters struck like very slow cobras, burying their venom-soaked fangs in blood-soaked batflesh. Sometimes the Overgorgon's hair worked in tandems, and the anacondas held the bats still so that the bushmasters could bite them.

More bats were gathering in the skies. Among them the Overgorgon discerned the outline of Death Bat, lord of the chiropterids and king of the dissident city of Xibalba. His beating wings distorted the starlight, rippling the night skies in which the spaceship of his god and father, Camazotz, no doubt dueled with the vessels of Quetzalcoatl and Ixtab in a reflection of the battle being fought by their children below.

Hell Jaguar breathed the thoughts of Death Bat, inhaling the psychic steam upon the chilled winds of the gloaming. "He's come for the Cimiamatl," he said to the Overgorgon, motioning her through the Eye of Kanaloa. "Tis more than just the Lemurians who lust for its black knowledge."

As the horde of bats bore closer, Hell Jaguar gripped his

ampullang with his clawed hand. A stream of napalm poured from the open mouth of the sculpture of Tezcatlipoca, saturating the entranceway to the temple. As the horde of bats drew closer, the mouth of Tlaloc spat a bolt of lightning into the napalm. A wall of flames erupted, blocking the entire entrance with an impenetrable conflagration that would burn for hours unless extinguished by another pyromancer.

Hell Jaguar turned and examined the foyer of the temple. Hanging aquariums filled with electric eels and glowing jellyfish illuminated the chamber.The corpses of teuthids were scattered across the stone floor, a mass grave of squidmen freshly slain by Tuatara Man, Selachia, and their Lemurian warriors. Inside the sculpture of Kanaloa, eight tentacles formed curving stairwells that led to the bottom of the mountain. At the center of the chamber was a large, circular pit. The Overgorgon stood at its edge, peering into the black depths of the Temple of the Squid God. It was like looking through the entrance of a bottomless alimentary canal.

Hell Jaguar's eyes flashed as he studied the innards of the temple with his cat-vision. He could see through the darkness to the bottom of the mountain, as clearly as if the entire temple were bathed in orange light. He tied the ollinchord to one of the dangling aquariums, then grasped the Overgorgon around the waist, his fingers entangling with her coral snake and rattlesnake pubic hair, and leapt into the abyss.

Like two spiders on a single strand of webbing, Hell Jaguar and the Overgorgon descended through the Temple of the Squid God, dropping silently past hundreds of chambers where squidmen toiled, copulated, and prayed to effigies and idols of Kanaloa. The air was putrid and slimy, saturated with evaporated milt and roe.

Eventually they came to the nadir of the mountain, where the throneroom of the Squid Messiah lay. The chamber was filled with squidmen, each bearing a coral sword. Beneath their domed, cyclopean heads their tentacles dangled over their broad shoulders, muscular chests, and chiseled torsos. Like many species of squid the teuthids were constantly changing colors, creating ephemeral patterns of camouflage in their flesh that shimmered and flickered like the scales of dying fish beneath a desiccating sun.

To one side of the chamber, atop a twenty-foot high dais, the

Squid Messiah sat upon a throne of seashells. Unlike his minions, the Squid Messiah was completely black and did not change colors. Holding a trident and a trawl in two of his caliginous tendrils, he watched over the devotees of Kanaloa with a glowing, violet eye.

The caverns were lit by hanging aquariums similar to the ones in the foyer, these containing mermaids with bioluminescent tails. A subterranean lake at the other side of the room was filled with more mermaids, these eyeless, colorless and translucent, like species of fish which have been deprived of the sun for generations and lost all evolutionary traits pertaining to light. Hydroducts leading deeper into the temple, to subterranean caverns miles below sea level, were plainly visible beneath the still, diaphanous surface of the pond. Although the cavewater was crystal clear, the bottom of the pool could not be seen.

Hell Jaguar and the Overgorgon hung from the ceiling, as silently as two lovers sharing a single Noose of Ixtab whilst enjoying a tantric ritual of erotic asphyxiation. Together, they spied upon the Lemurians and teuthids below. The Overgorgon glanced in the direction of the dais upon which the atramentous Squid Messiah reclined on his throne of seashells. Her psychometric scales could feel the snakeskin pages of the Cimiamatl pulling her in the direction of the dais, for it was the snakeskin of her grandmother, the snakeskin of Coatlicue, which the Mayan Book of the Dead had been written on. Lying somewhere beneath the dais, spiked through the cover of the eldritch tome, she could feel the giant quill, plumed with the feather of her father, Quetzalcoatl, and dipped in the blood of her mother, Ixtab, drawing her spirit forth like a lodestone. The exuviae of her ancestors were calling her, beckoning her in a tactile language that transcended the gulfs of space and time.

She turned to Hell Jaguar and whispered, "There's an oubliette hidden beneath the throne, and a door hidden inside the oubliette. Beyond it lies a labyrinth in which the Cimiamatl is hidden."

Hell Jaguar breathed in the viscid air of the temple. "There's something alive in that labyrinth, too. Something powerful."

"The Teuthsibyl. Powerful, but not invincible."

As the Overgorgon softly conversed with her lover, the Lemurians emerged from one of the stairwells. The speleomancer was the first to enter the chamber, having used his cave-magic to lead the Lemurians through the caverns and tunnels. The squidmen immediately swarmed upon him with the ferocity of feral animals, clutching at him with their tentacles, their tendrils tightly embracing and violently caressing his body. One of the tentacles wrapped itself around his head, attached one of its suckers to his eye socket, and pulled out his eye with a wet popping noise. Another encircled his waist and buried a sucker in his lower back. The sucker dug and burrowed like a leech and attached itself to his kidney. The tentacle jerked like a whip, ripping his kidney from his flesh. The squidman held both the extracted eyeball and the dripping kidney over its head, then wrapped another tendril around the spelomancer's chest, with a sucker just over his heart. It attached to his skin and began to pull, but before it could pluck out his heart Tuatara Man came to the aid of the cave wizard and severed the squidman's tentacle with his battle-saw.

As the speleomancer and his bear familiar scurried for the shelter of a tenebrous cranny to hide and heal in, and the lacustrimancer and his platypus dove into the refuge of the underground lake, a swarm of squidmen descended upon Tuatara Man. With a beam of purple light from his third eye, Tuatara Man lethally irradiated one of them. He thrust his staff into the eye of a second and decapitated a third with his battle-saw. Yet another squidman charged. Tuatara Man immobilized the squidman with a paralyzer beam from his third eye, then amputated his tentacles one by one and left him bleeding to death on the floor. Tuatara Man wrapped one of the severed tentacles around his staff. It blended perfectly with the excaudated tails.

The horde of bats had somehow broken through the wall of fire at the top of the mountain and were now descending into the chamber. Death Bat swooped down and stole the enoculated eyeball and derenalated kidney from the tentacles of the first squidman. His cinnabar fangs gleaming like blood-coated marble, Death Bat alighted upon the stone floor and swallowed the eyeball whole, then patiently masticated the kidney. Spit, blood, and urine dripped down his chin and onto his chest.

The bats immediately detected Hell Jaguar and the Overgorgon with their powers of echolocation. They swarmed, and as they descended, their bodies bulged and transformed into batmen, vampires and chupacabras. One of the shape-shifters flowed and coalesced into the form of the Chiropteress, Queen of Xibalba and consort of Death Bat. Her bat-winged labia beat as though preparing to detach from her flesh and fly away. Her three mouths opened and closed like animal snares possessed by demons. Like Death Bat, her fangs and claws were composed of blood-red cinnabar.

The Overgorgon hid behind her shield. Chiropterids slammed into it and fell to the ground. She lowered the shield and beheaded two batmen with her jade sword, then skewered another through the solar plexus.

Hell Jaguar's obsidian claws and fangs burst into flames. The razor-sharp obsidian blades along the edges of his macuahuitl blazed with the same fire. He began swinging the studded, club-like weapon in an infernal hurricane of death. Severed limbs and decapitated heads rained down like living meteor showers. Death Bat looked up. His crimson, glowing eyes interlocked with Hell Jaguar's orange, chatoyant gaze. As Death Bat beat his wings and lifted from the ground, Hell Jaguar lowered himself halfway to the floor and met the chiropteran king face-to-face. The Overgorgon leapt from his side and sprinted for the side of the dais.

Hell Jaguar and Death Bat wrestled in mid-air. Death Bat sank his fangs into Hell Jaguar's neck. At the same time, Hell Jaguar raked his flaming claws across Death Bat's chest. He head-butted Death Bat twice, dislodging his fangs from his throat, then swung forward on his ollincord and kicked him in the solar plexus with both feet.

As Death Bat flipped backwards through the air, Hell Jaguar released the ollinchord and dropped to the ground.Breathing a stream of fire, Hell Jaguar cleared a path to the dais, then bounded up its steps and tackled the Squid Messiah. The throne of seashells tipped over as Hell Jaguar drove the Squid Messiah through the wall behind the dais and into a hidden alcove.

As Hell Jaguar and the Squid Messiah battled, the Overgorgon climbed the side of the dais like a lizard. Her anaconda and bushmaster hair crested over the edge of the platform and lifted her like a mass of prehensile tails. She slithered into the small opening that had been exposed when the Squid Messiah's throne had toppled. Her hair splayed out, gripped the rim of the pit, and gently lowered her into the oubliette, then retracted like an anemone and disappeared into the secret dungeon along with her.

Following the psychometric vibrations connecting her to the Cimiamatl, the Overgorgon made her way through the labyrinth. A mob of draconids, herpetids, piscids, chiropterids and teuthids followed her into the maze and attacked. Her jade scimitar and coatlepantli shield quickly grew as red as Death Bat's cinnabar fangs. After she had slain the entire horde she switched the lever in the back of the shield, transforming it into a tzompantli, and filled the five rows of the miniature skull-rack with severed dragonheads, lizardheads, fishheads, batheads, and squidheads.

Using the sensory-pits and viper-glands in her head to navigate the corridors, the Overgorgon made her way to the library in the center of the labyrinth, to find the Cimiamatl waiting on an altar made of stone.

She stepped forward and reached for the book. A mote of pale moonlight fell across her hand. She glanced up to find a slanted psychoduct in the ceiling, reaching all the way to the top of the mountain. Through the long, diagonal shaft the Overgorgon could see a tiny bit of the eye of Kanaloa and, beyond it, a sliver of the eastern sky.

She turned her attention back to the book. Grasping it, she found it to be utterly immovable No matter how she pulled or pushed, the Cimiamatl didn't budge. She pried at the edges of the cover until blood caked her jade claws, but could no more open the book than she could lift it.

As she struggled, a tiny beam of light shined through the psychoduct and over the cover of the Cimiamatl. The Overgorgon raised her eyes. The moon was reaching its apex in the east, and as it did, the psychoduct was channeling the raw power of midnight into the chamber and onto the Cimiamatl. The shaft of yellow illumination opened the book with the twisting force of the Sinistral Moon. Like the ten-thousand wings of some fantastic bird, the pages of the Cimiamatl flipped back and forth, begging to be read. As it did so, the sound of wet tentacles and suctorial organs dragging over a stone floor echoed from somewhere inside the labyrinth. The Teuthsibyl was coming for her nightly lucubrations in the light of the Sinistral Moon.

The Overgorgon rose to her feet and reached for the book. As the penumbra of the moon aligned directly with the psychoduct, she lifted the Cimiamatl as though it were composed of nought but sky and dreams, revealing a large hole in the table where it had lay.She immediately began to back away as the amorphous head of the Teuthsibyl flowed through the opening like a bubble of hot gore.

The eye of the squid sorceress was an oracle, flashing with random scenes from around the Widdershins Earth: Kalanaga, the Chronolamia, sipping on soma in far-off India; Imhotep II, the Night Pharaoh, riding his black sphinx amongst the lost pyramids of the Western Sahara; Dagon Kong, Beast-Champion of Atlantis, wrestling a plesiosaurus in a spiked battle-pool; and hundreds of other visions, each lasting less than a second.

The Teuthsibyl continued to emerge from the altar. Her gelatinous, mucilaginous head squirmed upon a mass of one hundred tentacles. Each tentacle was lined not with suckers, but vagina dentata, gnashing like the fanged jaws of rabid animals.

Cradling the Cimiamatl in her left hand, behind the protection of her shield, the Overgorgon swung her jade scimitar. The Teuthsibyl lashed out with her tendrils at the same time. The Overgorgon flicked the switch of her coatepantli shield, transforming it into a tzompantli and catching the writhing tentacles inside the skull-rack. She closed it just as quickly, trapping a large mass of them inside. The Teuthsibyl constricted the muscles in its tentacles, lifting both the shield and the Overgorgon into mid-air. As the Overgorgon found herself hurtling towards the Teuthsibyl's gnashing, beaklike mouth, she struck with the celerity of a cobra and drove her jade scimitar through the oracular eye of the squid-beast.

A fountain of scalding teleplasm erupted from the eye of the Teuthsibyl as the Overgorgon withdrew her blade. Inside the teleplasm thousands of constantly-shifting images rippled and flashed like peyote visions, as psychedelic as the tears of of a weeping shaman. The monstrous sorceress staggered backwards and fell into the spreading pool of her own oneirolachrymose magma. Her flesh sizzled and popped like animal fat.

The Overgorgon stepped back and watched the teleplasm burst like lava from the Teuthsibyl's eye. After several seconds, she realized that the flow of kaleidoscopic ichor was neither slowing nor stopping. The room was already filled with more of the bubbling, boiling teleplasm than should logically have been contained in the

Teuthsibyl's body.The Overgorgon tossed her jade scimitar aside so that she could grip the Cimiamatl more securely, then fled back through the tunnels. The teleplasm continued to pour from the Teuthsibyl's eye, following the Overgorgon through the maze like a heat-seeking predator.

*

As Hell Jaguar slashed at the Squid Messiah with his burning claws, Tuatara Man ascended the steps of the dais. He snuck up behind Hell Jaguar, grabbed his tail with one prehensile dragonfoot, and began dragging the teeth of his battle-saw across it.

Hell Jaguar rolled over onto his back and kicked Tuatara Man in the groin with both heels. Tuatara Man staggered but maintained his grip on Hell Jaguar's tail. Hell Jaguar spat a fireball, but Tuatara Man countered it with a beam of purple light from his third eye. The two forces nullified one another. Hell Jaguar writhed on his back.

The Squid Messiah had regained his senses. He grabbed his trident, raised it over his head, and drove it straight for Hell Jaguar's throat. Hell Jaguar caught it with his hands, overpowered the Squid Messiah, and wrenched the trident from his grasp. He swung the trident at Tuatara Man, who blocked it with his staff and continued sawing Hell Jaguar's tail off. The Squid Messiah formed a temporary alliance with Tuatara Man, regrasping the trident while kneeling on Hell Jaguar's throat. Selachia climbed atop the dais and assisted in holding Hell Jaguar down, and then the impromptu coalition grew even larger as Death Bat and the Chiropteress joined them. Hell Jaguar snarled and hissed and spat fire. He twisted and wriggled upon the stone floor. His adversaries pinned him to the ground. Tuatara Man was now able to maintain a back-and forth rhythm with his battle-saw as he continued to sunder Hell Jaguar's tail. A few moments later, Tuatara Man triumphantly wrapped Hell Jaguar's excaudated tail around his staff.

Hell Jaguar roared, and with a strength born of primal fury flung Death Bat, Chiropteress, Selachia and the Squid Messiah from the dais. He leapt to his feet and charged Tuatara Man, snarling and hissing, feral and rabid, with vengeance on his tongue and hell in his eyes.

As the Squid Messiah,Selachia, and the Chiropteress and Death

Bat turned upon one another once more, the Overgorgon and the tsunami of teleplasm erupted from the hole in the dais. The teleplasm exploded like a geyser and rapidly flooded the chamber. The heat became unbearable as more and more of the boiling substance poured forth. Ankle-deep in the rising tide of scalding, oracular ichor, a sense of panic fell upon the chamber, and everything in it scrambled to escape.

The healed speleomancer frantically gesticulated and shouted a concatenation of spells, conjuring a new labyrinth of caves in the rock of the mountain. A cavern opened in the side of the chamber, and the speleomancer and his tiny bear, the lacustrimancer and his platypus, Tuatara Man, Selachia, and the rest of the surviving Lemurians dashed through the crumbling entrance that had been set like a bomb to cave-in behind them. Death Bat, the Chiropteress, and the rest of the shape-shifters transformed into smoke and floated to the top of the temple. The squidmen dove into the subterranean lake at the far side of the chamber.

Hell Jaguar grabbed the ollinchord, still dangling from the top of the temple, gathered the Overgorgon in his arms, leapt into the air, and rocketed back to the entrance of the temple.

The lava-like teleplasm rapidly rose through the entire mountain, licking like flames at the pads of Hell Jaguar's feet. Hell Jaguar and the Overgorgon ricocheted off the ceiling of the foyer. Hell Jaguar's flaming claws slashed the ollincord in half and they dropped to the ground. The wisps and clouds of smoke which Death Bat, the Chiropteress, and his vampiric minions had transformed into were floating through the wall of fire Hell Jaguar had created in the temple entrance. They passed through it as though by osmosis, revealing the method with which they had earlier passed through the impenetrable flames. Hell Jaguar watched the living smoke dissipate into the night.

Breathing in, Hell Jaguar sucked the nimbus of fire into his lungs, then led the Overgorgon through the entrance. Together, they climbed to the peak of the mountain for refuge as the teleplasm blasted through the eye of Kanaloa like an ocean of multi-colored ink being shot from the eye of a teuthid leviathan.

The Overgorgon hissed, and a giant macaw flew to her side a moment later. With the Cimiamatl safely cradled in her arms, she and Hell Jaguar climbed upon the back of the macaw and flew triumphantly back to Aztlan. After thousands of years, the Mayan Book of the Dead was returning home, to rejoin the Mayan Book of Life upon the Scales of Mictlan, to re-open the ancient cenote connecting the forces of the Widdershins Earth to the damnations and demonica of Cold Hell.

*

Hell Jaguar and the Overgorgon landed upon the balcony of the Overgorgon's jade ziggurat. After greeting the Toxisaur and his soldiers, they walked through the doorway of the Overgorgon's bedchamber, preparing to balance the Scales of Mictlan with the Cimiamatl. As they approached the table, however, they found that the Scales of Mictlan had been balanced in their absence.

For they were completely empty.

Hell Jaguar growled as the Overgorgon walked back to the balcony and interrogated the Toxisaur. She returned a minute later.

"The guards saw nothing. Tis impossible, and yet..." the Overgorgon paused.

A black butterfly was fluttering around the room. Hell Jaguar caught it in his paw and crushed it with his fist. Dark wisps of smoke drifted through his fingers and floated into the air. Hell Jaguar opened his hand. The black butterfly was gone.

The tiny cloud of smoke drifted through the door of the bedchamber and into the skies. Hell Jaguar breathed in a vast lungful of night and glanced at the Kajib Xalkat B'e in the corner. He could smell the spoor and psychic residue leading into the teleportation portal, a warm melange of smoke, wings, metamorphosis, and evil.

"Death Bat," he whispered, grim and stoic. "He has taken the Popol Vuh to the Vampire Pyramid of Xibalba."

The Overgorgon sighed. "Then our quest has most surely mirrored the opposing rotations, the circular karmas, and the cyclical reincarnations of the Widdershins Earth and the Sinistral Moon," she lamented. "We have regained the Book of the Dead...but we have paid for it with the Book of Life!"

To be continued...

www.ingramcontent.com/pod-product-compliance
Lightning Source LLC
Chambersburg PA
CBHW060437180626
46817CB00007B/2864